Praise for
The Bridal Pleasures Series

A Duke's Temptation

"A sinfully sexy hero with a secret, a book-obsessed heroine in search of her own happy-ever-after ending, a delightfully clever plot that takes great fun in spoofing the literary world, and writing that sparkles with wicked wit and exquisite sensuality add up to an exceptionally entertaining read worthy of 'Lord Anonymous' himself."   —*Booklist* (starred review)

"With humor and charm, sensuality and wickedness, Hunter delights."   —*Romantic Times*

"Ms. Hunter's Boscastle series is one of the few historical romance series that I read. You'll find lively characters, unusual plots, and an underlying sense of fun."   —Fresh Fiction

"An unusual duke and a naive country gentlewoman sound like a typical historical romance, but Ms. Hunter makes it so much more. These characters turn the ordinary into something special and kept me glued to the book."   —Night Owl Romance

continued . . .

"This is the first in what looks to be a very promising, and extremely seductive, new quartet. Most of the focus is on the main couple, Samuel and Lily. This is as it should be; however, a bit of danger and suspense makes enough surprise appearances to keep things intriguing. Few can resist a novel by Jillian Hunter!"

—Huntress Book Reviews

More Praise for the Novels
of Jillian Hunter

"One of the funniest, most delightful romances I've had the pleasure to read." —Teresa Medeiros

"An absolutely delightful tale that's impossible to put down." —*Booklist*

"A sweet, romantic tale . . . full of humor, romance, and passion. Historical romance that is sure to please."
—The Romance Readers Connection

"A lovely read." —Romance Reader at Heart

"Enchanting . . . a fabulous historical."
—*Midwest Book Review*

The Bridal Pleasures Series

A Duke's Temptation

JILLIAN HUNTER

A Bride Unveiled

The Bridal Pleasures Series

A SIGNET SELECT BOOK

SIGNET SELECT
Published by New American Library, a division of
Penguin Group (USA) Inc., 375 Hudson Street,
New York, New York 10014, USA
Penguin Group (Canada), 90 Eglinton Avenue East, Suite 700, Toronto,
Ontario M4P 2Y3, Canada (a division of Pearson Penguin Canada Inc.)
Penguin Books Ltd., 80 Strand, London WC2R 0RL, England
Penguin Ireland, 25 St. Stephen's Green, Dublin 2,
Ireland (a division of Penguin Books Ltd.)
Penguin Group (Australia), 250 Camberwell Road, Camberwell, Victoria 3124,
Australia (a division of Pearson Australia Group Pty. Ltd.)
Penguin Books India Pvt. Ltd., 11 Community Centre, Panchsheel Park,
New Delhi - 110 017, India
Penguin Group (NZ), 67 Apollo Drive, Rosedale, Auckland 0632,
New Zealand (a division of Pearson New Zealand Ltd.)
Penguin Books (South Africa) (Pty.) Ltd., 24 Sturdee Avenue,
Rosebank, Johannesburg 2196, South Africa

Penguin Books Ltd., Registered Offices:
80 Strand, London WC2R 0RL, England

First published by Signet, an imprint of New American Library,
a division of Penguin Group (USA) Inc.

First Printing, October 2011
10 9 8 7 6 5 4 3 2 1

*This book is dedicated to Susan Boyle
and to all the unsung heroines
she has inspired.*

Chapter 1

Monk's Huntley
England 1808

*M*iss Violet Knowlton had suspected for years that something was wrong with her. It wasn't until her thirteenth summer, however, that the hidden flaw in her nature came to light. Before then she had considered herself to be an obedient girl, a fortunate one, even though she had lost her parents so long ago she had no memories of them to mourn their loss.

Her aunt and uncle, Baron and Lady Ashfield, had cocooned her and raised her as their own. They had moved from bustling Falmouth to the obscure hamlet of Monk's Huntley to shelter her from the wickedness that she had been warned waited outside the door to snatch up an unwary girl.

As Violet grew older she would stare out her bed-chamber window and wonder what form this wicked threat would take. Would it be a man? A beast? She had lived under the impression that all girls were in danger of this unknown menace. If only her guardians had explained why they would sometimes stop talking when she entered a room unannounced. If only they had confessed that they meant to protect her from herself, she might have understood that she could never let down her guard.

It was a cause destined to fail.

It was two months before her thirteenth birthday when she looked from her window and first noticed the boy in the abandoned graveyard that lay between her uncle's manor house and the woods. Twilight had fallen, and the boy seemed to be engaged in an energetic duel, although for the life of her, Violet could not see his opponent.

Three days went by before she spotted him again. This time it wasn't quite dusk and she realized that he was fighting alone. After that she began to keep a vigil, propped on a stool, hoping for a glimpse of his intriguing figure.

She couldn't have described him in any detail to anyone. He looked tall from her vantage point, furtive and full of energy. He wasn't a ghost. She saw him once in the daylight, charging past the crypts with a sword over his head. He ran as if his life were something out of an adventure novel, as if he had dragons to slay or that meant to slay him.

Sometimes he appeared and disappeared like a wizard before her eyes. She wondered who he was and where he lived and why he was not afraid to play in the churchyard that everyone else in Monk's Huntley knew to avoid. She spent hours wondering about him, because she was lonely and despaired of making friends with the other young ladies in the village. The girls who'd grown up in the parish refused to allow a newcomer like Violet into their circle. The harder she tried to impress them, the more they drew away from her, until she gave up trying.

Her closest female companion, in fact her only one, was Miss Winifred Higgins, the governess Violet's uncle had hired at the spring fair. She was a comely redhead with a beguiling warmth, and just as Violet was starting to feel close to her, Miss Higgins revealed a startling confidence of her own—she had lied to Baron Ashfield about her credentials. She was not a twenty-year-old etiquette school graduate experienced in the moral guidance of young girls.

As it turned out, Miss Higgins had never attended school and had run away from home. While Violet sat on the garden wall sketching dragonflies, her governess was being led astray by the bricklayer's son in the hedgerow. She swore to Violet that this was true love.

"How old are you really, Miss Higgins?"

She stared at Violet. "Nineteen."

"Honestly?"

"I shouldn't have told you anything," Winifred said, her eyes scornful.

"I told you about the boy."

"Don't go near him," Winifred warned her. "At least

not by yourself." She frowned. "I'm almost eighteen. I suppose you're going to tell your uncle that I lied."

"No." Violet couldn't imagine losing her only female friend. "Are you going to tell him about the boy?"

"I haven't seen any boy yet."

"But you do believe he exists?"

Miss Higgins shrugged. "Why not?"

There were advantages, Violet learned that summer, to having a governess who was not only negligent in her duty but in one's debt. Soon Winifred granted Violet the small freedoms that had previously been forbidden her. She did not complain when Violet walked barefoot in the garden. She allowed her ward to wander farther from the manor grounds to sketch, until the day they walked to the slope that overlooked the church ruins.

They stood in silence, staring down at the rows of moss-stained graves that had looked oddly romantic from Violet's window. They stood in the shade of the tall yew trees that by tradition guarded the deceased, and Winifred whispered, "Why would anyone choose to frequent a place like this?"

"To find buried treasure," a cheerful voice answered from behind them.

Winifred gave a scream that was shrill enough to awaken an army of ghosts from their eternal slumber. She swayed in the ankle-high ferns that covered the slope. Violet caught her by the arm. She might have screamed herself had she not recognized the stout young gentleman standing behind her, a shovel balanced on the shoulder of his brass-buttoned coat.

It was only her neighbor Eldie—Eldbert Tomkinson—
the son of the parish surgeon. He talked to her every
Sunday after church and often came to the manor to
play chess with her uncle. He could repeat entire poems
backward. He had drawn a historical map of Monk's
Huntley on his bedsheet.

Violet thought that he was too clever for his own
good, although, to his credit, he said he believed that
she had seen a boy sword fighting in the churchyard.
But he wasn't that boy, and for a moment she could not
help feeling disappointed that he was only unexciting
Eldbert.

"What is he doing here?" Winifred whispered,
studying Eldbert's shovel in suspicion.

"He's convinced that there's buried treasure in the
graves, but he's afraid to look by himself."

"I am not afraid," Eldbert said. "I need another person to hold my map and read my compass while I dig,
if you want to know the truth."

None of them had ever ventured this close to the
ruins.

It was only a matter of days before Violet and Eldbert
met again and combined their courage to slide down
the embankment into the churchyard. Violet landed
against a grave with her pencils and sketching book intact, Eldbert, his shovel, and his small map beside her.

It was also only a matter of time before their mutual
neighbor and nemesis, the Honorable Ambrose Tilton,
realized he had not seen them lately and set out to
learn why. As the heir to his father's viscountcy, Am-

brose would soon be regarded as a prize catch among the unmarried maidens of Monk's Huntley. In Violet's opinion, however, he was a mean-spirited spoilsport.

Violet tolerated Ambrose for Eldbert's sake. She never understood why Eldbert put up with Ambrose's taunts and condescending smugness, until finally Eldie let it slip that Ambrose took regular thrashings from the older boys at school and was too ashamed to tell his father or the schoolmaster.

"But he's big," Violet said in disbelief.

"He's afraid," Eldbert said. "Some boys just are, and you ought to feel sorry for him, Violet."

So Violet did, except when Ambrose made a point of being the most obnoxious person in England. "Are you looking for that boy with the sword again?" he shouted down the slope. "He doesn't exist, you know! Neither does that buried treasure! I hope you realize how stupid you look!"

The boy *did exist*, and Violet was determined to find out who he was, although she wasn't sure she would have been courageous enough to explore the church ruins without Miss Higgins standing guard on the slope, and Eldbert beside her. She certainly would not have ventured into the sunken remains of the private mausoleum where the earl and his household had been laid to rest over a century ago.

"Do you want to go into the catacombs?" Eldbert asked her.

"No. Isn't that where the plague victims are buried?"

"Yes," he said, brushing a lock of his cropped black

hair from his spectacles. "The grave diggers piled them one on top of another."

"How ghastly."

They moved as one, stealing between clumps of grass and cracked gravestones. Violet read only a few of the names and epitaphs on the tombs that she passed. She refused to believe that death ended like this, in decay and abandonment. She was glad that Eldie's mother had been laid to rest in the burial grounds on the other side of the village.

His voice startled her. "This would be the River Styx," he said, poking his shovel at the stream that meandered into the skeletal remains of the roofless chapel and down the steps that led into the subterranean vaults. An enormous stone pillar had been positioned across the entrance. She gazed down into the airless black crypts and felt a shiver go down her back. It wasn't a shiver of fear. It was of excitement.

"Well, if this is the River Styx, then we are standing at the gate of the underworld, and I hope that nobody is home."

He turned his head. "What is that noise?"

She listened to the sounds of the trickling stream and her heart beating and then ever so faintly heard the scraping of metal against stone. "I think something is living in there, Eldbert," she whispered.

"A fox, probably. Or restless spirits. Maybe something worse. Let's explore another day."

"We're not supposed to be here, anyway."

"No," he agreed, and pulled her up the stairs by the

hand. They had made it to the top and stumbled into the yard when a grinding echo rose from the depths of the sunken vault. Eldbert started for the embankment. Something compelled Violet to turn.

"Eldbert," she whispered. "Look. It's him."

The boy's head was lowered when he emerged from the vaults. But as he climbed the steps he grew tall and straight. He swaggered through the tufts of grass toward her.

She was too stunned to move. His blond elf locks hung below a strong chin. From where she stood it seemed that his eyes caught the light like crystals. He was dressed oddly, in elegant nankeen trousers, a striped shirt, and a ragged yellow jacket that he wore with such panache it could have been an ermine-lined cloak.

Eldbert bumped up against her, his voice low with panic. "He's from the pauper palace."

"From where?"

"The *palace*," he said. "Let's get away as fast as we can."

She felt her sketchbook slipping to her side as Eldbert nudged her again. Eldbert was right. He was always right. The boy might be intriguing, but that didn't mean he was polite, and as for being from the palace, well, she couldn't hold that against him.

"I'm sorry if we disturbed you," she said quickly. "We only hoped to make friends. I've seen you sword fighting and I was so impressed that . . . that . . . My name's Violet Knowlton, and this is my neighbor, Eldbert Tomkinson. We shouldn't be here at all."

The boy said nothing. In fact, he appeared so unmoved that she wondered whether he had understood her. She waited a moment. She wanted to run, but her instincts warned her it was too late. She had hoped to make a friend. It was obvious that he did not return the feeling.

But then his eyes changed. Color flickered behind the cold silver. His thin lips curved into a smile. "My name is Kit," he said in a courteous enough voice, but before she could let out her breath, he drew the sword that had been concealed beneath his tunic and leveled it at her shoulder. "I think I'll have to take you hostage."

Eldbert dropped his shovel. "What has she ever done to you?"

He glanced up briefly. "Mind your business."

"Run, Violet," Eldbert urged her. "Fetch my father and the servants while I hold him here. Fetch Miss Higgins if you can find her."

The boy gave a mocking laugh that indicated he wasn't intimidated in the least by Eldbert. "Well, go on," he said to Violet. "Why don't you take your sister's advice and run home?"

"You don't need to be unpleasant," Violet said without considering the consequences. "I said that we only came here to make friends."

"And I said that I was taking you hostage, in the vaults, and there isn't a thing that Guts and Garbage can do to stop me."

At that insult to Eldbert, Violet finally came to her

senses, leaping into action before she could consider the consequences. She snapped off her shawl and flung it in her would-be abductor's face. "I'm sorry that I ever watched you. I don't wonder that you're alone in this awful place. What good is it to ply a sword against invisible enemies?"

Kit lifted his sword to disentangle the shawl, but the fringe had wrapped itself around the hilt. No matter how deftly he plied the weapon, the bits of wool refused to detach, until in the end the girl, who had no understanding of what a dangerous person she was dealing with, snatched it free and gave him a withering glare.

She wrapped the shawl back around her shoulders with a dignity that made him feel dirty and ashamed. He recognized her as the girl who watched him from her window, and knew that she would have reported him to the workhouse by now if she meant to. She served as an audience of sorts for his sword practice. She was better company than the dead rivals Kit summoned from the vaults for frequent fencing matches. The ghosts wouldn't hurt him. The parish overseers would if they caught him wasting work hours.

The overseers liked flogging boys to the bone, or hanging them upside down for a night, or putting them in solitary incarceration. Kit hated that punishment the most, especially when the warden sneaked a few rats into the cell to make the offender less lonely.

Kit had lived in the workhouse ever since he was taken from the foundling orphanage almost twelve years ago, when he was two. It was recorded in the workhouse registry that an orphanage nurse had found him when he was a bundle of squalls, abandoned and wrapped in a fox-lined cloak outside the orphanage door.

Now he was allowed out three hours every other day to gather stones and serve as a scarecrow in the old farmer's fields. He came to the churchyard for peace. He wasn't sure why the catacombs and lopsided tombs attracted him, aside from the fact that they concealed a drainage tunnel that led to the workhouse.

A century and a half ago plague had swept through Monk's Huntley, sparing only a few families. The cemetery lay under a curse. Nothing but grass and toadstools grew beyond the shade of the encircling yew trees, and these fungi Kit beheaded with a vengeance as soon as they cropped up.

Sometimes he staged a great sword fight for the girl's benefit. She was far enough away that she might not be able to tell he was a fourteen-year-old pauper. Or that the sword hidden in the crypt was really a farmer's hoe and not a Toledo steel blade.

She was pretty enough, with dark hair, sparkling eyes, and a clear voice. Her face reminded him of one of those brooches worn by the nice old charity ladies who visited the pauper palace.

The inmates never got a chance to eat any of the custard tarts and meat pasties that the old ladies baked for them, though. The wardens confiscated the food baskets, and that was that. So let the girl at the window look. Looks cost nothing. It was the touching Kit couldn't tolerate. He'd learned how to defend himself at an early age against the calloused hands that stole under his blanket. The day would come soon when he'd either rise up and fight or he would run away. He'd given himself until October. It was run or be sold to a stranger as an apprentice when he turned fifteen. The workhouse didn't give a pauper the luxury of choosing his future.

He frowned at the girl. "I wasn't serious about taking you hostage. Not with this." He threw the farmer's hoe over his shoulder. "It was a game. Sword fighting is a game. I wouldn't have hurt you. Go home."

"I'm sorry," she said.

"For what?"

She bit her lip. "For ruining your secret."

Kit was certain that he would never see her again.

The first time he'd seen her in the window he had thought she was an invalid. Then he'd speculated that she was an heiress from London being held for ransom. No one in his right head would look for a missing girl in Monk's Huntley.

After a few weeks he concluded that she was being locked up as punishment for disobeying her parents. He had felt sorry for her. He had come to a lot of conclusions about her before the moment she became his friend.

And not a single one of them turned out to be true.

Chapter 2

$\mathcal{F}$our days later Ambrose discovered Violet and Eldbert's secret. Ambrose suspected the pair of them were up to something, and it irked him to no end to be excluded from an activity in what he considered to be his domain. Ambrose took orders from no one, except his mother, who scared him witless, and his schoolmates, whose bullying filled him with anger and shame.

He nearly had a fit when he found out that Violet and Eldbert had not only ventured into the forbidden churchyard to befriend a boy from the workhouse, but that the boy was teaching clumsy old Eldbert how to fence. Violet was sitting upon a gravestone, of all the disgusting places to sit, threading clover from the slope into a crown.

The thin fair-haired boy noticed Ambrose first. His eyes narrowed in hostile recognition, as if he knew who Ambrose was, which was as it should be. Then he straightened in a stance that seemed to challenge everything Ambrose stood for.

"What are you doing here?" Eldbert asked in a masterful voice that he'd never dared to use before this day.

Something had changed. No. Everything had changed. Violet and Eldbert had always played the games that Ambrose chose. But now Violet rose from the gravestone, and a few clovers slipped from the crown she had woven for . . . a rough boy, a poor one, a nobody, a—God bless—a boy who was wearing the missing pantaloons that Ambrose had been accused of misplacing only last week.

"What are you doing?" he sputtered, shaking his head in disbelief. "Why are you associating with—"

"The Knight of the Unconquerable Sword," Violet said, stealing a look at the other boy. "You're not allowed in his realm unless you follow his rules."

"Rules? Rules? I am to follow a beggar's rules, am I? A beggar who"—his face turned purple—"is wearing my stolen trousers? You stole them off the laundry line!" He hopped up and down in howling indignity. "Go home, the two of you, or I'll tell my mother what you've been doing."

"No," Violet and Eldbert said in unison. Eldbert added, "If you tell, our friend will get in trouble."

Ambrose's jaw dropped as the other boy reached back for the sword lying across one of the graves. "That belongs to your father, Eldbert!" Ambrose exclaimed. "It—"

"You'll have to promise to keep our secret if you want to join us," Violet broke in sweetly. "Won't he, Kit?"

But Ambrose and Kit were locked in a staring battle

that ended only when Eldbert said, "If you keep our
secret, Kit will teach you how to fight, Ambrose, and
no one will ever hurt you again."

"I can't carry a sword to school."

"There are other ways to fight bullies."

Ambrose returned the next afternoon with two of
his father's smallswords.

They met whenever they could that summer, two on
each side to compete in treasure hunts using the maps
that Eldbert had drawn. The only true find they made
was friendship. Violet invented enchanted kingdoms
and drew pictures, exasperated that the boys rarely
held still. Kit had taught Ambrose the rudiments of
sword fighting and how to throw and duck a punch,
skills he had perfected in the workhouse yard. Although Ambrose was as obnoxious as ever, he had
given one boy at school a black eye and admitted reluctantly that he had Kit to thank.

Four friends, Violet thought with satisfaction, frowning in concentration over her sketchbook. Five if she
included Miss Higgins, who was spending more time
with Violet since she had discovered that her bricklayer was marrying another girl in September.

One afternoon Kit got careless. He was showing off at
swordplay for his friends, and by the time Violet's governess realized it was time for tea, Kit could not gather
more than a few stones from the field. Before he knew
it, dusk had fallen.

The older inmates at the workhouse claimed the tunnels after dark. He would lose his privileges of underground passage if he broke the rules. Besides, he felt like a human being after being in Violet's company. He liked to keep that illusion of integrity, at least until he returned to the palace.

But now, because of his dallying where he didn't belong, he would have to walk through the woods and hope he could sneak through the main yard before supper. Which would be a bowl of old piss. If no one covered for him, he'd get flogged until he bled through his shirt. The pain of it would be bad enough, and he didn't know how he could keep his outside friends from finding out that he lived like a mongrel, for all he tried to impress them.

To add to his mounting woes, he realized he wasn't alone in the woods. He heard whispering from the undergrowth up ahead. He slowed and swung himself into the crotch of a sessile oak. If anyone thought to jump him, he didn't have to make it easy. He could swing down, kick one of them in the nose and the other in the thingamabobs. He waited. *Shit*. He counted three heads in the thicket.

Then after another moment he realized that he wasn't the intended victim. A middle-aged gentleman in a short cape crested the footpath. He carried a walking stick under his arm. He looked to be enjoying a leisurely stroll. He appeared to have no inkling of the three men lying in wait for him. Kit might have whistled out a warning if he didn't have his own worries.

There was nothing to do for it but twiddle his thumbs while the oafs divested the gent of his pocket watch and whatever else he was fool enough to carry in the woods.

None of my business, Kit thought, and crossed his arms behind his neck.

The three darted out with all the subtlety of wild boars. One butted the older fellow in the belly. Another charged from the rear. The third, who had a meat cleaver, went for the gent's knees.

It was going to be a slaughter.

"Here, little piggies!" Kit shouted before he could stifle the impulse, reaching into his pocket for a palmful of stones.

He threw hard and fast, positioned on one knee. The three obliged themselves as targets by looking up to locate his hiding place. So did the victim, who upon Kit's closer assessment appeared neither as unaware nor as helpless as Kit had assumed.

His eyes pinned Kit for an instant, as if he knew who he was. Of course, by then it was too late to do anything but join the fracas. He would as soon get flayed in a decent fight as in the yard.

He rose from his position in the tree, bracing either hand to propel him into flight. He was almost to the ground when a flash of silver caught his eye, and the gent's walking stick transformed into a lethal-looking sword.

The blade flashed in the falling dark, and the first assailant's arm flowed bright red. Kit hurled the remaining stones stashed in his pocket for the hell of it, laughing as the three failed thieves ran away. "Pitiful," he mused. "Amateurs."

"Indeed," said a deep voice in the dark.

Kit's nape crawled with foreboding. He turned, curious despite himself, to study the walking stick before he met the man's eyes. "The morons never had a chance. Nice work, mister."

"I have seen you in the graveyard," the man said slowly. "Are you not afraid of being caught?"

Kit stumbled over a stone.

"What is your name?"

As if it mattered. As if anything mattered except that because of this man he was going to lose the only friends he had ever made in his miserable life.

"I am Captain—"

Kit didn't wait to hear another word.

He ran.

Violet realized that she seemed ungrateful. It was her birthday, and she had walked into the parlor after breakfast to find a dancing master waiting for her.

Her uncle cleared his throat. "This is your present from us, Violet."

"Thank you," she said, staring past him to the window. She could see Eldbert lurking in the rosebushes. He was motioning her to come outside. She made a face.

"Violet," her aunt said in embarrassment. "You've

been asking your uncle for dance lessons ever since we moved here."

"I know, but . . . does it have to be today, Aunt Francesca?"

"Why not? Are you unwell?"

"I think I might be."

"Then excuse yourself this minute. Do not get the master ill when he has traveled so far to give you lessons. Dr. Tomkinson said at church there is—"

Violet darted to the door before her aunt could change her mind. She loved dancing. She did want lessons. But not when she was too miserable to care about performing the proper figures of the cotillion.

Kit hadn't appeared in the churchyard for three weeks. She watched for him from her window every morning and every night, as she had before she was certain he existed. Eldbert braved a daily walk through the churchyard to the edge of the woods with his father's telescope to scan the palace outskirts.

"Did you see any sign of him?" Violet asked over and over. She couldn't help but ask, even when she knew that Eldbert would have told her if he had.

"There were too many people milling about in the yard," Eldbert replied. "It looked as if a procession of coaches were lined up outside the gates. As if visitors had come to tour."

Ambrose scoffed at him. "Honestly, Eldie, who'd want to tour what is practically a prison?"

"A prison?" Violet said in horror. "I thought it was—"

"A palace?" Ambrose regarded her in despair. "You don't really think there is anything palatial about a workhouse? Next thing I know you'll tell me Kit's convinced you that he's on holiday when he sneaks about the churchyard. He's a born liar and a braggart."

"He never bragged to me about anything," Violet said numbly. "At least, not about where he lives. It isn't a prison."

Eldbert threw Ambrose a warning look.

And Ambrose ignored him.

"Who do you think starts life in a foundling orphanage?" Ambrose asked Violet.

"Well, orphans, of course. Unfortunate children, like me, who have lost their parents."

"Chance children," Ambrose countered, folding his arms like a satisfied genie. "Lawbreakers and little bastards."

An unbecoming pink infused Eldbert's cheeks. "I lost my mother. Are you calling me a name?"

Ambrose looked past Eldbert to Violet, who knew that she ought to cover her ears for what was to come but couldn't make herself. "Watered-down porridge for every meal," he said. "Hiring you out to strangers. Whippings. That's the workhouse life."

"Kit has never complained to us of being hungry," Violet said, her voice warbling. "Not once. He's never asked me for anything to eat." At least, not out loud. Yet now that Violet thought about it, Kit had never refused one of Eldbert's ham sandwiches, either. Violet had thought it was polite of Kit to wander off to eat.

But had she once considered the possibility that he was starving? That his sharp-boned face had been a sign of a deprivation he was too ashamed to admit?

"You're the one who's lying, Ambrose," she said with conviction. "You have envied Kit since the day you saw him. He's better than you with a sword. He's handsomer, more noble, more—"

"He doesn't *ask* for anything because he steals what he wants," Ambrose replied. "Good grief. He stole my pants. He's a beggar, a thief, and a liar."

Eldbert made a fist and drew back his arm. "Don't look, Violet," he said, pulling himself up to an impressive height that made Violet wonder whether he had grown overnight. "I shall address this insult to Kit's honor."

Violet would have protested if an all-too-familiar voice had not called her name from the top of the slope. She glanced up distractedly and recognized Winifred amid the sheltering stand of trees.

Reluctantly she picked up her skirt to heed the summons. Eldbert threw his punch the moment she turned away. She heard Winifred calling again, a compelling urgency in her voice. "Your uncle is coming, miss! He's been looking for you everywhere!"

She gasped, ducking on instinct as Eldbert's fist extended over her head for another punch and caught Ambrose on the chin. She cared not a jot about the clumsy battle that ensued. She was too upset about Kit's disappearance.

Violet reached Winifred's side as the baron huffed

through the coppice to the top of the slope. He stared at his niece and her governess for an unmeasured interval, as if he sensed something were amiss and could not name it.

"What on earth are you doing this close to the churchyard, Violet?" he demanded.

Violet could not lie to him. Miss Higgins, however, could—and did.

"She heard Eldbert and Ambrose fighting, sir, and tried to intervene."

At any other time the baron would have said, "Twaddle," but the sight of Eldbert limping up the slope with a bloody nose stole his attention. "Dear, dear," he said. "I hope you got in a good one, Eldbert."

Violet touched her uncle's arm. "Uncle Henry, have you ever visited a workhouse?"

He glanced back toward the churchyard before allowing Violet to lead him to the manor path. "Yes, my dear. I have."

"Was it as horrible as Ambrose says?"

He hesitated. She looked up at him and waited. He was an honest man, and she knew that she could believe whatever he told her. "There are few places on earth as hellish as a workhouse, Violet. Pity those who must live there and depend on our charity."

"But children are well treated there, aren't they?"

"Some are. Most aren't. There are twenty-three of them sleeping to a room."

"And beatings?"

"Yes. Beatings."

"Why isn't it stopped?"

"The parish needs funds to build a decent school and hospital to take care of the sick, and to separate the children from the criminals."

"I didn't dream anything like that could exist," she said in despair, looking off into the woods. And with her newfound knowledge, her innocence gave way to a compassion that would influence the course of her life.

One of the wardens had caught Kit climbing over the locked gate and gave him a blow across the head that turned his vision red. "So Master Cockroach has been good enough to come 'ome, and by the gate this time. You've had it now, Kit. You'll be in lockup soon, my boy, or sold to the first bidder. You're almost of the age."

They flogged him in the yard early the next morning. He bit his tongue so he wouldn't cry out. It only made it worse for the younger boys who were getting beaten at the same time. Stupid though it seemed, the thought of Eldbert and Violet took some of the sting away. He'd tricked them into thinking he was invulnerable. Now he had to trick himself.

The cane came down harder. He buckled, and a hand caught hold of his shirt. The seam tore at the shoulder. *Bugger it.* Violet and Miss Higgins would be embarrassed. *Don't think of them. Stop.*

Prison.

Workhouse boy. Dirty little beggar.

Give me another chance. I was born in sin and I don't know why, but I swear I'm good inside. I know it doesn't show. I know that I'm all blow—

"Get up," a voice said, and filthy water hit his chin.

He closed his eyes. Better now. He couldn't see any faces. He couldn't see anything at all.

Summer was coming to an early end. Kit turned fifteen. He was always on edge and felt as if he were being watched. Every day one of his pals at the house disappeared or died. He knew he was next.

He frowned at the sketch of him that rested across Violet's lap. "Stop doing those."

She glanced up. "Are you all right?"

"Why wouldn't I be?" he asked, covering a cough in his fist.

"Your face is flushed. And your eyes are red."

"I'm fine. Don't draw pictures of me. You always have to make me look like a prince or a knight. Make me a nobody."

The warden diagnosed him with the measles the next day. Kit wished the illness would kill him, but it didn't. He recovered faster than his workhouse friends, but he still felt rotten almost a fortnight later when he sneaked to the churchyard to see his friends.

"What is it, Kit?" Violet asked him as they watched Ambrose and Eldbert fencing among the trees.

He noticed that she hadn't brought her sketchbook,

and he felt bad for that. But not as bad as when she stood, her eyes glassy, and put her hand to her face.

"What's the matter?"

She dropped her hand. Then she started to cough and sway on her feet. "Oh, God," he said. "Eldbert! Ambrose!"

The boys came running. By the time they arrived, Violet was shaking and holding her arm up to cover her eyes, whispering, "Why is the light so bright? It's never this bright down here."

"What have you done to her, you filthy beggar?" Ambrose asked in panic.

Violet swayed on her feet, one arm outstretched. "I've caught the plague," she whispered. "I feel like I'm dying."

Eldbert stared at her in fright. Ambrose turned an ungodly shade of gray and took off for the woods.

"Help me, Eldbert," Kit said, sweeping Violet up in his arms. Violet white and sickly was preferable to what he saw at the palace, and he had done this to her. "Where is Miss Higgins?"

"I don't know," Eldbert said, stumbling after Kit's hurried strides. "Where are you taking her?"

"To her house."

"But they'll—"

"Look, can you at least carry her feet? If she dies, it will be on me."

"Die? She can't die. I had the measles a few years ago, and I survived. My father said it's spreading through the parish again. But . . . Violet can't die."

For the rest of his life Kit would remember that scene. He ran up the slope and toward the Tudor-framed manor. The butler, standing at the door, sent him a look of gratitude and gathered Violet in his arms. The baron burst from the house with murder in his eyes, and behind him a lady—the baroness, Kit guessed—gave a wail of despair.

Kit watched for Violet at her window, and knew it would be his fault if she died. He and Eldbert kept a vigil outside the garden gate of Violet's manor, until one day she appeared at the window and gave a weak wave.

"Ye gads," Eldbert said, passing Kit his telescope. "She looks hideous."

Not to Kit. She looked lovely and alive.

A week later Ambrose caught the measles. He hacked and ran a raging fever and afterward blamed Kit for imperiling his life. Miss Higgins, having been infected years ago, did not fall ill.

Their small band met for the last time one late afternoon in early August. They had managed to sneak off only because the baroness was helping Eldbert's father visit sick families in the parish. Kit studied Violet's face and thought that even her unwholesome pallor would not stop men from falling in love with her. Eldbert and Ambrose were being sent away to school. Violet wouldn't have any friends soon, he thought.

"I'm going away, too," Kit said.

She looked across the grass, her gaze stricken. "Where?"

"I'm being sold," he said. "There's a bill posted on the workhouse gate if you'd like to buy me."

"You're being—"

He hated himself for having told her the truth, even if it was for her own good. A girl like Violet had no business playing with dangerous boys like him. She was so naive, he would have stayed in this godforsaken parish to keep her safe if it were within his power.

"You'll be a blacksmith or a chimney sweep's apprentice if you're lucky," Ambrose said, sounding half-sympathetic. "Has anyone bid for you yet?"

He could have pushed Ambrose's arrogant face into one of the graves. "Yes, as a matter of fact. It isn't official, but it looks as if I'm being apprenticed to a cavalry captain."

Ambrose snorted, unimpressed. "You mean the old drunk who thinks that his son haunts this graveyard?"

Kit pulled a stone from his pocket. "He doesn't drink now," he said, daring Ambrose to defy him. "And he knows his son is dead. He was killed at war."

Violet had turned away, tears in her eyes. "When are you going, Kit?"

He tossed the stone into the air and caught it. His throat hurt, and he thought he was getting sick again. "I don't know."

"You could be a worse apprentice," Eldbert said, adjusting his spectacles. "A dentist could have bought you. I wouldn't mind being apprenticed to an officer myself. It isn't an easy life, being the son of the parish surgeon." He reached into his coat and took out a letter opener that Kit guessed had come from his father's desk.

"What is that for?" Ambrose asked, sitting up at attention.

"It's for us to seal our pact of friendship in blood and agree that we shall all meet again in ten years."

"What should we call ourselves?" Violet said, looking up at Kit.

He smiled at her. "The Bleeding Idiots." He frowned at Eldbert. "You aren't giving her a scar?"

"Don't worry, Kit," she said.

He turned his head. He felt an inexplicable urge to kiss her hand and knew that for her sake it was a blessing that he had to go away.

They enacted the ritual at the thin stream that trickled amid the crypts. Ambrose shrieked the loudest when he pricked his finger, not as much from the pain but from the blood that dripped onto his trousers. His cry drew Miss Higgins from her post on the slope to scrub at the spot by the stream with a stone, Lady Macbeth in a mobcap, muttering, "I'll lose my job if I have to explain what I allowed under my guard. The four of you are incorrigible."

"Five," Violet murmured.

Six, actually, if one counted the child Miss Higgins had no idea she was carrying.

Chapter 3

The Marquess of Sedgecroft's Benefit Ball
London 1818

*K*it strode across the private stage of the Park Lane mansion. In one hand he gripped a rapier, which he was using to mark last-minute directions; in the other he held the program for tonight's performance:

MEMORABLE SWORD FIGHTS IN ACTUAL
AND
LITERARY HISTORY

Presented by
Master Christopher Fenton
and
the twelve pupils of his
Academy of Arms

whose names are listed
in order
of
performance

He searched the backstage shadows. He counted
eleven students, two assistants, and a footman who belonged to the house. The youngest, the brashest, and
indisputably the best of Kit's students, Pierce Carroll,
had not arrived. It was an hour before the performance.
Kit started to pace, a habit that he knew drove his assistants to distraction. But it was either pace or skewer
the closest moving object to the wall.

He had never played to such a grand assembly before. His nerves felt as taut as the violin strings being
tuned in the ballroom. He'd taught fencing to dukes,
numerous other aristocrats, and an unconventional
lady actress or two. He'd staged plenty of impromptu
sword fighting performances in the street and at intimate parties. Still, this would be the first time he put
his skill as a *maître d'armes* on display to the beautiful
world.

His challenge tonight would be to make his students
appear to be masters in their own right. Teaching true
gentlemen to look heroic was how Kit made his living,
and it was a decent one for a former pauper. With any
luck Lord Bidley would not lunge off the stage into the
lap of the voluptuous viscountess who had been pursuing Kit for the last three months.

Carrying a sword may have no longer been the

height of fashionable dress. A pistol might have surpassed the sword as one's favorite weapon. But a man's boast of owning a well-honed blade and knowing how to use it never went out of style.

He stared through the curtains again. Guests had begun to settle in their seats, and candlelight blazed across the stage. Who in the hell had lit all those candles? What if one of his pupils decided to emulate the trick Kit had once rashly demonstrated in a tavern, extinguishing the flames with one swoop of his sword?

The mansion would go up like a matchbox. Kit's greatest performance would be his last. The monies collected tonight for charity could not touch what it would cost to repair a palatial mansion in Park Lane.

"Sir! Sir!" a frantic voice called from backstage.

Kit pivoted, lowering his rapier as he recognized the gaunt senior footman who, next to Kit's patron, the Marquess of Sedgecroft, and his wife, appeared to be third in command of the spacious mansion. His name was Weed.

"Has anyone seen the young master? Has he escaped this way, perchance?"

Kit stared at Weed in complete bafflement. It was true that he instructed pupils in various stages of development, but none of them— "Oh, *that* master," he said with a laugh. "Master Rowan?"

Rowan Boscastle was the Marquess of Sedgecroft's son and heir, a rambunctious youngster who was Kit's most challenging student. Like most little boys, Rowan had an affinity for swordplay and untimely disappearances. "He isn't back here," Kit said with certainty, motioning his assistants, Kenneth and Sidney, to his side.

"What is it, sir?" asked Kenneth, a broad-shouldered young Scotsman.

"A missing child."

"The *heir*," the footman said with emphasis.

"I shall find him," Kit said, and handed his rapier and program to Sidney.

"How?" the footman demanded.

"I used to be good at hiding." Kit took off the cape that had belonged to his father, Captain Charles Fenton. He wore it only on special occasions, to bring him luck. "You know the order of the acts if I am late."

Kenneth folded the cape over his arm. "Are you sure you don't want to put on your mask and padded jacket for this adventure? Remember your last lesson with Master Rowan."

Kit hesitated as he recalled the incident. It was the only time that he had been injured by a foil. "Good idea."

Miss Violet Knowlton had spent two hours chatting with her future husband's acquaintances and clients, but she hadn't spent two solid minutes with the man himself. She would have thought Godfrey remiss in his duty had she not known how important this evening was to him. He was so eager to prove himself a gentleman worthy of selling goods to the ton that at times it was a relief to escape his company.

Violet was not always in a mood to charm and flatter Godfrey's customers—in fact, to a merchant, everyone in England was a potential client. She felt ashamed to admit that being nice on command quite exhausted her.

In fact, she felt ashamed that instead of appreciating the marriage proposal that her aunt had conspired to secure, she had begun to wish it had never been arranged. Her aunt had sacrificed so that she and Violet could come to London, certain that here Violet would find a better husband than in a lonely parish. The wedding was to take place in two months. Godfrey wanted a small ceremony to which only important guests were invited.

Violet had accepted Godfrey's proposal more to please Aunt Francesca than herself. Uncle Henry had died two years ago, and her aunt had become restless in her grief. The pair of them had traveled for fourteen months straight.

"We don't have to move for me," Violet had insisted.

"What is there in Monk's Huntley for us now?" was her aunt's mournful reply. "There are no other decent young men left in the village. It has become a . . . grave."

Violet knew that her uncle's death had darkened her aunt's perspective. Even so, she could not completely disagree. Monk's Huntley grew lonelier for her every year, and yet Violet had been loath to leave it.

"Maybe we'll make happy memories there one day again," she said. "Eldbert and Ambrose will come back one day when they inherit."

"But you would never marry either of them, would you?" her aunt would innocently ask whenever the two gentlemen were mentioned.

"No, I wouldn't," Violet would answer, and then she and her aunt would end up laughing at the very idea.

"It's good to laugh again, Violet," her aunt said on one occasion. "Neither of us has laughed much since arriving in London."

It was true. The baroness had busied herself contacting old friends who might suggest a suitable husband for Violet. It wasn't until they met Sir Godfrey Maitland while buying umbrellas at one of the shops in his emporium that Violet took any interest at all in courtship.

She should have known that a romance sparked during a rainstorm was bound to fizzle before it caught fire. Her aunt approved of Godfrey's good manners and common sense. He was anything but a rake, and she and her aunt couldn't live on the baron's inheritance forever.

"Are you certain you're up for the sword fighting display, Aunt Francesca?" she asked in concern as her aunt rose from the couch of the retiring room. Francesca had grown frail in the last few months, and Violet worried about her all the time. She was the only family Violet had left.

"I shall be fine. Go and have a footman find us seats that are not too close to the stage."

"Of course," Violet said, and as she reached the

door, she glanced back. Godfrey had been taking fencing lessons for months and was about to perform in tonight's benefit.

"Off with you!" her aunt said.

So off Violet went, asking a young footman to show her the way, which he did until he was summoned by an older footman on an undisclosed emergency. "Wait here, miss," he said. "I shall be right back."

But after a few moments Violet wandered into an unlit antechamber that led to a staircase carpeted in rose and gold tones. Before she could change direction a small boy bearing two swords shot through the door and charged up the stairs, dropped one of his weapons, and vanished from sight.

"Excuse me," she called after him, bending to pick up a battered wooden sword. "I think you'll be missing this."

He didn't come back.

She straightened, swinging the well-worn weapon at the wall. It must have been a first toy. The grip felt smooth with use; not a splinter snagged her glove as she ran it along the short blade.

She gave it another experimental thrust. "Stay back, all of you," she instructed the peacock feathers that trembled in the pink vase that sat on the alcove table. "Let me pass and I promise to keep your whereabouts a secret. But you—"

She restrained a cry as a man in a fencing mask and padded jacket flew toward her through the curtained alcove adjacent to the feathers. "Don't say another word," he said, holding up his hand in warning. "Just between the two of us, the feathers can't be trusted."

She backed up a step, clutching the wooden sword. "Who . . ." Had she interrupted a part of the evening's performance? Was this a rehearsal or an actual act? She stared at the foil in the stranger's right hand. There weren't any other players in the vicinity.

But then again she was drifting about in a mansion that was owned by a member of the infamous Boscastle family. Her maid had warned her that the blood running in their veins must have been brewed from a love potion, and that their influence was contagious.

She stood in hesitation for a moment before instinct drove her back into a dark alcove. The swordsman paused, pivoting to study her with an intensity that made her grateful she could not see his face through the mask.

"I've made a fool of myself, haven't I?" she whispered.

He shook his head gallantly. "It's those treacherous feathers. They try to waylay me every time I go by here."

She sighed, burying the sword in her skirts. There was no point in hoping he hadn't seen it. "I feel ridiculous."

"Not at all," he said slowly, lowering his foil. "We have an escaped heir on our hands. It's a situation that tends to bring out one's protective instincts."

She felt a pleasant sting of familiarity jolt her. His voice held a sultry ring that infiltrated her awareness.

Whether he was acting or not, his sense of mischief was contagious. In fact, he might seem dangerous if he hadn't engaged her so easily. "In that case you're going in the wrong direction. The heir went up the stairs. I assume this was his sword."

He stared down at the wooden sword she had lifted into the light. "One of them. I hope he didn't attack you with it."

She smiled. "He was in such a rush, I don't think he even saw me."

"Small boys can be dangerous."

"Yes, I know." She handed him the sword. "Good luck in your quest."

He laughed, gave her a courtly bow, and reversed course. "*Merci, mademoiselle.* Forgive me if I startled you. And please forgive any unseemly giggles and shrieks of horror that you may hear when I find the culprit."

"Of course," she murmured, her gaze following his supple form as he climbed to the landing.

Something in his playful manner appealed to her. Her upbringing urged her to ignore him. But an unusual impulse overrode that cautious voice. It had been ages since she had been involved in lighthearted intrigue. It had been longer still since she had felt the least bit unrestrained. She couldn't picture Godfrey chasing a disobedient son during a party unless it was to discipline him.

Come to think of it, she could not picture Godfrey's children at all—a disconcerting thought, as she wanted a family, with all the warmth and noise and bother that children would bring. She had always wanted to be a mother, but why she should think of such a thing now, in the presence of a stranger, was perplexing.

The swordsman stopped in the middle of the stairs and turned. She felt him staring back at her through his mask. Of course, *she* had been staring at him, too. It wasn't every evening that one encountered a strong-limbed swordsman chasing the heir to a marquessate through a West End mansion. Still, for all Violet knew such events were commonplace in aristocratic homes.

"Are you lost?" the man on the landing inquired politely. "I didn't think to ask when I burst out onto the scene like Punchinello."

Violet retreated farther into the protective darkness of the alcove. She knew she ought to make an excuse and leave, but his courtly charm beguiled her. Even if it was part of a show, it was an enjoyable one. The stairs drew attention to his height and the width of his shoulders, to his lean torso and long, muscular legs. The mask lent him a mysterious appeal, and perhaps it also gave his voice that seductive pitch. The lowness of it enthralled her. "I think I have taken a wrong turn," she confessed.

"Where did you want to go? Not that I'm an expert on this house."

For a moment she was embarrassed that she couldn't remember. "I was supposed to be finding seats for the performance," she answered after a pause he was polite enough not to comment upon.

He dropped down a step. From the short distance

between them he radiated a danger that sent an arrow of warning straight to her heart. She shivered involuntarily as he let a long silence build before he spoke to her again.

"In *that* case," he said, "I will look for you from the stage. And when I ask for help from the audience, I hope that you'll volunteer. There is a seat in the second row, the first one from the center aisle, that will be reserved for you. Shall I show you the way?"

Violet shook her head and tried to gather herself. What had come over her? A stranger holding her spellbound. "I'm not an actress."

"I wouldn't have thought so for a moment."

"I'm hopeless at learning lines. I—"

He slipped down another three steps with an agility that appeared to be instinctual. "You don't have to say anything."

"But to stand up in front of the entire house? With everyone staring at—" She stopped. No one would be staring at an ordinary miss like her. He was one of the attractions tonight, and looking at him, she didn't wonder why. "I don't have the confidence," she admitted. "I wouldn't be able to repeat my own name."

"You don't have to." He gave a careless shrug. "All you have to do is stand up when I appear in the aisle and let me rescue you."

"From what?" she asked in the amused curiosity that her aunt had often predicted would get her in trouble.

"From marrying a villain."

"Ah," she said softly, as if she believed a word he said. "And how will you do that?"

"I'll swoop you up onto my horse while you are standing at the altar." He leaned back against the rosewood staircase railing. "Then all you have to remember is to put your arms around me and hold on tight."

"Put my arms around you?" she said with an incredulous laugh. "In front of the whole of Mayfair?"

"Well, it is for charity."

"And I suppose you are going to ask me to rehearse in private?"

It was his turn to laugh. "I wasn't. But if we had the time, I would be more than happy to oblige."

"That is terribly generous of you."

"It's no trouble at all."

"Perhaps not to you," she retorted, shaking her head.

He was silent for a moment. "I think you have the wrong impression. I don't ask just any lady I meet to take part in my act."

"Well, then, thank you for the honor."

"You still don't believe me."

"Does it matter?"

"I think it might. I think I've just been insulted."

"Some ladies might consider your offer insulting."

"Only if it was the kind of offer that you think it was. Which it wasn't."

She narrowed her gaze. "How do I know that?"

"I'll pay you fifty pounds if you can find another

lady in the house who can honestly claim that I offered her that chair."

"As if I can go about asking! And don't you have to find the missing heir?"

"I know where he is. He's waiting for me to pretend I'm in a panic."

Violet released a sigh, fighting the inexplicable urge to carry on the conversation. For all his banter, the man looked untamed and prone to stirring up trouble. He had certainly stirred up something inside Violet that she should have resisted.

She forced herself to turn. She was in no position to match wits with a stranger, no matter how attractive he might seem. "If you'll excuse me—"

"May I look for you later in the evening?"

What a persistent rogue. "It's probably not a good idea," she replied over her shoulder.

"I'm going to anyway," he said as she lifted her skirts to walk away. "Just remember—it's all for charity."

She wavered. There was something in his manner that tempted her to take another look.

Was she so vulnerable that she would fall prey to the first scoundrel who approached her at a party? She couldn't even see his face, and yet she felt as if she knew him. Well, he *was* performing with her fiancé. Godfrey might even have made friends with the rascal at the fencing academy; not that Godfrey enjoyed much of a social life outside his emporium.

"Miss Knowlton!" a feminine voice called from the end of the corridor. "I have been searching for you all over."

Violet spun around. Her hostess, Jane, the honey-haired Marchioness of Sedgecroft, beckoned to her from a gilt-paneled door. "Your aunt felt a little unwell."

Violet hurried toward her, relieved that the attractive stranger on the stairs had taken his cue to disappear before Jane could spot him. "What happened?" she asked the marchioness in concern.

"I was talking with her, and suddenly she complained of feeling light-headed." The marchioness took her hand, staring past Violet for a moment before she resumed her explanation. "Our physician has already examined her and given her a mild sedative. He couldn't find anything wrong, but with your permission he will visit her later, in a week or so."

"Perhaps I should take her home."

"I suggested that and she became very upset. Why don't you let her rest a few hours? I have the finest physician in London here tonight. I didn't want to alarm you. But I thought you ought to know."

She followed the marchioness up another private flight of stairs to an interior drawing room where two under footmen flanked the door. Her aunt rested on a chaise. She looked so pale and delicate that Violet's heart stopped for a moment.

"Aunt Francesca?"

Francesca's eyes fluttered open. She regarded Violet

with a frown. "Oh, dear. I think I've caused a fuss. You haven't missed Godfrey's performance, have you? He's worked dreadfully hard to impress everyone."

"There will be other times for Godfrey to impress us," Violet said firmly, sitting on the chair that the marchioness's under footman had brought for her.

"Your niece is right," the marchioness said. "The sword fighting display is marvelous, but it does not have a calming effect upon the senses. My son has been attacking the staff ever since he watched his fencing master rehearse last week."

"Swordplay, when done properly, is very romantic," Aunt Francesca said with a wistful smile. "Violet's uncle was wearing a sword when I first met him. Did I ever tell you that, Violet?"

"I don't think so," Violet said.

"There are many things I kept from you, Violet. But only because I meant to protect you."

"You *have* protected me. What is this fuss about?"

Aunt Francesca nodded tiredly. "You shouldn't be here with me. You have a new guardian now. He'll be looking for you in the audience. Go, and applaud him. And, Jane, see to your duties. You have a party to give. I shall not spoil everyone's fun."

Jane laughed. "I've had more fun in my day than a lady is allowed. Anyway, you and your niece will be back for other parties. I never met your husband, madam, but he was kind to my father when he was ill and by himself in Falmouth."

"Henry had a good heart," Francesca agreed. "Now enjoy the evening, please, or I shall feel dreadful about it."

"I like your niece," Jane said with a smile. "I might borrow her to take her shopping while she's in London."

"Please do," Francesca said. "She needs to be around someone young and full of life."

"I have to warn you of one thing," Jane said as she motioned Violet to the door. "I am known to be a little wicked at times, although I've quieted down somewhat since marrying the marquess."

Violet was shocked at her aunt's reply.

"I have made her a little too quiet for her own good."

Jane laughed again. "I can remedy that."

Chapter 4

$\mathcal{K}$it's assistant Kenneth spotted his master the moment he mounted the backstage stairs. "There you are!" He cut a swath at sword point through the pandemonium of fencing students, servants, and actors before his master could be claimed by another distraction. "How nice of you to join us, sir. We have twelve minutes left until the opening act. Lord Montplace has developed stage fright and is cowering in the curtains. Mr. Dawson has forgotten his lines, and I cannot find the dagger for *Hamlet*—"

He broke off to draw a breath.

Kit bent as a second assistant removed his mask and threw a black silk cape around his shoulders. "Then there will be a change in the last act." He motioned to the two gentlemen in cockaded hats who stood in the opposite wing, awaiting the stage director. "Mr. Jenner, practice passing your left foot again. No, no. Your *other* left. Do not expose your shoulder like that. Oh, for the love of—"

"The last act, sir," Kenneth prompted him. "Are you referring to Pierce's performance or the one in which you pick Tilly out of the audience and rescue her from the baron who killed her family?"

Kit frowned. "Leave that seat empty. It's only fair that I select a random guest from the audience to bring onstage."

"Does this random damsel have a name, sir?"

"I assume so." Why hadn't he asked her? Why had he practically walked her into the wall and warned her not to trust the feathers? She'd been too easy to tease.

"What do I tell Tilly, sir?"

"Promise her the pearl earbobs that she saw on Ludgate Hill."

"Master Fenton! Master Fenton! Pierce is going on and we don't have the dagger!"

"Damn it," he said softly. "I saw it a moment ago when I—"

"Here it is, sir!" his dresser interrupted, vaulting between the stage pulleys.

Someone bustled through the curtains from the stage, revealing the scenery of a Roman temple. As far as props went, Kit thought it convincing enough, except for the street vendor's wheelbarrow that sat between the two false pillars.

"Did they sell hot cross buns in ancient Rome?" he asked with a scowl.

"Well, I can't imagine why not," Kenneth said; then, "Ah, here comes Mr. Carroll now. And in costume. That's one disaster averted."

Kit stared down into the theater. Most of the seats had already been filled, except for a few in back—and the first one in the second row off the center aisle. Footmen hovered about offering the guests champagne and wine. That was good. A slightly foxed audience was easier to entertain. Too much alcohol, however, and there would be the inevitable fool jumping onstage in the middle of a sword fight.

Kit drew back. There was no sign of the mystery lady he'd met in the hall. He should have thought to remove his mask to get a better look at her. All he could remember was that she had dark hair and a reproachful smile and wore a lilac-gray gown that wrapped around her enticing curves like twilight.

It wasn't that he dallied with every pretty woman he met. God knew he'd almost been late to the performance, and he wasn't sure why he had stopped to tease her. Something about her had caught him by surprise. He didn't happen upon a lady whisking a wooden sword at the wall every evening. Especially not one with a tempting silhouette and dark eyes that sparkled with secrets and a mouth that he wanted to make smile and to kiss at the same time.

She reminded him . . . of whom? He searched his mind.

Damnation. She hadn't been one of the maidservants who made a fuss over him whenever he visited the house for lessons. He didn't think she was one of the young ladies who took tea with the marchioness from time to time and watched him fence with Master Rowan.

But he felt as if he knew her.

Which, of course, he didn't.

If she had a desire to meet him again, she had only to pick up a program to find his name. It wasn't as if he would be hiding in the wings all night.

The audience clapped and stood as the curtains closed on a scene from *Hamlet*. The master of ceremonies appeared onstage and promised over the uproar that more swashbuckling acts would follow after a brief intermission, and that any subscriptions bought tonight from Master Fenton's academy would be donated to charity.

Pierce Carroll, the academy's newest pupil, was still taking a bow when Kit vanished backstage and hurried into the retiring room. For a moment he expected to see his mentor and adoptive father, Captain Charles Fenton, hunched over a stool, criticizing and praising Kit in turns. He'd been dead four months now. But it didn't seem that long ago that he'd bought Kit's indenture, and Kit had thought it was the end of him. Instead, it had been the beginning.

There wasn't any doubt that he and Fenton had found each other at a low point in their lives. Fenton was a bastard when he drank, and Kit gave him hell in return. But he thought about Fenton all the time.

Tonight he swore he could feel his presence. He swore he could hear his father's voice. *Live with passion. Fight with honor. And look over your shoulder every now and then.*

Look over his shoulder?

Was that meant to be a warning?

His father didn't answer.

Another voice intruded on his thoughts.

"They love you, sir." Pierce slipped inside the room, his face lean and clean shaven. "Did I do well enough?"

Kit grabbed one of the damp towels on the dressing table and rubbed it over his jaw. "You know you did."

Kenneth poked his head in the door. "Sir Godfrey is on next!"

Kit buckled on the sword belt that his valet had thrown at him. "Remind him that the light in Pierce's lantern is alive. He is not to fling his cloak anywhere near the curtains. Encourage the audience to hiss when Pierce sneaks on the stage and to applaud when Sir Godfrey wins the duel."

"Yes, sir."

"And . . . have any messages been sent to me in the past hour?"

"Messages? Oh, yes, sir. The senior footman of the house has sent word that the marchioness thanks you for finding the young master for her."

"Oh. Good."

"And some other guests are inquiring about the availability of private lessons through July. A member of Parliament wishes to take up the sword again, at his wife's encouragement. Seems your swordplay lit a dying spark, sir."

"Splendid." He wasn't averse to additional income, nor to enhancing the romance of the sword. But he *would* appreciate having the privacy to stir up a little passion in his own life.

"Actually, Kenneth," he admitted, shying away from the brush his valet bore toward his head, "I was thinking—*ouch*—of a more personal message, from—"

The valet's brush stilled, caught in Kit's hair. "Ah. A liaison?" Martin said, eyeing Kit over the lowering brush. "Well, why didn't you say so in the first place? There were a legion of them. I sent the footman packing and tore up the messages. We don't want those nasty women around here."

He ducked the valet and swung around in disbelief. "You did what?"

"You said we should never let a flirtation distract you from a lesson, duel, or performance. I thought I'd be doing you a favor by keeping your mind on course. Wait. There was one message that I promised to give you."

"Well."

The valet lowered his voice self-consciously. "The viscountess said—"

"That's enough, Martin. She isn't the distraction I was hoping for."

By the time Violet was convinced that her aunt felt better, she had missed all but the closing acts. Not wanting to disturb anyone, she took a seat at the back of the theater. The audience seemed in high spirits, speculating in whispers what the finale would include. The master of ceremonies was taking bids for a midnight duel with the sword master, all the proceeds to benefit an orphanage or hospital of their choice. It sounded like fun, Violet thought, and if she had a decent purse, she might have bid herself.

She wouldn't have been the only lady in the audience to do so. The sword master counted plenty of female followers.

She studied the stage, wishing she had been able to find a closer seat. Judging by the set, a candlelit altar and church interior, it seemed like the next scene would be a romantic act. What part would the masked rogue she'd met tonight play? Had she missed him? Godfrey had talked only about his own role. In fact, he'd talked about it so much that Violet felt she *had* seen it. Or she could convince him she had.

"Ladies and gentlemen! May we have silence in the theater?" The apron lights dimmed. The crowd hushed. "Thank you," the master of ceremonies said. He paused to acknowledge the marquess and his family in the upper gallery. "And now for our finale, we require one brave young lady from the audience—"

A commotion broke out across the theater. Countless white-gloved hands crested the air like waves. One of the footmen behind Violet said to another, "If only the army could get volunteers that easily."

Volunteers for what?

The master of ceremonies selected a blond woman in a pale yellow dress from the second row. Sighs of disappointment escaped the ladies not chosen. Violet regarded the empty seat with a wry smile. First seat on the right from the center aisle. Well, it hadn't taken the rogue long to replace her.

She sat forward, interested to see what mischief she had missed. Would she regret her decision to remain uninvolved? Probably not. She had grown remarkably staid in recent years. Like most young gentlewomen she had learned that a lady obeyed the rules, or broke them to her rue.

The act turned out to be an adventurous escapade that delighted the audience, performed in high-spirited energy. A black-garbed swordsman paraded a white stallion through the theater and up onto the stage to rescue an unwilling bride from a wedding altar. A lively duel between the rescuer and the enraged bridegroom and his retainers ensued.

Violet noticed two assistants waiting at the end of each aisle to catch the horse and its rescued bride, who dismounted as skillfully as a cavalry officer. Of course it was all staged. The rescued damsel worked for the scalawag dancing the villain across the stage at sword point.

To Violet's frustration he moved too fast for her to get a clear look at him. Strong chin. Limbs as flexible as a dancer's. Dark silky hair with glints of gold. She felt her skin tingle in recognition.

Just because he'd flirted with her in a hallway? And what part in this performance had he expected her to play? Not only an onstage role, but a private one, no doubt. A backstage affair. Godfrey would have a word

or two to say about *that*. Furthermore, he would have
died of shock if Violet had ridden a horse through the
theater, her ankles exposed to the audience.

*All you have to remember is to put your arms around
me and hold on tight.*

In that moment, if she could have reached the
swordsman, she might have done exactly that.

The action onstage commanded her attention. But in
less than a minute the mood of mischief darkened to
menace. From behind the pews of the chapel innumerable enemy soldiers sprang up like dragon's teeth to
challenge the stolen bride's defender. Violet soon forgot this was a performance.

She barely noticed when a footman ushered a late-
arriving guest into the seat beside her. The swordsman
leaped over the pews with his back to the church altar,
his enemies forcing his retreat. One by one, he beat
them down until at last he stood against a stained-
glass window, trapped, outnumbered.

Violet frowned, caught up in the outcome. The figure onstage represented chivalry, vulnerability, and
the unconquerable power of right. He exemplified
the courtier who refused to bend to any power but
one who treated his subjects with grace. How could
this brave knight find victory? It looked as if he were
done for.

She cringed as an enemy swordsman disarmed
him, slashing a bloody wound from the shoulder of
his tunic to his hip. She knew perfectly well it wasn't
real blood. But she and several other ladies gasped all

the same. His sword clattered to the stone floor of the chapel.

How at the last hour could a defenseless hero win?

All appeared to be lost.

He fell to his knees, his silky hair covering his face, blood running from his wounds.

Was the audience to be left unsettled and helpless, with even a theatrical triumph denied? The hero they had championed could not die at an altar, grace and victory snatched from his hand.

The light that pierced the stained-glass window behind the fallen knight faded. The stage went dark. Violet felt the uneasiness that gripped the audience.

The knight could not fail. Evil must not win.

The curtain closed on his unmoving figure. Was it over?

"For God's sake," one gentleman muttered, "get up. It cannot end like this."

"Get up!"

"Get up!"

The audience chanted the words with righteous anger, with passion. Their voices resounded to the painted medallions of the soaring plaster ceiling. The swell of emotion that swept through the small theater mounted until Violet's very pulse echoed the same refrain.

Get up. Get up. She knew it wasn't real. And yet she believed in the hero's pain with all her heart. *Get up. Get up.*

Show us it can be done. Give us courage. Help us. Stand up for what is right.

It's only an act, she thought. *The fallen swordsman was just trying to make an assignation with me. Of course he isn't going to die.* The cheeky rogue had the vigor of a dozen men.

"Get up," she whispered, her voice joining the others. And as she spoke an image from long ago stirred in her mind. "Get up," she said, shaking her head in frustration as the image subsided before it could take shape.

He reminded her of . . .

The curtains opened again. Mist swirled around the warrior, who slowly rose to approach a massive anvil in which was embedded a sword.

Appearing from the wings to flank him at either side came a dozen knights in foot chains. One dared throw him a pair of gauntlets. A second wiped the blood from his shoulder with a cloth. Two others defied their captors by struggling free and helping him put on a tunic. A fifth knight—heavens above, Violet thought, stifling a giggle, it was Godfrey—knelt at his side.

When the knight stood, the audience held its collective breath. And when he pulled the stone from the anvil, he rose above disgrace to defend those who could not defend themselves. The sword glittered over his head. It shone as he lifted it to the cheering audience, a young Arthur in a satin tunic. It rang as he broke the chains that bound his knights.

Violet sniffed. He reminded her of every girl's hero, she supposed. A man who could chase a child through a house when he was about to perform the show of the season and *not* lose his patience. A man who even managed to plot an after-performance rendezvous.

A legendary hero or a consummate artist? Perhaps it didn't matter. Tonight he had staged a call to arms to help the downtrodden, using the romance of the sword to inspire. Never mind that he had inspired romantic notions in the ladies watching him, Violet included. She gave a sigh.

No wonder Godfrey bragged that he was one of only twelve students chosen to perform. And what dreadful timing for Violet to miss his important scene. She would never hear the end of it.

The end.

She blinked.

The Marquess of Sedgecroft had come onstage to deliver his final words.

The crowd cheered wildly. Grayson Boscastle, the fifth marquess, was a gregarious lion of a man, beloved by London society despite, or perhaps because of, his previous sins.

"We are all of us tonight a privileged class," he addressed the audience. "We have dined on the food prepared by the finest chefs in England this evening. We have been well entertained. And we have no doubt spent more hours pondering our evening dress than we have the beggars we passed on our way to the tailor's or the mantua maker's. But for your generosity, the destitute, the downtrodden, and I thank you. And for the heart-stopping sword duels in which my son is eager to engage me, I thank Master Fenton and the dedicated students of his academy."

Master Fenton.

He appeared at Sedgecroft's side, the epitome of sensual elegance. Violet couldn't take her eyes from him.

She wished she hadn't come here tonight.

A horrible pain had pierced her heart. It took her a moment to work out what she was feeling, but then she knew. It was the pain of wanting what could never be.

To think she had been instantly attracted to that gorgeous and graceful man. How shocking of her. Virtuous Miss Violet Knowlton should never have even contemplated such a romance.

It was better to consider this a case of infatuation at first sight. Did she believe such a thing was possible? But how else could she explain the strange connection she had felt to him, as if she had known the alluring Fenton all her life?

There was a simple explanation.

She had fallen in love with a romantic hero, as had so many ladies in the audience.

Christopher Fenton.

The name wasn't familiar.

He took three bows to thunderous applause.

And then quickly disappeared from the stage.

Chapter 5

$\mathcal{V}$iolet noticed that she wasn't the only member of the audience mesmerized by the performance. Several guests remained in their seats, staring at the deserted stage. Even the gentlemen could be overheard lavishing praise on the dramatic spectacle.

"Yes, yes," one said. "I know it was nothing but an illusion. Well, illusion and skill and hard practice. But with the world as disillusioned as it is, what is wrong with a night of forgetting what one may face tomorrow? We need to be uplifted to carry on."

Violet silently agreed. Illusion. Yes, knightly tales and gentlemen fighting off street ruffians made for good drama.

"He *is* magnificent," a woman whispered in the shadows somewhere behind Violet. "I vow he's seduced the entire house. It isn't fair. I spotted him first. Now every lady in town knows who he is."

"Be quiet," her companion said with an embarrassed laugh. "He might still be backstage and listening."

"Good. Then I can make him an offer. It's said that his sword can be bought."

Violet rose to her feet in indignation. How dared this vulgar woman ruin all the lovely feelings that his performance had awakened?

She turned. She knew better than to venture an unsolicited opinion, but before she could stop herself, she blurted out, "Isn't he known for his chivalry?"

The two ladies stared at her in annoyance. The first, flawless in a costly cream silk gown, smiled. "Would you like me to let you know when I find out?"

The other woman sighed. "There's no need to taunt her. She looks as fresh as a May queen."

Violet lowered her gaze, surprised at her outburst. *She's wrong,* she thought as the ladies exited the theater, laughing all the way. *He can't be bought. Not like that.* At least, she hoped he couldn't.

"I'm not fresh, either," she muttered, turning again without looking where she was going.

"Excuse me, miss."

She blushed. Not only had she walked into a footman, but it was the same one she had lost earlier in the night. "I'm so sorry."

"It's quite all right, miss."

In fact, she was so flustered that she started when she felt a firm hand turn her by the elbow toward the door. She wasn't quite ready to join the rest of the party. She needed a moment more for her daze of emotions to settle. She wanted to linger just a little longer in a world where a happy ending was assured.

The magic would wear off by morning. It might be gone before she reached the carriage and returned home. Except . . . there was still a ball to attend, and dancing always brightened her spirits.

She cast a wistful look at the empty chair in the second row and looked up into Sir Godfrey Maitland's smug face. "Well, what did you think?"

"What a wonderful entertainment."

He was still wearing his sword and theatrical garb, glancing about every few seconds to acknowledge a compliment from guests who recognized him as one of the players. "And my act?"

"I missed your performance," she said quickly. "But I saw you at the end."

"You did what?"

"After Aunt Francesca took unwell, I didn't know—I went the wrong way and—"

"You missed *my* performance?"

She nodded slowly. She wasn't ready to tell him about the interlude in the hallway with his fencing instructor. In hindsight it was fortunate that she hadn't given her name or engaged in any flirtatious gestures that could have been carried back to Godfrey.

"Well, you wouldn't have wanted for anything to happen to my aunt for the sake of a little sword fight. And the marchioness was so kind—"

"The marchioness?" He drew her away from the

crowd of chattering guests that spilled out into one of three halls. "You spoke to her in person?"

"Yes, Godfrey. She took Aunt Francesca upstairs into—" A small group of ladies and gentlemen broke between them, tossing back apologies as an afterthought. "I did mention that my uncle befriended Lady Sedgecroft's father in Falmouth years ago."

"Yes, but I didn't realize she would go out of her way to return the favor," Godfrey said. "This might end up being the best thing that has ever happened to us." He gripped her arm and pulled them back into the flow of traffic. "I don't mean that Francesca is unwell, of course, but that you've strengthened your connection to Sedgecroft's wife and I have been invited to a private party—"

Violet looked past him, her attention diverted. A commotion had erupted at the end of the hall; a surge of energy swept through the air, and she felt herself caught up in its undercurrents. Some excitement had attracted all the young ladies to the masterful figures posed on various steps of the marble staircase.

"It's Fenton and his players," Godfrey remarked in surprise. "They're being interviewed, and I'm supposed to be part of it. You don't really mind, do you, Violet, if I leave you alone with Francesca for an hour? I've been invited upstairs."

"How pleasant for you, Godfrey."

"It's an exclusive affair for the gentlemen who performed or contributed heavily to the benefit."

She widened her eyes. "So there won't be any actresses or wives?"

"As if a woman of your beauty and virtue had reason to be jealous of another."

"Just remember these are business connections," she said under her fan.

"I'll do my best," he said softly against her cheek. "And you remember that we're going to another fencing competition at Hyde Park the day after tomorrow. *This* time you *will* watch my performance. I shall see you shortly at the ball. Don't forget to be agreeable to anyone you meet.

"If anyone should ask where I am on your way out," he added, "tell them I am attending a private party with Sedgecroft and Fenton."

Against her will Violet glanced over the crowd to the figure who had turned to mount the double staircase. He was dressed simply, in a white linen shirt and tight black pantaloons. She couldn't see whether he was wearing a sword or not, but as the other players were, she thought he might be. He was attractive, nonetheless.

Fenton. He shook his head when a gentleman offered him a champagne flute. He appeared to be searching the crowd for someone. She assumed that this time it wasn't a lost child.

Perhaps he'd been in an unguarded mood when she'd met him earlier. He didn't look as playful or approachable now. But then, he was caught in a crowd, and everyone seemed to be vying for his attention.

Any other man would have been exhausted after his strenuous performance.

He still exuded enough vitality to charge the room.

Was it possible that he was looking for a way to escape, or for her? No. She was a ninny for letting the thought cross her mind. How many times had her aunt told her that one lady was never enough for a rogue?

"Do you want to meet him?" Godfrey asked her unexpectedly. He must have noticed the direction of her gaze. Then, before she could answer, he lifted his arms over his head. "Fenton! Over here, by the door!"

Fenton turned in Violet's direction.

And Violet caught a tantalizing glimpse of his face before he noticed Godfrey waving his arms like a windmill, and glanced the other way.

Oh, dear.

Whomever he was looking for, it wasn't Godfrey. In fact, Violet felt embarrassed on her fiancé's account. He acted at times with a sense of entitlement that tempted her to pretend she didn't know him.

He had seemed pleasant during their short courtship. A well-mannered gentleman who would make a faithful husband. But little by little she had seen glimpses of a callous heart behind what she feared was superficial charm.

The sword master's gaze met hers for a moment as he looked back toward them. As his eyes brushed over her, a peculiar awareness coursed through her blood, as if she had been turned upside down and set back on her feet.

"Who is he again?" she asked in a hesitant voice, knowing what the answer would be.

"What?" Godfrey swung around, lowering his arms to stare at her. "Fenton. Christopher Fenton. I have mentioned him countless times. He's performed in private for the prince regent."

"Has he?" Violet asked, hoping she looked properly impressed, and not like a lady who had been invited to participate in one of Fenton's performances.

"Do let me go now, darling. The other gentlemen have already gone upstairs to the gallery. It's like a private club, you know."

"For scoundrels."

"Honestly, Violet. What a remark to make. I hope you will refrain from expressing comments like that to anyone else. It isn't typical of you at all. I suggest you stay away from the champagne. It must be more potent than it tasted."

Kit studied the clock in the corner of the candlelit gallery. The private chamber was known for the high-society seductions that had been sparked within its walls. He knew he should consider it an honor to be invited to mingle with the chosen few whom it pleased his host and patron to bring together for a brief interlude before the ball, but there wasn't a woman in the room who drew Kit's interest. He avoided looking at the viscountess in cream silk who half reclined in shameless invitation on the brocade sofa. She made it obvious what she wanted. Her eyes had been undressing him all evening.

He felt like stripping off a shirt and striking a pose with the other Roman statues against the wall. He wondered how attractive she'd find him if she knew the truth about his past.

The shame of it had discouraged him from any lasting relationships with the gentlewomen he'd met.

"She's a bit obvious," an amused voice said over his shoulder. "Why don't you put her out of her misery and arrange a liaison with her for later in the night?"

He turned to Sir Godfrey with a wan smile. "She happens to have a husband."

"And you aren't eager to put your dueling skills to the test?"

"Not without a better reason. Besides, sir, you've taken lessons long enough to know that I counsel self-control."

"I can't argue with that."

Not since petitioning to earn his diploma as a *maître d'armes* in France with his adoptive father's influence had Kit allowed himself to be provoked into a genuine match. It would take an unthinkable insult for a master to issue a rash challenge. It would be a disgrace to kill someone unskilled. He'd decided years ago that he would rather peddle dreams to adventurous students than murder another man to prove his superiority.

On occasion, though, a challenge arose that could not be ignored. Some brash fool needed to show the world how exceptional he was.

He dealt with these unfortunates once or twice a year. The match usually involved a prodigious quantity of spirits and a woman who looked prettier through a pair of drunken eyes than she did the next morning. But Kit had seen too much sin in his life to find adultery the least bit appealing.

Of course, as a maestro, he was not above a friendly crossing of the blades when challenged, for a few extra pounds. It never hurt to pad one's pockets.

Sir Godfrey took a deep swallow from his goblet. "You won the crowd tonight. I believe you could have your choice of nearly any woman in London as your bed partner after that rousing performance."

"Now, that is an exaggeration," Kit said with a laugh. Even if it were true, there was only one woman who came to mind. He didn't know her name. He hadn't had the wits to ask, but he knew that she wasn't in this room and that she hadn't been the type to fall for a scoundrel's flirtation in an empty corridor. Nor had she accepted his invitation to take a seat of dubious honor in the audience.

He couldn't explain why he'd felt drawn to her, as if he could talk to her as a friend.

Sweetness, sensual appeal, and an instant sense of compatibility in the same woman. Kit didn't meet many ladies like her. His lovers and friends tended to fall into distinctly separate groups. He had to wonder what she was doing at a party like this. She seemed over her head.

But then again, Kit didn't belong here, either. He

gave lessons to gentlemen. He wasn't one of them. Tonight he had entertained the ton on a grand scale. For
all their accolades, he remained a commoner who depended on men like Sir Godfrey to earn his living.

"You executed the cloak-and-lantern episode without a flaw," he said, resisting the urge to look at the
clock again. "Not one hesitant move. I daresay a thief
would think twice about assaulting you."

"A pity that the lady I wanted to impress missed my
performance. All because of her doddering old aunt."

Kit pretended to appear sympathetic. The truth was
that he liked Sir Godfrey a little less every time they
talked. He had a double-sided nature that included de-
meaning the aristocrats he envied and the lower classes
he employed in his business affairs as a merchant. He
saw sword fighting as a means to impress others, not
as an art. An intelligent man, but not a particularly
kind one.

Godfrey gestured with his goblet to the far wall.
"Do you have any notion how much those Roman statues cost?"

Kit liked new objets d'art when he could afford
them. But then he wasn't an aristocrat. He couldn't sit
on his arse all day admiring ruins. He had to work for
his bread.

"I don't even know if they are real," he said honestly.

"It wouldn't matter much to mortals like us if
they're fake," Godfrey replied. "Replicates go for a fortune on the retail market. The past is all the rage. Do

you know how my fiancée has asked to spend the next few days?"

"Visiting the museum?" Kit guessed.

"That would be an understandable activity," Godfrey said. "But no. She is begging to see an exhibit of ancient tombstones. Can you imagine? A beautiful lady willing to pay to poke about a stranger's grave."

"As you say, it is the rage." What Kit really wondered, and then for only a moment, was what kind of woman would measure up to Sir Godfrey's ideals. "Why are you indulging her, if I may ask?"

"You may, since I brought up the subject. I am besotted with her. I was quite surprised when she agreed to marry me, and even then she did so with reluctance. There were three other men in competition for her hand. She chose me." He drained his goblet. "Or rather, her aunt did. I had to convince the old lady to pick me."

"Because you were . . . ?"

"Because I had the best manners and I was not a rake. When you meet my betrothed, perhaps you will understand why I was desperate to have her."

"Is she that beautiful?"

"Yes. She's an heiress, too, which doesn't hurt, if you take my meaning."

When Baron Ashfield died, Francesca lost the best friend she had ever known. Her father had chosen young Henry for her when she was seventeen and

Ashfield was serving in the army. A sensible arrangement, Papa insisted, and Francesca had wept for weeks because she loved the vicar's nephew, and if that was not a *sensible* choice she could not imagine who was.

She had cringed when she met the baron, an ungainly man twice her size who rarely spoke, and then in halting half thoughts that made her question his mental faculties. It was only after three years of marriage that he confessed how dearly he loved her.

She had been languishing in bed, despondent after the last of four miscarriages and the realization that she would never carry a child. She had never suspected a man could be capable of such grief or emotion. "Please, Henry, one of us must remain calm."

"Well, then, Francesca, it will have to be you," he had said in a choked-up voice, "because you have brought me to my knees. I loved you the minute I saw you. I loved our lost children when you conceived them and—"

"Why did you not tell me this before?"

He'd hung his head. "I was afraid that you would take my affection for you as a sign of weakness."

She had placed her hand on his shoulder. "Am I that much of a Tartar that I cannot be told the truth?"

She had never noticed that his eyes brightened whenever she paid him attention. She had been so preoccupied with imitating the aloof marriage of her parents that it hadn't occurred to her that it was possible to build abiding love upon affection. Upon a basic friendship.

He'd looked up quickly. "Yes," he had said, "you are. And you are going to ruin Violet's chance for genuine happiness with all your fears."

Now Francesca sat with the other matrons in a quiet corner of the brilliantly candlelit ballroom. *What have I done? I was so worried that a rogue would take advantage of Violet's nature that I pushed her into Godfrey's arms. Why did you leave me to make this decision, Henry? Why did you have to die before I had to decide? Why did you have to die at all?*

Sir Godfrey *had* seemed to be the ideal suitor, a match that aimed neither too high nor too low. He was a self-made merchant who led a circumspect life. She had wanted Violet to have a stable marriage and surround Francesca with grandchildren before she died. She had not realized, however, that Sir Godfrey counted on her being dead before such a time.

Tonight, when Francesca had taken her turn, she had heard the truth revealed in Godfrey's voice as he questioned the physician outside the door. The marchioness had summoned him from backstage, against Francesca's wishes.

"How long can she go on?"

"That is not for you to decide, sir."

"She cannot live forever, can she?"

"Forever? No, sir. But she is in good health, as far as I can tell. It is grief, in my opinion, that has weakened her."

She knew she wouldn't live forever. Her only purpose was to help Violet find the happiness Violet's mother had thrown away during her short life. Anne-Marie's ghost would never stop haunting Francesca if she broke her vow to protect Violet.

She had chosen Sir Godfrey for Violet for all the right reasons.

Was it unreasonable to hope that a righteous marriage would come of her good intentions?

Had she been wrong to value reputation above love? It was natural for a man to hope for an inheritance, wasn't it? It wasn't possible that Godfrey was marrying Violet solely for the money she would soon have.

Sudden quiet enshrouded the ballroom. Francesca turned, distracted, to watch the couple who had been announced at the door.

A broad-shouldered gentleman in black crossed the ballroom, a lady in flowing pink silk holding his arm. The entire assembly seemed awestruck by the formal entry of the party's host and his elegant wife, the Marquess and Marchioness of Sedgecroft.

According to gossip, which Francesca gleaned primarily from her maid, the marquess had once been considered London's most notorious scoundrel. Perhaps he still was. It was rumored that he had fallen in love with the bride who had been abandoned at the altar by his cousin. No. That was not right. The marchioness had botched her own wedding.

Faugh. London and its scandals. Francesca thought that Jane was an enchanting woman. The evening, she reminded herself, was a benefit performance. The look of unadulterated devotion that Sedgecroft gave his wife appeared genuine to Francesca's eyes.

A fresh wave of excited whispers swelled.

Francesca sat up to locate the source of the furor.

Another man had followed the marquess into the ballroom.

He was a man whose presence caused chairs to be scraped back, footmen to straighten, ladies and gentlemen young and old to vent approving sighs.

Francesca wished for a quizzing glass. Was this the marquess's son? She compared the two attractive figures in silence. No. They were too close in age, even for prematurely sewn oats.

Cousins, perhaps. The marquess motioned the younger man into his intimate circle.

Perhaps, if not for the matron beside her, Francesca would have withdrawn back into her thoughts. But the lady, who clearly meant to be kind, leaned toward Francesca and said, "I almost miss the danger of the past century's duels. At least one could address an enemy with dignity and skill."

Francesca studied the young man who had caused such a stir.

He did not possess the arrogance of a peer. He looked, in fact, rather unassuming, possibly amused to find himself the center of attention.

He was lithe, light on his feet. He wore the plainest clothes of any gentleman Francesca had observed that night. A flowing shirt of fine linen. Dark breeches of an indeterminate fabric. And yet an irresistible elegance radiated from his person.

He was indeed a young man who drew one's notice—to Francesca's surprise he seemed to have caught even Violet's attention. Francesca half rose from her chair, as if she could act as a barrier before this questionable connection.

Too late.

The handsome newcomer had also noticed her niece.

He had turned his back on the marquess and was cutting a path toward Violet as precisely as a pair of tailor's scissors through silk. And it was Sir Godfrey, the man meant to protect Violet, who appeared to be summoning him to her side.

Chapter 6

The chamber players began to warm up their instruments after Kit followed his host into the ballroom. The Marquess of Sedgecroft had insisted that Kit attend the dance. Kit could not refuse. As Sedgecroft said, "You are the hero of the hour, Fenton. My guests paid to see you perform. Your performance is not quite over."

Agreed.

The orchestra started to play, and the melodious notes of violins, flutes, and French horns competed with the chatter of guests in the ballroom. The clamor rose as Sir Godfrey approached Kit with a brunette in lilac-gray silk on his arm. Godfrey said something over the music.

Kit didn't understand a thing through the blood that rushed to his head.

He stared at Violet and only a moment passed before he recognized her. He would have known her in the hall if it hadn't been for his mask and the dark shadows and the decade that had changed her. He stared at her and felt himself as challenged by her presence as he had the day she had first confronted him in the churchyard. He knew he was expected to make some polite response. But she was beautiful, and he was soaking in the sight of her after too many years.

Sir Godfrey had bragged of her charm. This could not be the first time a man had faltered when introduced to her. It was better to say nothing and appear awkward than to give her away. She would be shamed if Kit revealed that she had befriended him once upon a time when he was a beast and she was a lovely girl.

Now he was a larger beast and she was a lovelier woman. Some things never changed. Could he still convince her that he was worth her company?

"Master Fenton?" a voice said, and he ignored it.

Did Violet recognize him? No wonder he'd been attracted to her in the hall. No wonder they could talk to each other like old friends.

"Fenton?" the voice repeated.

There was so much to say, and yet discretion forbade that Kit say anything at all. Violet was the prize that one of his students had pursued and won. Godfrey, of all persons. A petty man whose only charity was himself. How in the hell had that happened? She had to be marrying him for his money. But that didn't seem like the Violet whom Kit had known.

The warmth and wicked remembrance that glowed in her dark eyes acknowledged their secret pact from childhood. He turned, irritated at the voice that finally intruded on his thoughts. Sir Godfrey was getting on his nerves.

"Master Fenton," Godfrey said, "may I *again* present to you my enchanting fiancée, Miss Violet Knowlton. Master Fenton is my instructor, Violet. In fact, he will go down the dance with you while I accompany Lady Heyville. She is one of our best customers, you will recall."

Kit turned back to Violet, inclining his head. "It is my pleasure," he said meaningfully.

"No," she said, her voice strong. "It is mine."

"An honor then," he said.

Then they looked each other in the eye, and the blood that had rushed between Kit's temples hit him in the center of his heart. And he was grateful that there were other people standing around them, because he might have said or done something unpardonable otherwise.

"Be on guard, Master Fenton," Sir Godfrey said with a pleasant smile as he walked away. "She dances like a dream."

Kit stared spellbound at Violet.

Of course she did. She was a dream. He'd dreamed about her so often that it wasn't surprising he felt as if he'd known her when he saw her in the hall with the toy sword. Violet had been the chink in his armor before, and maybe she still was. She had always looked a little lost to him, as if she were a deposed princess in need of a protector. But talk about the damned leading the damned.

She might have been brave to venture into the churchyard, or more likely she'd been driven by a desire for friends. But now that Kit was old enough to ponder the past, he realized she had put herself in a vulnerable position.

Hell. She was still vulnerable. Who had been taking care of her all these years? It was a good thing he hadn't been as dangerous then as he'd pretended he was. Now was another matter.

He smiled, knowing she'd be offended if she could hear his thoughts. He had managed to offend her tonight without even trying. His lonely girl. Why else had she made friends with a pauper? Lonely or not, she was who he dreamed about when he felt most alone.

She had been his morning star, and he had found her in the dark again.

She shook her head, her eyes lowering as Godfrey disappeared. "I should have known it was you," she said, releasing a rueful sigh. "I never could resist your swordplay."

"Dear God, Violet," he said in an undertone. "How could I not have realized it was you in the hall? You look much the same, but you're so beautiful—"

"Meaning that I wasn't beautiful before?" she asked, her voice amused.

"Not in the way you are now," he said, his eyes drifting from her face over her curvaceous form. "And I never thought about you like that before." But he did tonight, God help him. The sight of her was going to feed another decade of dreams.

"You're quite handsome yourself," she said with a quick smile.

He shook his head. "It might be a good thing I didn't recognize you right away. I probably wouldn't have been able to perform. I would have impaled someone on my sword if I'd known you were watching."

She laughed at that. "I doubt it. You controlled that sword as if it were part of your arm. I admire you more than I can say. You've come a long way, Kit. From a workhouse in Monk's Huntley to a mansion in Mayfair."

"It doesn't feel like it right now." He still wanted to be the center of her attention. "What are you doing in London?"

She sobered. "Getting married."

He glanced across the ballroom, his face disapproving. It couldn't be. "Not to the haberdasher?"

She frowned. "That isn't very nice."

Neither was the haberdasher. And now Kit had another reason to dislike him. "Isn't that what he is?"

"He started out as a haberdasher," she said. "But he owns the entire emporium and plans to buy another arcade."

"Well, joy to the world," Kit said. "That's just what it needs."

Violet arched her brow. "I can see someone still has a little of the wicked left inside him."

"That might be true," he admitted. "But God knows I'm better than I was before."

"After what I saw of you tonight, I'd have to agree.

How did it happen?" she asked in a whisper. "When I last saw you, I wasn't sure how you were going to end up."

"That's a kind way to put it. What you mean to say is that you weren't sure I wasn't going to come to an end."

"No. I didn't."

"We all thought that I was done for, Violet."

"I was half convinced your departure would be the end of me, too," she confessed.

"Well, thank God it wasn't," he said with passion. "You've turned out finer than anything I could have hoped for."

He wished his heart would stop racing. There had never been anyone else like her in his life. "If you give me a chance, I'll tell you more after the dance ends. That is, if it ever—"

The chamber music built to a majestic swell and broke across the ballroom before Kit could finish. Footmen lowered candles in the outer girandoles and escorted onlookers to chairs. Gentlemen discarded their dress swords at the last instant and handed them off for the safety of the other dancers.

Kit shook his head and moved closer to her, realizing that the other dancers were lining up for him to lead. Meeting Violet on the night of his grandest benefit almost made him believe in destiny. He wasn't sure whether she ought to view it as good fortune or not. Or whether she'd want anything to do with him after this.

Careful.

Watch your opponent.

Parry.

Save your best move for the last moment.

Except that she had saved him a decade ago. She was anything but an opponent. Every fight he'd won since then was dedicated to her. He didn't want to engage her in a duel—he wanted to engage her in another kind of battle, one that didn't have to come to a bad end, or end at all. This was a night for charity. Could he plead that he needed her again?

"Do you remember the 'Bleeding Idiots'?" she asked.

He pretended to look puzzled. "Is that a division of the infantry?"

"Pardon me," she said so softly that he had to lean toward her to listen, and his chin grazed the lush hair that her pearl comb could barely tame. "I must have mistaken you for another misfit."

He glanced up, staring around the ballroom as if he were vaguely bored, detached, when every thread that held him together was stretched tight in restraint. "There is no mistake," he replied at last. "I am, indeed, the misfit you made a pact with. But I think we're going to have to dig a little deeper into our history than the last day we were together."

"Oh?" she asked, intrigued.

He nodded. "I think we should relive the first one, when I took you hostage."

The dance began.

* * *

If Violet had never before appreciated all the dance lessons her aunt had given her, she did now. She needed to rely on craft or Kit would break her concentration. He was a physical man, unaffected and compelling in his mere presence. She would have been awed by his masculinity even if he weren't the friend she had never forgotten. But their friendship added a secret intimacy, a whisper of spice to their reunion. She wanted, wickedly enough, to touch him. To stare into his eyes.

How was any privacy possible in a crowded ballroom?

They crossed hands and swirled through the line. Violet glimpsed the surprised faces of the guests they passed. She felt sorry for them. It was all she could do to keep up with her partner herself. "I have a feeling we aren't doing this dance properly," she said breathlessly. "What is it patterned after?"

He skipped back a few steps, made a bow, and turned the other way. "The last duel I fought in Paris."

"It isn't."

He looked at her, lifting her hand for the arch. "No." He grinned. "It was in Spain. I had just gotten my first sword and I thought I could fight anybody. Needless to say, I lost the duel and had to learn a Gypsy dance as part of the deal."

She laughed, catching her breath. "Do you know what is most amazing about tonight?"

"That we didn't recognize each other in the hall right away?"

"No. That your swordplay draws a crowd and that you started out practicing with a hoe."

"I'm good at improvising," he said with a rueful grin.

"I think you must have a metronome hidden in you somewhere."

"You don't seem to have any trouble keeping up," he noted.

"I can control my motions," she said, "*most* of the time. It's one thing to anticipate music heralding a change in a direction when it's an established dance. But it's another to be able to follow your lead. In what direction, if you don't mind my asking, are you trying to lead me?"

"Out of the ballroom, if I can."

"With everyone lining up behind us?"

He broke into a laugh. "I didn't consider that."

"You opened the dance."

"Does that mean I can decide when to end it?"

"No," she said quickly, afraid he was capable of anything. "Don't do that."

He gave her a hard stare. "Not even if I start another one right away?"

She stared back at him, his face caught in the prisms of the crystal chandeliers. She was tempted to say yes. "And then what would happen?"

"Another dance?"

"Until we wear through our shoes?"

"Doesn't time stop on a night like this?"

"Not unless you can make it do so." And if anyone could, she thought, it would be him. He teased her senses into a tempest. A flurry of emotion, of hope and loss, rushed through her. He made her forget who she was supposed to be, the lady she had become. He'd left his mark on her heart, and it had never healed.

He was Kit, and yet he wasn't.

She had looked at him before through a young girl's eyes and had seen the champion she had needed to see. She hadn't known until it was too late that he had needed her, too.

He had been abandoned, beaten, and abused, and become valued in the shallow world. She searched his face. She thought she saw a few remnants of boyish hope beneath his attractive veneer of cynicism.

It was overwhelming to look at him all at once. It hurt to think of how much he'd survived and how well he hid it. A decade had darkened his fair hair to ash. The angles and hollows of his face had filled out with a man's character, giving it a chiseled strength. He had to have become strong inside, too. But he'd always been strong.

And he'd earned the right to his cynicism.

"Well," he asked, the devil lurking in his eyes, "am I still menacing enough to scare away crows?"

She felt warmth tingling through her veins. "After what I saw of your dashing show tonight, you're impertinent to ask. The ladies flocked to you."

"You didn't flock to the chair I saved," he said, staring into her eyes. "I kept it empty for you until the last moment."

His voice weakened her. She would have loved to fling herself against his solid chest and have him alone for these few moments. But the world had discovered him for the wonderful treasure he was. Her handsome friend.

There had never been anyone like him in her life. And if he kept staring at her she wouldn't be able to dance another step. But at the same time she knew all eyes were on them and she must maintain her respectability.

She peered over his shoulder, desperate to break the tension between them. "Where is your bride now, by the way? Did she run off with someone else already?"

He shook his head. "I've waited for ages to see you again. I don't want to waste what's left of our dance talking about anyone else."

"London fell in love with you tonight—"

"How long will you be here? I'm not interested in the rest of London right now."

She needed to slow their pace, to deflect the intensity between them, to drink lemonade. Her heart was beating too fast against her stays. "All this time," she said, "I was afraid that you had been misused by the man who bought you, or that something worse had happened. I hoped you'd be treated well—"

"Who told you I wasn't treated well before? I lived in a palace, didn't I?"

"I didn't understand, Kit."

"Why should you have?"

"I do now."

"It wasn't your fault. You were good to me."

"You were a demon, and you broke my heart when you went away."

His smile pierced her composure. "I didn't have a choice. I was a wretched little beggar, and things could have turned out worse. I was adopted. And I was given an education. Can't you tell?"

She smiled up at him with sudden affection. "That's why I didn't recognize you. It was the polish."

His lips curled into a provocative smile. "Then it wouldn't shock you if I really did lure you off to have you to myself?"

"It wouldn't shock me, but Godfrey would probably get the vapors. As would my aunt."

He blinked. "Your aunt is here?"

"Yes, she's watching us, too."

"Then I'll have to change my plan."

A couple wove around them, laughing helplessly, out of time; Kit and Violet laughed, too, as they went down the dance, ladies on one side, gentlemen on the opposite, until Kit arrived at the top of the line.

"You dance well," he said to Violet, releasing her hand to exchange partners.

She took a breath. She danced well enough, but fencing had rendered him as flexible as a ballet dancer. It took vigor to perform the intricate figures and patterns as well as he did.

She knew the names of each step—glissade, chassé,

the jeté, and assemblé. But it didn't matter. His energy surpassed hers. He made his living with his physical prowess. She saw Godfrey wave at her once, then gallop off in another direction. Her aunt was perched, appraising, on the edge of her chair, and goodness only knew what she thought.

Violet was with Kit, and a wonderful disbelief overwhelmed everything else.

He was healthy, vital, confident. To think she had cried herself to sleep for weeks worrying about him.

Did he remember all their adventures? To look at his fine figure she couldn't imagine that he'd ever been flogged. He was a master-at-arms. How had it happened? He had become Master Christopher Fenton.

"My uncle died two years ago," she said, and thought he could not hear her.

He missed a step, recovered, and wove back in the line without anyone being the wiser. "I'm sorry. I suspected as much but was afraid to pry. I went back to Monk's Huntley for the first time only two months ago. There was a caretaker at your house, but he was hesitant to talk to me."

"We left after Uncle Henry was buried," she said, and offered no further explanation. She wouldn't ruin this moment by revealing that her friendship with him had given her aunt and uncle a raging fit. How could she admit that her guardians had found their secret association so appalling that they were afraid to let her out of their sight? Or that Ambrose had confessed everything to his mother? Violet had felt ashamed for disappointing them, and guilty that Miss Higgins had been sent away. Yet here she was dancing with the forbidden boy who had become a fencing master, with not only her aunt but her betrothed as their audience.

Even now she couldn't reveal that she and the dashing Fenton had kept company in their youth. And yet if she could, she would have happily followed him on another misadventure—and not cared whether she made it home in time for tomorrow's tea.

But she wouldn't. She bent to the rules now. Her aunt had made sure that she had not fallen into a wicked rake's hands. And she was all her aunt had left in the world. Her aunt had tamed violet's unladylike inclinations. Until tonight.

Chapter 7

$\mathcal{K}$ it had not earned his diploma in Paris without learning to master his emotions. He hadn't impressed his professors by thrusting at the first insult. No one in the ballroom would have guessed from watching them that his dance partner had kept alive the spark of humanity that had survived his workhouse years.

For all his proficiency with weapons, Violet had gotten through his guard. No duelist alive could have struck him such an unseen blow.

It was a fairy tale in reverse.

To hold her, however briefly, in his arms, forbidden to acknowledge their past, tested everything he had learned. Ten years had separated them.

Enough time to realize how much she had meant to him. She'd made him feel he was capable of anything at the lowest point in his life.

He had so many questions to ask her, so much to

explain, but a dance didn't last forever, no matter how complicated he made the steps seem. She danced with expression. Her arms floated with the grace of angels' wings. The fold of her elbow took on an eroticism that would keep him awake the rest of the night.

She mirrored him move for move. Their bodies pressed back-to-back. His blood surged at the fleeting contact.

Touch. Tease. Withdraw.

The quick nudge of her shoulder against his hinted she hadn't become as demure as she appeared. It required all his concentration to stay ahead of her.

She bent her arms in an arc, staring up at his face. She flowed from one step into another. Pliant but straight. Erect from the waist to the shoulder.

A dangerous exuberance coursed through his veins. If they moved this well together during a dance, he thought they would set any bed they shared on fire. It was a shame he would never know.

Her eyes shone in the candlelight. He wanted to pull her into his arms and ask everyone else in the ballroom to go away for a few hours. He wanted to ask her what had happened to Eldbert and Ambrose, and did she know that Miss Higgins had settled down here in London as a seamstress and that she and Kit often reminisced about Monk's Huntley?

But he realized that the dance was ending and that another man was waiting to claim her in the formation of dancers. He stepped closer to Violet, hoping to keep her to himself for just a little bit longer.

He reached for her shoulder and stopped.

She looked up again. What could he say? He could hardly whirl her off the floor and into his half world.

"I had hoped you wouldn't grow up to be a rogue," she said quietly.

"Which implies that I wasn't one before. But I was."

"No, you weren't. I shouldn't have said that."

"But it's true," he said, grinning. "I was on my best behavior around you. What I did at the workhouse is— Well, those aren't stories for your ears."

"I don't think you were ever that bad."

"I stole Ambrose's trousers. I lied when I said I had found them in the grass. I deceived you the day we met. You defended a liar. And I let you."

Violet's expression did not change. In fact, Kit questioned whether she'd even heard his confession, until she shook her head and smiled. "They looked far better on you, anyway," she said, and a moment later another dance began around them, couples taking their places in the line. They drifted to the edge of the floor. "Fine, then. You always were a rogue. I knew you had stolen the trousers all along."

"But you liked me anyway?"

"Yes. I did."

"Why?"

"You were alone like me, and adventurous, and even though you didn't want it to show, you had good in you."

He stared at her, his smile impudent. "Is that why

you flirted with me in the hall before you recognized me? For the good in me?"

She flushed. "Not exactly. The way I remember it, you flirted with me first."

"But you flirted back," he retorted. "And I could have been anyone, for all you knew. I had a mask on. You didn't."

She shook her head. "No. There was something different about you. I couldn't think what it was. It didn't occur to me that I might know you."

"You do know me."

"Not really."

"Well, we could renew our friendship in private, if you're willing."

She smiled reluctantly. "I don't think so."

"You're tempted. I can tell."

"Maybe I am. But that doesn't mean it's a good idea, or that I will act on it. My aunt has a positive phobia of rogues."

"I promise I won't ravish her. Or steal her trousers."

"Don't make fun of her, Kit."

His eyes darkened. "I'm not. I wouldn't. But—does she still remember me?"

"I'm not sure how much she remembers, but as you and I didn't recognize each other right off, I doubt she'll place you."

"All right." He shook his head, letting her think he'd given up. "I understand. There are too many people here tonight."

"I'm sorry, Kit. It's—"

"When *can* I see you again?" he asked her softly. He thought that if he had more time he could spin it out into a possibility—of what he didn't know. She had given him a chance before. Perhaps it could happen a second time. But he knew he couldn't lose his dream again without at least a kiss between them.

"Don't ask," she whispered. If he asked her to meet him again, she wouldn't be able to refuse. "Not now."

"Five minutes, that's all," he went on, completely ignoring her reluctance. "In the room off the hall where I saw you earlier."

"I don't think I even remember where it was."

"Ask a footman to show you to the rose reception room. Only five minutes. I beg you."

"I can't ask a footman to . . ." In her mind she pictured herself walking straight there. Walking straight into trouble's arms, her aunt would say.

He straightened in a masterful stance. "There's so much more that I want to know about you."

He waited and decided that she would not come.

There's so much more that I want to know about you.

I must claim a kiss, too.

There was more to it than that. There were more things than he could possibly explain in one evening, but it was a place to start.

He didn't want her to think he was a rake, but that was what he looked like. He merely wanted to see her without an audience. A kiss could seal the past, or it would open an endless avenue of doors for the future. Violet would forbid it, of course. He wouldn't force her to kiss him.

But already he knew he couldn't let her marry the haberdasher. Hadn't the man confessed he desired Violet's inheritance as much as he did her love?

Damn the past, he thought as he waited for her in the rose reception room, where only a soft lamp burned. Damn the future, too. *Give me a kiss, Violet, and let the present take us where it will. Refuse me, and I won't ever ask again. But don't pity me. Don't kiss me because you felt sorry for me once.* He wanted anything but her pity now.

The instant she appeared at the door he took her by the hand, closed the door, and swept her up against the wall. Her skirts rustled in the silence until she stilled. For several moments neither of them said a word. She stared up at him as he outlined her cheek and chin with his fingertips.

She laid her head back against the wall, as if offering him the hollow of her throat. He bent and pressed his mouth to her throbbing pulse. He touched the tip of his tongue to it and felt her quiver. "I must be in shock," she whispered unevenly. "I wouldn't be letting this happen otherwise. Meeting each other here tonight was such a . . . surprise."

He gave a low rumble of laughter. "That's rather like saying that the Great Fire of London was a surprise."

Her eyes danced with irony. "This is a very different reaction from the one you gave me when I first offered you friendship."

"I buried that boy in the vaults ten years ago when I left. He's dead."

"He isn't dead to me," she said, her voice deep with emotion. "Nor does London seem to think so. And you know it."

He smiled. She was still a passionate supporter. "The problem," he said, "is that London doesn't know me. Not like you do."

"Nobody knows about your past?" she asked after a pause.

"There are some people, yes. The Boscastle family, for instance. I couldn't in good conscience work with Lord Rowan without being honest about my life. For most people it's enough to know that I was Captain Charles Fenton's son, and that we were two head-strong swordsmen who respected the blade and our bond."

"It isn't a sin to be born in poverty."

"Haven't you heard? The destitute deserve to suffer. But there's something *you* have to know. It wasn't my choice to leave you."

"I understood that later," she said. "I wish I could have done something to keep you there."

He shook his head. "I'd have gone wild. I might have hurt you. I might have gotten involved with some very nasty people, indeed."

"What really happened after you left?" she asked, regarding him with the smile that made him forget she was forbidden to him. Her smile used to calm his temper when they were younger. It still affected him, but nothing about her calmed him now. She was voluptuous and bewitching; she was waking up all the demons he had put to rest. "All I remember is that you were apprenticed to a cavalry captain and that Ambrose said he drank because his only son had been killed at war."

"It was true," Kit admitted. "He became something of a recluse after his son died. He drank and went out only when other people weren't about. He used to watch me through the woods at times when he was foxed and think I was his boy's ghost. Then I met him in the woods one day and he knew I was real and from the workhouse."

Violet frowned. "Did he turn you in?"

"No. I got caught because I was careless. He went to the parish board and asked if I was up for sale. The bill had already been posted on the gate. He saw it and bought me."

"Oh, Kit. Please say he was kind to you."

He shook his head, not looking at her. "I expected more of the same treatment from him that I'd had at the workhouse. I planned to steal his money and run away at the first opportunity. Before it came Fenton adopted me. Overnight I was not only a swordsman's apprentice; I was his son."

"Then he *was* kind," she said in relief.

His eyes glittered. "The first thing he told me the day he brought me home was that if he could train a regiment, he could train a rat."

"A rat? I suppose you got in a fight."

"Of course we did. I ran away that night."

Her eyes widened. "In Monk's Huntley? Where did you go?"

"To Eldbert's house, but he was asleep. His father's groom took me back to the captain in the rain."

"I wish he'd told Eldbert."

"I made him swear he wouldn't. I didn't want to look like I was desperate. I did have some pride."

Violet breathed out a sigh. "And everything went well after that?"

He laughed. "Hell, no. I mistrusted the situation. He was an officer, a master-at-arms, and a lonely man who was haunted by the happiness he'd once known in Monk's Huntley. I, as you know, was a little swine. When we set sail from England, I knew I'd been bought cheap to be resold to foreign pirates."

She raised her eyes to his. "That's what Ambrose said had happened. And that the pirates would auction you off."

"I never saw a single pirate. If I had, I'd have probably asked to join them."

"Ambrose also predicted you'd be made into a eunuch."

He lifted one brow. "I can prove that prediction false if you're curious, but it wouldn't be a gentlemanly act."

She blinked. "I think I'll take your word on it. Where did the ship take you?"

"To Majorca." He grinned. "When we reached port I

spotted a bearded man in a scarlet cloak standing on the dock. I said, 'I'm not getting off the ship. Drown me like a cat for all I care. But catch me first.'"

"You were difficult to catch in those days," she said, shaking her head.

He smiled grimly. "Well, he did, but it took him three hours. That night we rode on donkeys over cobbled streets and up into winding hills to a hut where I watched how a sword was made. Soon after that we went to France so that I could study for my diploma."

"A sword master," she mused. "I should have thought of that. How many duels have you fought?"

"To the death?"

"Oh. Perhaps I shouldn't have asked. I don't want to know, do I?"

"The answer is none. I'm not saying there haven't been times when I came close. But I made a promise to my father that I wouldn't go off half-cocked at the least offense. He had a falling-out with a friend in France when they were brash students of the sword. It ended in a duel."

"He killed his friend?"

"No. But he severed the man's hand at the wrist so that he could never be the swordsman he was. My father was drunk and regretted it all his life. The chevalier never forgave him and called him a coward for not killing him instead."

"But he treated you well."

"So did you," he said.

He studied her face and fought the hunger that he felt. If only she wouldn't look at him like that. As if she believed in him. As if perhaps, secretly, she believed that their old friendship could be revived into . . . an abiding passion? Love?

Her vulnerability must have drawn many suitors. She had the beguiling gift of being a good friend. She listened and even now she didn't judge him. Oh, how pleasantly sweet it felt to be himself again.

He smiled. "And what have you been doing in the last decade or so?"

"Nothing as exciting as you."

"No? I doubt that."

She laughed. "Well, I've never left England, for starters. My aunt and I have been traveling for the last year. I've done charity work, and I have you to thank for opening my eyes to a world I didn't see before we met. And . . . I learned how to dance and how to use a fan to discourage advances."

His gaze held hers. "My compliments to your dancing masters. I assume you went through a battalion of them. You had me breathless in the ballroom, but then I can't blame all of that on the dance."

"I *was* breathless."

"Where is your fan to discourage my advances?" he asked slowly.

She glanced past him to the floor. "It's hard to see when one is pinned to the wall. I have a feeling I dropped it when you took me in your arms."

"My apologies."

"And my compliments to you on a painless disarmament."

He was surprised at the force of desire her artless words unleashed. "It isn't painless from my viewpoint."

"Your weakness doesn't show," she whispered innocently.

He gave a laugh. "It's all in the training. I hide it well. A sword master learns to manipulate those around him."

"I have heard that some ladies practice a similar technique."

"Which is?"

"I think it's provocation."

"Yes." He stared into her eyes. "A refined and ancient battle strategy that I admire. Not every woman can employ it to her advantage."

"I'm so proud of you, Kit," she said in a soft voice.

He gave a disgruntled sigh. "You're marrying one of my pupils. It does not feel like a mark of success."

She nodded vaguely. "Yes, I accepted his proposal last month."

"Only last month?"

She hesitated. "Yes."

Not hesitating, he took her face between his hands and bent to kiss her ever so softly on the mouth. He could have devoured her. Instead his lips settled on hers. She breathed a soft sigh, lowering her gaze. He glanced down at her lush breasts, straining against the delicate seams of her silk bodice. She had accepted him at his worst. He was afraid to show her that in some ways he was still desperate. And that in others he had become a master. "Why did you choose him?" he whispered, wrapping his hands around her waist.

She looked at him through her half-closed eyes. "Your hair is darker than I remember, and my aunt chose him for me. Is that what you wanted to know?"

"How do you—"

He kissed her so deeply that she buckled. He caught her, pinning her to his body for a brief moment of bliss before he gathered her in his arms. She stared up at him with a bewildered smile, whispering, "What are you going to do if someone comes?"

"I swear," he muttered, his grasp on her tightening, "that I will kill the first person who enters this room."

She lifted her head in alarm. "What if that person happens to be the marquess or his son?"

"Well, of course I'm not going to hurt a child."

"What if it's one of your pupils?"

"Like Godfrey?" he asked, his eyes narrowing.

"What if it's my aunt?"

Kit turned pale at that thought. "In that case I'll have to let her kill me. Sit with me a moment." He led her across the room to a long chaise hidden in a discreetly curtained niche. No one could ever accuse the marquess of not providing enough convenient places to make mischief in his house. "We need more time. We need to be alone. We need—"

"—to breathe," Violet said, her hand lifted to her bodice. "I am too tightly bound tonight."

"Take my breath," he whispered, lowering his face to hers.

"That doesn't help. Every time you kiss me, I feel like I'm going to pass out. Being near you makes me go faint, Kit."

"You won't faint." He rubbed her wrists through her gloves, glancing back at the door. He detected movement below the stairs, the clatter of glasses, a footman approaching. In a house like this, fortunately, the servants were trained to look the other way during an indiscretion.

But he couldn't even think of the name Violet in the same sentence with a word like *tryst* or *indiscretion*. He could not think clearly at all.

Oddly, what he did think about was all that he and Violet had gone through together. Violet breaking out in the measles, Kit certain he had killed her as he carted her off inelegantly to the baron at the manor house. He could still hear Lady Ashfield wailing in panic. And how could he forget Violet standing up to Ambrose, insisting he treat Kit with respect or go away?

She was the one responsible for Kit's redemption. Her friendship and faith in his goodness had given him the strength to survive the workhouse. Would his repayment be to ruin her? She twined her hand around his neck and coaxed his face toward hers. He could have stretched out beside her and spent the night talking about whatever came into their heads. Or maybe just kissing.

Why did she have to belong to someone else?

Why did that someone happen to be one of Kit's best-paying pupils? Not the most talented, mind you, not even one he particularly liked, but there was an implied contract between pupil and master that Kit was fairly certain did not include a clause that allowed a discount for ravishing a student's bride-to-be.

"Kit, stop brooding for a moment, and look at me."

He smiled slowly. It was good to hear her scold him. "Godfrey doesn't know anything about your past, does he?" she asked him urgently.

"No. Only few close friends—"

He stared down into her eyes. An ache pulsed to life deep inside him again. "I won't tell anyone I knew you before. It never crossed my mind."

"I wasn't thinking only of me, Kit. You've made a name for yourself. Nothing should spoil that. I'm happier for you than I can hold inside me."

"Then leave him," he said bluntly.

"Leave him?" she whispered, her eyes evading his. "I've only just agreed to marry him. We cannot do this. I have to go."

He knew he could not stop her. Their kiss aroused not only his sexual nature but his conscience. Taking her virtue would only prove what the workhouse warden had prophesied the day that Kit had walked out the gates: He could not be redeemed at all, and in the end he would drag everyone who believed in him to hell.

She lifted the back of her hand to his cheek. It was

an ambiguous gesture, wistful and inviting at the same time. "Kit? Kiss me again, and then I must go."

He lowered his head, his mouth slanting over hers. He felt her lips soften, and for once he wished he had not become a man who listened to his conscience. He felt her lips part, and he forgot everything except the sweetness of her mouth. The ache he had denied thrummed from his fingers as they glided down her shoulder to her breasts. She warmed his blood, like winter fire and fine wine.

He felt decadent, drunk on this small taste of her. She kissed with a sweet passion that could enslave him.

"Kit," she said in a deep voice.

"Is this our first kiss or another farewell?"

She shook her head, her fingers sliding across his mouth, to stem his questions or to end their kiss, he wasn't sure. He was too desperate to prolong their contact to work through it.

"I've thought about you, Kit."

"Don't go yet." He straightened, calling on self-denial, discipline, whatever weapon was at his disposal.

He heard her breath catch and felt remorse shiver down the nape of his neck into his soul. Dying inside, he pulled her hand from his mouth, kissed her gloved knuckles, and lifted her to her feet from the chaise and through the curtains. Slowly her gaze lifted to his.

He studied her as if she were a dueling opponent and his life hinged on her next move. He studied her face for nuance. He listened to the cadence of her breath for innuendo. A deadly rival if ever he had met one. What did he see in her eyes?

Wounded innocence? No. Violet stood on higher ground. She had never wasted her time seeking anyone's sympathy. An invitation? Kit would not insult her nor delude himself on that account.

What he read in Violet's expression cut deeper. He might not have imagined her brief response to him, but whatever she felt beyond poignant resignation she would not encourage.

She had protected Kit when he was a vile, obnoxious youth. It was his turn now to protect her. He might not be a gentleman, but he had earned a place.

He walked her to the door and checked that the corridor was empty before he let her go.

In the past he had remained hidden in the churchyard and watched her run through the woods until she reached the top of the slope and he knew she was safe.

Now he stayed in the shadows and waited for her to reach the well-lit corner, where she would turn and disappear. He swallowed hard as she hesitated, glancing back over her shoulder as if she still could not quite believe what had happened tonight.

He drew a breath, willing his body to settle down.

He had left an ugly impression on her the last time they'd been together in Monk's Huntley. It killed him, remembering how he must have looked to her. Helpless. Humiliated. Worth less than an animal being sold.

Part of him had never wanted to see her again. The

other part desperately wanted her to see what he'd become.

When he fell asleep later tonight, it would not be locked in a solitary cell, nursing a hard blow to the head. He wouldn't crawl through a tunnel to reach his rooms. He was his own man. He was free. And if he wanted to stay up until daybreak thinking about the woman he had kissed, he would do so.

But for all of his accomplishments, he was still a thief. If he wanted her, he would have to steal her from another man.

Chapter 8

$\mathcal{A}$unt Francesca, stubborn beldam that she was, had insisted that she felt well enough to stay to have pastry with the other matrons and that she would go home with Godfrey and Violet.

Sir Godfrey had stared at his betrothed and his fencing master on the dance floor and could hardly believe the compliments he heard. Guests seemed to be comparing their improvised country reel to everything from a Hungarian courtship ritual to a pagan Highland dance. He half expected someone to arrange Fenton's swords across the floor for this highly . . . Well, Godfrey wasn't sure how to describe the dance.

Improper to ignore the music and make up one's own steps at a party of this importance. Only the lower classes would dance like . . . He gaped at Violet, her head thrown back, her laughter unaffected, those dark curls escaping her pearl comb to caress her white skin. *Suggestive.*

Her behavior suggested many things to Sir Godfrey.

None of which he cared to ponder. Violet was virtue incarnate.

And Fenton? From what Godfrey knew of him, Fenton led a decent life.

He insisted that his pupils study hard and avoid trouble. Those who did not adhere to the code could not attend the academy. He was Godfrey's secret hero. He was the strong but gentle brother Godfrey had always wanted in place of the two stupid brutes who throughout his youth had bashed him around for sport.

But that was in the past. The brutes could kiss his rump. Godfrey anticipated that his business would double in the weeks before the ton left London for their country estates. After Fenton's well-received spectacle of sword mastery, the sales of lanterns and walking canes that Godfrey had stocked in the emporium would increase. He had given away all his cards to the well-heeled philanthropists who had asked about his affairs. A news reporter had even introduced himself and promised a nice mention of Godfrey's arcade in the paper.

The dance was almost over. Godfrey felt as if he were aging by the minute. The way they danced . . . It just wasn't done. The manner in which Violet and Fenton moved. Goodness. It went beyond insouciant. It bordered on dangerous.

What if one of them tripped the other and fell? Godfrey had practically put out his back performing with that lantern tonight. Where did Fenton find the energy to dance like that?

In another half hour or so he would be comforting

Violet over her aunt's failing health and making plans to take over the country manor in Monk's Huntley. Godfrey could not imagine himself living in an old pile that faced a graveyard, but it would do for Violet and their children on the occasional holiday. The deed was paid off. And Violet did seem to harbor a strange attachment to the place.

"We can't sell the house, Godfrey," she had told him repeatedly. "Not until you see it."

He felt an embarrassing fondness for her. Other people admired her, too. He noticed quizzing glasses raised to study her and Fenton. *Bless her*, he thought.

Violet is only using her gifts to advance us. She is too refined to be drawn into an encounter with a common swordsman. But she wasn't above dancing for a benefit.

And Fenton might be common, but it wouldn't surprise Godfrey to hear that the man had been raised to an honorary appointment or some such tribute in the future. The marquess wanted to employ him as the family's master-at-arms. If Fenton accepted, Godfrey would not be surprised. He might even ride on Fenton's coattails, if there was profit to be made.

His spirits elevated, Godfrey decided he would wait until after the dance to chide Violet. It wouldn't be fair to spoil the moment. After all, he wouldn't want society to get the impression that she and Fenton were actually conducting a . . . He was at a loss as to what his fiancée and fencing master were doing.

Undignified? Not with dignitaries imitating their inventive figures and looking altogether damned ridiculous. Had Violet been tippling? Not unless she did so in secret. Furthermore, no one on earth but Violet could aspire to pirouette in midair like a spinneret.

Bless her, he thought again. Violet was only dancing with Fenton because Godfrey had asked her to. She would never act like the giddy debutantes in the ballroom who were still oohing and ahhing over Fenton's excessive display of chivalry.

Violet's manners had sent Godfrey into a swoon the first day they had been introduced.

"Sir Godfrey, I believe," a deep voice said from above him, and he looked up into the gregarious face of the Most Honorable, the fifth Marquess of Sedgecroft, his influential and wealthy host. "Is this an inopportune time to mention a small matter of business?"

Godfrey bowed so deeply that his nose touched his knee.

"Are you certain that you don't want me to stay beside you the rest of the night, Aunt Francesca? It is a strange house, and you cannot see well in the dark."

"I see more than you think I do, but no, I do not wish you to stay." Her aunt spoke quietly from the bed, where she rested against a pile of pillows. "Not if you cannot hold still for me to sleep. Why are your cheeks damp? Have you been crying?"

"I went outside in the garden while you were undressing. It's starting to rain."

"You went outside at this hour? Let me feel your

head. How often have I told you that it is unhealthful to stand in the damp after a strenuous activity?"

Violet swung around the bedpost, lowering herself to her aunt's side. Francesca's fingertips pressed against her forehead before slipping down her nape to test for fever. "How am I?" Violet asked, restraining a grin.

"Too full of energy for a young lady who should have worn out her shoes. Ask Delphine to make you a mug of skimmed milk to settle you down."

"Yes, Aunt Francesca," she said, dancing back to the door and almost escaping before her aunt said, "Is that all it took to make you happy? A rogue's attention at a ball?"

Violet managed a smile. "I don't know what you're talking about."

"Did I miss more than the performance tonight?" her aunt asked in soft reproach.

"Taking into account the Boscastle history for infamous affairs, it is possible that we both did."

Aunt Francesca frowned, folding her hands over her Bible. "Go to bed, or at least go to your room. Do not set one foot outside again at this hour. I should think you've had enough excitement for the night."

"Yes, madam."

"Close the door, Violet."

"Yes, madam." And she almost did, curtsying and twirling straight into the lady's maid that she and Francesca shared.

"Is everything all right, miss?"

"Yes, Delphine." She glanced back in embarrassment. "She's ready to sleep."

"Shall I help you out of that gown?" Delphine asked.

"I can manage. Just listen for my aunt in the night. Perhaps one of us should sleep in here."

"Definitely not," Francesca murmured, her eyes sealed shut.

Violet lowered her voice. "She felt light-headed at the ball, but a physician attended her and said she was fine. Probably only overcome by the excitement."

Delphine nodded. "I wouldn't have been able to sleep for days before or after an event of that social importance. It's too much at her age."

It was too much at Violet's age—especially when Kit had turned an exciting enough social event into a forbidden reunion. Violet doubted she would sleep much herself tonight. She might not even be able to sit for a minute straight.

She shook herself and hurried off to her room to change for bed. The small chamber felt stuffy, and she was warm from dancing and kissing Kit. She kicked off her shoes and wandered to the window, pushing it open to breathe in the night air.

A light smattering of raindrops cooled her burning cheeks and caught like diamonds in her unbound hair. Where did he live? She looked out across the church spires and glistening rooftops that rose above the gaslit square. Was he close to her, in fashionable Mayfair, or in the dangerous East End? Why was she still tempted to run outside and find him in the dark? Why was he still the most fascinating person in the world?

She wanted to know everything that had happened

to him since she had last seen him in the churchyard. If only they could meet openly, not share wistful passages of their lives in secret.

She would love to hear all the details of how his passion for sword fighting had become his profession.

She was sure that her life would seem dull in comparison, which was what a lady's life should be. How relieved she was to discover that he had been compensated for what he had overcome. And that Ambrose had been wrong when he swore that Kit would find trouble wherever he went.

Instead, he had carved out for himself a dignified calling. The captain he called his father had given him the legacy he deserved.

He had admirers galore.

And he had kissed her. *Oh, God.* How he kissed her. She would never recover from the thrill of his mouth upon hers.

A chorus of irreverent male voices broke her reverie. She listened for a moment and struggled to close the window as a carriage clattered past the quiet square.

She would not be whistled at by a group of inebriated gentlemen rattling home at this late hour. And drunken they must surely be, to judge by the off-key singing that announced their approach.

She drew the blinds and slowly undressed for bed, slipping into her robe before she hung up her gown and carefully folded her gray silk gloves into a drawer. It was only then that she felt a bit of paper tucked deeply into the seam of her left glove. It was an embossed trade card.

She held the card to the light to read the inscription.

Christopher Fenton
Maître d'armes

And at the bottom of the card, beneath his Bolton Street address, he had scribbled: *My sword belongs to you.*

A rogue, indeed. For all she knew he had passed out several such cards at the party.

What if Delphine had found the card first? She smiled unwittingly.

What if Violet had removed her gloves at the party and the card had dropped onto someone's plate? What if she had left her gloves in Godfrey's carriage?

She could never acknowledge in public what Kit had meant to her.

They had never met until tonight. It was the way it must be. She had come too far to conduct herself in an improper manner with the object of a childhood fascination.

She was a lady who would fulfill her aunt and uncle's dream for her. She would be the wife of a wealthy, well-respected merchant who took fencing lessons because it was a gentleman's art, and Sir Godfrey Maitland valued gentility as much as he did gold.

And while she might yearn for so much more, it could never be.

Chapter 9

It rained lightly as Master Fenton and his entourage packed up their equipment and set off in Kit's lumbering coach from the Park Lane mansion for the fencing academy.

Some of the scenery he had used was on loan to the salon from Drury Lane. Kit packed up his swords before anything else. He could replace stage props if he had to, but a sword recorded the history of its owners. It kept a memory of every drop of blood it had drawn.

Some swords, it was believed, harbored a curse if they had not been used in an honorable fight.

Tonight he'd used the sword that he and his father had watched being made in Spain, and it had brought him luck. It had brought Violet back to him.

He lived minutes from his small salon, a situation that was convenient but afforded little privacy. By the time the assembly unloaded the coach, Kit would have only an hour or two before his other pupils began arriving at the salon for lessons.

He decided halfway home that he'd rather walk than travel in the crowded carriage with not only his two assistants, but Tilly, Kenneth's wife, and another student who had asked to ride with them.

"Who is she?" Tilly asked quietly from the window as he jumped onto the curb.

He looked at her in surprise. "Impertinent servant, did I say I was going to visit a woman?"

"Evasive master, I saw you dancing with one."

"You weren't supposed to be in the ballroom at all after your rescue."

She grinned, her chin resting on her wrist. "Nobody even noticed me. I only took a peek from behind the orchestra door. I don't believe I've ever seen prettier figures in a French cotillion, and half the couples got lost on the floor trying to keep up. She looked lovely from a distance. You looked nice together; that's what I thought."

"For a wench you think too much."

But Violet had looked lovelier up close, and if Tilly had sensed how engrossed Kit had been with a virtual stranger, then he wasn't as careful as he'd meant to be, and someone else might have noticed. At a party that spectacular, however, the little flirtations that occurred would soon be forgotten.

It wasn't even what had happened later in the reception room when he'd been alone with Violet that would have raised eyebrows.

It was their prior friendship.

"Go," he said, motioning the coachman forward with his cane. "No more spying on me tonight, Tilly."

"Do you love her?"

"How could I love a lady I've never met before tonight?"

"That's what I wondered. May I give you one piece of advice, sir?"

"No. Absolutely no advice."

"You looked lovely at the ball, too. There's no one who can move me to tears with a mere bow. You've the devil's elegance, I vow."

"Heartwarming words. I shall embrace them to my bosom evermore. Now, good night."

"But you ought to learn the proper steps to a dance if you wish to impress a lady like her."

"I beg your pardon," he said without a glimmer of emotion.

"What's her name?" she called as the carriage rolled away.

"It's—" None of her concern.

None of his, either. For all it mattered, Kit should think of Violet as Lady Maitland, the title she would take upon marriage. Sir Godfrey's wife.

He vented a deep sigh of displeasure. She could have chosen better. He understood the reasons for the match. Sir Godfrey might be a pompous ass. He might not claim the most impressive credentials in London. But he had been born above a foundling.

He frowned at the raucous laughter that arose from his receding carriage.

Would he have been happier if Violet had been engaged to a man he did not know? Violet did not need his approval to marry anyone.

If Kit had met her before she had accepted Sir Godfrey's proposal, he might have been able to influence her decision.

But he could hardly present himself at her aunt's door, explaining that he was the boy who had brought disgrace to her niece, that he had once lived in the workhouse near her estate, and would her ladyship be so kind as to listen to his opinion on the matter.

Even now he was not considered by good society to be presentable.

He glanced around, distracted by the fall of boot heels somewhere down the street. A man in a black coat veered from the corner and hurried toward him.

Kit's hand closed around his sword cane, but he made no attempt to shrink back on the sidewalk. Pity the poor sod who thought to assault a master-at-arms.

He narrowed his eyes. The pedestrian resembled Pierce Carroll, one of the pupils who had performed at the benefit tonight.

He swore to himself as the distance closed. The man didn't resemble Pierce.

It *was* Pierce, bustling straight toward him with a guileless smile that made Kit feel like a mother goose whose fledglings shadowed his every step.

He swung down his cane in annoyance. The last thing he needed was a pupil hanging on his arm.

"Sir," Pierce said, pushing back his beaver-trimmed hat in respect, "do you mind if I walk with you?"

Kit shrugged. "Suit yourself. I'm not heading in any particular direction." He walked on, not encouraging conversation.

"Did I do well tonight, Mr. Fenton?"

"I told you that you did. It was probably the best rendition of Hamlet's rapier-and-dagger switch that I've ever seen."

Pierce loped at his side. "I didn't think you'd be alone tonight. You could have chosen any lady at the party for company."

Kit laughed drily. "I wouldn't go that far."

"Everyone was enchanted by your dance with Sir Godfrey's fiancée. She's more than beautiful, don't you think?"

Kit hesitated. It crossed his mind that Pierce was either the biggest moron he had ever met or was trying to provoke him into confessing something he would regret. Fortunately, it took more than that to piss out Kit's tallow.

"She's staying with her aunt in Cavendish Square," Pierce added, one foot in the street, the other on the pavement.

Kit shot him a considering look. Pierce appeared to be all of twenty. "How do you know?"

"Sir Godfrey took me home once in his carriage and made a detour to show me the place."

"Why don't you buy your own transport?"

Pierce grinned. "I wouldn't have any money to pay for your exorbitant but essential lessons."

Kit refrained from making a rude remark about the young man's expensive habits. Pierce dressed well, but Kit knew little about his personal affairs. As a rule Kit minded his own business—and did not pry into his pupils' private lives. To his misfortune they did not always return the courtesy.

"I didn't realize that you and Sir Godfrey moved in the same society," he said.

Pierce looked past him. "I wouldn't call us close friends. But we've gone out for the occasional pint after practice. I can't see for the life of me why any woman as—" He veered into Kit, and Kit shoved him aside without a second thought. "Sorry. I know we are not supposed to malign our fellow students."

"You gossip like a girl."

"I don't fight like one," Pierce said, hanging back a moment.

Kit didn't respond. Fine swordsmanship tended to engender respect among students, not counting the infrequent professional jealousy that ended in a deadly duel.

For the most part, men who had studied diligently to earn their diplomas had enough sense not to challenge an equal.

But not always.

He recognized in relief the familiar landmarks that led to his dwelling house. The hackney driver who occupied the spot two doors down nodded as he passed. The pawnbroker's shop was closed, but the corner tavern had drawn the usual crowd.

He counted five vehicles lined up in the street. He could smell burned cheese and uncorked champagne as he pounded up the steep stairs to his rooms. Laughter and light. His lodging house might not be as elegant as a Park Lane mansion, but it wasn't a basement in Seven Dials, either. He opened the door onto the crowded parlor.

He felt Pierce at his back, peering into the smoky warmth of the room. "And I thought you led a monk's life."

Kit shook his head. "This is the usual madhouse after a good show. Champagne, criticizing one another's performance, and—"

"Women," Pierce said, standing in the door before he followed Kit inside the parlor. "May I come in?" he asked after a brief hesitation.

Kit turned away as a friendly voice called, "Maestro!" and several glasses of port rose in salute. Seven other guests stood celebrating around the hearth, and the remaining assembly had not even arrived.

"Clean your sword before you leave," he told Pierce. "And no fencing on the stairs. It gives the landlady fits."

"Aren't you going to toast at least once?"

"I toasted enough for one night. I'm going to bed." He strode from the parlor toward his bedroom without any fanfare, and those he knew best knew better than to beg him to stay.

Sometimes he couldn't stand the disorder and the noise.

But it would be worse to be alone. At least no one ever came barging into his bedroom without knocking, excluding the overamorous actress, or wanton lady who took his lack of interest in a casual affair as a challenge.

Kit was highly particular where he sheathed his sword.

He washed, undressed, and fell across his bed.

He could hear shuffling and snoring, a blade tapping from the adjoining room until right before dawn, when a deep silence descended. In a half hour the first person on his feet would put on the kettle for tea. It wasn't long after joining the academy that a new pupil learned the master lived anything but an adventurous life.

As if he kept a mistress in every room, he thought absently, and the ache in his shoulder spread through his body, a body accustomed to being denied its needs.

But as daylight broke Kit didn't feel like denying himself; it shocked him to realize that he could fall victim to desire. He mocked other men who could not control their sexuality. He wasn't as strong as he believed.

He simply had not encountered the woman he couldn't resist. He closed his eyes and saw Violet's passion-flushed face.

He felt her lips open beneath his, and her breasts, soft and heavy, molded to his chest.

A tremor of want raked his spine and burrowed into the marrow of his bones. Did she toss in the dark, yearning to be touched and tasted and caressed in every erotic way he could invent?

Why should she marry an inept pupil when she could have the master instead?

He drifted back off to sleep. Would Violet dream about him, too?

A bellow from the staircase jolted him out of bed.

He jumped up, ran across the room, and opened the door. "What the bloody hell?"

His landlady stood before him, shaking with rage. "I run a reputable lodging house! If you can't stop those young bucks from creating mayhem in the middle of the night, then I'm tossing the lot of you—"

She blinked, looking down the length of him in awestruck silence.

Kit frowned. "Look, Mrs. Burrows, I'm sorry that the little bastards have disturbed you. It won't happen again."

She smiled. She tittered. He thought she might be tipsy. Then she looked down again. "It's no trouble, sir. Sorry I barged in on your repose. I know you worked hard tonight. Very hard, indeed."

And it was only when her gaze dropped for a third time that he realized what had made her go all noddy in the noggin.

He wasn't wearing a nightshirt. He wasn't wearing anything except the sword with which nature had endowed him. So much for his honor.

* * *

The prostitute stroked her knuckles idly down her customer's shoulder. Annoyed, he shrugged off her touch and rolled onto his back. "Did I displease you?" she asked in a detached voice.

He glanced at her with an appreciative grin. She might have been inquiring whether he'd like his liver with onions or plain. Now that he took the time to give her a second look, he realized that she bore a slight resemblance to the young woman who had captured Fenton's attention at the ball. No doubt she was a cheap imitation, but then, he hadn't been offered free entrée into London's most exclusive brothel.

Fenton had. But the master held himself to a higher standard. An ordinary whore would never suit him. Who would? Another man's betrothed?

"Is that blood on your shirt?" the harlot asked, sitting up to stare at the dark smear on her hand.

"Probably."

"Well, I didn't scratch you. And if you claim that I did, I'll deny it. I thought you said you'd been in a performance? That's real blood, for your information. I'm not as stupid as a sheep, and if you stain the bedding, the proprietress will double my fee. She only gave you a good price out of the charity of her heart. And what that means, mister, is that I'm basically letting you do me for—"

"I'll pay whatever she asks," he said, throwing himself on top of her naked body before she could utter another word. "Your voice displeases me. You should try to sound like a lady. You could pass for one in the dark. Now close your mouth. And open your legs."

She gazed up at him with a professional aloofness that heightened his desire. "One does what one must. It isn't always pleasant to pretend. But then, it's part of doing business."

She gasped as he thrust into her; his body took advantage of hers as his mind moved ahead to other avenues. She deserved whatever price she demanded. She had not only given him a good toss—she had inadvertently led him to the door of Fenton's destruction.

As soon as he had spent himself again, he got up and dressed, his black coat over his arm, his beaver-trimmed hat in hand.

"You're welcome, mister."

He did not bother to answer. He was sick of answering to the name Pierce Carroll. He was tired of tea parties and honor and pretending to care about humanity. He intended to celebrate his twenty-seventh birthday in Paris at the end of the month. But first he intended to pay an outstanding debt in his father's name.

He wanted the redress to be as public and humiliating as possible . . . a dishonorable end to the principles and illusion of power that Captain Fenton had passed down to *his* son.

Chapter 10

$\mathcal{V}$iolet and Lady Ashfield spent the next day at home. Violet sat quietly writing thank-you letters to the marquess and his wife for the previous evening's entertainment. Her aunt interrupted her every other minute to read an observation of the ball that she had come across in the papers. Violet managed to hide her curiosity by concentrating on her penmanship. But her heart jumped each time Aunt Francesca mentioned Kit's name or praised his performance, and she sighed in relief when Francesca at last finished.

"There is no description of the opening dance that you and that fencing master performed so well, Violet."

Or of the kisses they had shared so wickedly a little while later. Violet put down her pen, at a loss as to how to respond until she looked up at the mantelpiece clock.

"It's time for luncheon," she said hastily, rising from

the desk to ring the bell. "I can't believe we've sat an entire morning without even a biscuit between us."

"Ah, here is another mention in Domestic Observances—"

"Shall we have Chablis and cold chicken again? I fancy a slice of beef pie, but perhaps that should wait for—" She turned as Twyford appeared at the door. "Oh, I didn't even have to ring. We are starving, Twyford," she said. "And not particular about what you bring as long as it arrives soon."

"Yes, miss. Your luncheon is on the way. I thought that her ladyship would wish to enjoy these during her meal."

He entered the room, bowed before the baroness, and presented her with a delicate nosegay of anemones, roses, and bellflowers interspersed with sweetly fragrant shoots of honeysuckle. "They are from Godfrey," Francesca said as she read the card before dropping it in her lap. "With his grave wishes for my recovery."

"How thoughtful." Violet frowned at the faint sneer that flitted over the butler's face. "Twyford, would you be so kind as to bring us a small vase?"

"There is one in the cabinet behind you, Violet." Francesca lifted the nosegay dismissively to her niece, her face averted. "He may as well have said to save these for my grave."

Violet nearly dropped the flowers onto the carpet. "What on earth do you mean by that?"

Francesca glanced away with a guilty look. "Nothing. It is my black mood, I suppose. Death comes closer every day, and I am not prepared to meet it with grace. Put these in water before I die."

Violet unlatched the cabinet and brought out the vase for the footman who had just come into the room and deposited a silver luncheon tray on the table. "You are *not* seriously ill, and the best physician in London said so. You must stop feeling sorry for yourself."

Aunt Francesca nodded. "Don't listen to me. Sir Godfrey means to be kind, I suppose. Is he taking us to the park later today?"

"Our drive was planned for tomorrow," Violet said in a gentle voice. "He had business affairs at the emporium today."

"Whose idea was it to visit a tumuli exhibit?" Francesca asked with the bluntness allowed only the young or those of advanced age.

Violet motioned the footman to place the vase on the table. "It was mine. It wasn't Godfrey's. We won't go if it upsets you. It's a morbid idea, and I don't know what I was thinking. It sounded interesting when I read about it in the paper. I think we should go to the library or shop for your new pelisse. Why is it so dark in here?"

The footman went immediately to the window to adjust the curtains so that more light could penetrate into the room. Aunt Francesca appeared frail and her skin translucent as she raised her face to gaze outside. The thought entered Violet's mind that her aunt would not die unexpectedly one day. She would fade away one moment at a time.

"I wondered," Francesca said in a hesitant voice, "if your interest in this exhibit didn't have something to do with your earlier attraction to the old churchyard in Monk's Huntley."

Violet smiled to cover a sudden stirring of guilt. How much did her aunt remember of those times? Violet had never been sure what Miss Higgins had confessed before she was dismissed. Silence during times of family scandal was golden indeed.

"I liked to sketch, as you remember," she said. "The yew trees and the overgrown graves reminded me of a forest that had fallen under an enchantment."

Francesca sighed. "I vaguely remember one of your sketches. You drew a very detailed picture of a young king or prince—I can't recall. I'll have to find it for you."

"I was an awful artist."

"There was something poignant about your drawings," her aunt replied. "They seemed to tell stories that I could not understand. You were a fanciful child, Violet. Thank the stars that you have outgrown the age of temptation and have become a practical young woman."

Practical.

If only Violet believed in her heart that her aunt spoke the truth.

"You are practical, aren't you, Violet?"

"I like to think so."

"You weren't tempted last night—"

"To do what?"

Twyford reappeared in the doorway. "We have a visitor, madam. It's the Marchioness of Sedgecroft."

Violet resisted running into the hall to escape her aunt's line of interrogation. "Well, do bring her in."

For a moment Francesca had entertained the most fanciful thought. She had expected Twyford to announce that their visitor was the dashing rogue who had danced with Violet at the ball. Her heart had gone still.

Even she had recognized a romance when it unfolded before her. Perhaps she should have found an opportunity to explain to Violet why she had to be on guard at all times.

But what if the truth only put ideas in Violet's mind?

Did Francesca want to open a Pandora's box to the past? Why did Violet or anyone else have to know that she was illegitimate?

May it please heaven that Francesca would take the secret of Violet's scandalous origins with her to the grave.

Miss Winifred Higgins drew off her gloves and shushed her nine-year-old daughter so that she could finish reading the paper she had purchased on her way back from the market. Winifred worked for her sister, who was a mantua maker on Bond Street, and brought home daily mending to pay expenses. "It's about our performance last night, love. Let Mama read in peace for a few moments."

"What performance?" her daughter asked, stretching out on the rug with her assortment of fashion dolls, pattern magazines, and pocketbooks.

Winifred pushed aside the sewing she'd left on her chair. "The one that Master Fenton and Mrs. Hawtry had us make costumes for."

"King Arthur and Hamlet?" Elsie rolled onto her elbow, pearls, ribbons, and bugle beads scattering across the rug. She regarded her mother with an absorption that was not returned.

Winifred nodded, leaning closer to the coal fire to read. "Yes, yes, yes. Listen, Elsie."

Elsie turned back onto her stomach and stared into the fire.

"'In a series of elegant vignettes Fenton and his academy revived the chivalry and romance that the world has lost. The audience was left in awe at his display of this dying art and its principles of self-discipline and code of conduct. Fenton was at once enigmatic, dangerous, and elusive in his various parts. He won hearts with a sword that is said rarely to spill blood.'"

A tap at the door interrupted her reading. "Oh, dear. That'll be Mrs. Sims wanting the shift I haven't finished."

"Shall I send her away, Mama? I'll tell her you've gone out to buy thread."

"Don't you dare open that door unless I tell you to. You have no idea who might be on the other side."

"Winifred," a deep male voice whispered. "It's only me."

Elsie jumped up. How she moved so quickly without decimating her doll assembly Winifred never understood. "It's Master Fenton," she said in excitement as her mother intercepted her in the middle of the floor. "Can't we let him in?"

Winifred pressed her ear to the door. "Who is it?" she whispered through the thick wood.

"Another bleeding idiot. Open up, Winnie. I've news you have to hear."

She unlatched the door, barely allowing him to dip inside before she locked it again. She looked him over, sighing with the fond pride she would feel for a favorite brother or cousin. No one wore clothes as attractively as Kit. He was a tailor's delight, and bless his wicked heart, he helped Winnie out with a few pounds here and there, even though he would never be wealthy in his profession.

"Come in. Mind you don't get cat fur all over your coat. Elsie, put on tea, pet. I've read the paper, Kit. News indeed."

"That isn't all."

He sat, arranging himself in an elegant way that detracted from the fact that the sofa legs wobbled under his slight weight. He waited to speak again until Elsie disappeared into the kitchen. "She's here. Violet is in London. I saw her last night. It took only a moment before we recognized each other and . . ." He hesitated.

"Violet?" Winifred felt chills run down her arms.

"Violet Knowlton. She came to the performance in

Park Lane. I opened the dance with her. We pretended to be strangers. She's a lady, and even though last night I was rubbing shoulders with the marquess, I couldn't acknowledge in public that she and I once were friends. God knows I could have ruined her life."

"*You* danced with Violet?" Winnie lowered her pricked finger to her lap. "She came to London to see you perform at the ball?"

He shot her a rueful look. "Hardly. From what I gathered her aunt brought her here on a husband hunt, and to no one's surprise, it was a success."

Winifred looked from Kit's face to the fire. She couldn't guess by his expression how he felt, but something unguarded had slipped into his voice. Vulnerability. As for herself . . . Violet's arrival was welcome news. "What did she look like? Who is she marrying? Did she speak of me at all?"

He laughed, reminding her of the unrestrained young rascal he had once been. He was still a rascal, but one who kept his wicked nature under a tight rein. "I don't remember everything we spoke of. I don't even remember whether she spoke to me first or I to her. She's beautiful, Winnie. Her hair is dark, and her eyes are—" He broke off. "And her—"

"Her what?" she interrupted, too eager to care about his hesitation.

"Her fiancé is a merchant. Sir Godfrey Maitland."

Winifred managed to hide her dismay. "Oh." She had heard her sister mention the name, and not in a kind voice, either. "Fancy that. Good for her, eh?"

He shrugged, not answering.

"Is he a fine gentleman?"

He straightened his legs. "He's been one of my pupils for a few months."

"Then he must have good in him. Fenton's does not train just any riffraff."

"Only paying ones." He made a face. "He's all right. He's no Angelo, but then, neither am I."

Winifred sniffed. "No. You're better. But tell me more about Violet. Is she happy?"

"I would imagine so," he said after a pause that hinted to Winifred that *he* wasn't. "Don't all women look forward to their wedding day?"

"No," she said without hesitation. "Some dread it. Some plot to escape. The Marchioness of Sedgecroft, whose ball you attended, sabotaged her own wedding to the marquess's cousin. Well, that's the gossip, anyway. I shouldn't have repeated it. I know you're giving the young lord lessons."

"I don't think Violet is plotting anything but her future husband's social connections," Kit said, obviously only half listening to her.

"Oh. He's one of those."

He shrugged. "You know what it takes to stay in business."

Elsie bustled in, balancing two mugs of hot tea on a tray. "You are a good girl," Winifred said, and thought, as she did countless times every day, that she did not deserve the obedient child she had borne out of wedlock as a result of a rash affair.

"Are you going to see Miss Knowlton again, Kit?" she asked him as she took her tea.

He shook his head. "That's up to her. I won't embarrass her in public. And I doubt she'll want to see me in secret again."

Winifred studied him with a worried frown. "I'm sure she wants nothing to do with me."

"If I do see her again, it will probably be when she is with Sir Godfrey, and I will have to be careful what I say. It didn't seem to me that she held anything but fond memories for our days in Monk's Huntley."

Winifred stared at his profile. He wasn't quite a gentleman, but she knew of no finer young man in London.

And Violet was to marry a merchant. Sir Godfrey Maitland. *Goodness*. Winifred had assumed that Miss Knowlton, as beautiful and vivacious as she was, would have attracted a young nobleman, or at least a suitor who sounded a bit livelier. A suitor like—no, no. Master Fenton and Violet. Lady Ashfield would drop toes-up at that.

Anyway, who was Winifred to give advice to the lovesick? She had borne a wonderful child out of wedlock, and now Elsie would grow up in the shadow of her mother's shame. The regret of it ate at Winifred's conscience. So many doors closed to Elsie because of her mother's sins. Baron Ashfield had been right to dismiss Winifred for being a negligent governess.

For months after her dismissal Winifred had refused to accept any responsibility for her situation. She didn't connect her perpetual lies and disregard for duty to what had befallen her. She was unemployed because Baron Ashfield was a miserable old bugger. Violet was to blame for being a wicked girl and not an obedient charge. The bricklayer who seduced Winifred in the woods had never intended to marry her.

It was only after Winifred gave birth to his illegitimate daughter that she felt the first genuine pangs of conscience. As her guilt grew, her grudge against Baron Ashfield and his family began to recede. Soon Winifred wished for a chance to prove herself worthy of a young girl's care.

"Mama. Look. I've made a wedding dress for the master's lady."

Winifred's eyes misted as she stared at the drawing her daughter held before her. "This is lovely, dear. Did you copy it from one of Auntie May's magazines?"

"I made it myself."

"Do not lie to me, Elsie. I shall put you right to bed if you do."

"I am *not* lying," Elsie replied with conviction. "I drew it earlier. I would have shown you, but I was allowing you and Mr. Fenton your privacy."

"Privacy? We were *only* talking, Elsie. You do understand that much?" God forbid that Elsie should think Winifred had taken to entertaining men in the afternoon. It was bad enough Winifred sewed gentlemen's smalls to bring in a few shillings, or that Kit had a reputation as a rake when he resisted one pretty bint after another, a few of them titled, who threw themselves at him, to no avail. He and Winnie knew each other too well for any romance.

"You'll have to see her again, Kit," Winifred said. "Even if it's only to give her my kindest wishes. You will do that, at least, for me?"

A smile tightened his lips. "I know what you're trying to do."

"And?"

"And it's hopeless. We've outgrown those times. Our games. She's going to be married."

"It isn't hopeless. It had to be destiny that you met at a ball like that."

"Destiny?" He put his tea on the side table.

"Yes," Winifred said.

He stood, laughing, his coat falling in impeccable folds. "*Our* destiny, yours and mine, is to work hard and be grateful for what we have gained."

"Where's your spirit of swordsmanship, Kit?"

He took a coin from his pocket and tossed it to Elsie. "What kind of swordsman would I be if my intentions were obvious to the world?"

"Intentions? Oh, Elsie, give him back that coin. Kit, I will thank you not to train my daughter for street begging."

"May I train with the sword, Mama?"

Kit cleared his throat. "It's time for me to go. I'm standing guard at school today."

"Be careful, then," Winifred said, and when he was gone, she picked up the unmended shift and studied the tear with an expert eye. She might have made a mess of her own life, but she had developed certain virtues and talents along the way. No seamstress in London could mend a rent as expertly as Winifred. She had salvaged many a costly gown from disaster with her needle. She was good at putting things back together where they belonged. Patching up so that no one could tell there had been a separation in the first place.

"Mama." Her daughter's small hand on Winifred's shoulder momentarily distracted her. "Do you need the pattern books and another candle?"

"No, pet. Search under my basket of buttons for the good pen and our best paper. Are you too tired to write two short letters? If you do, I promise I shall buy you the prettiest dress you've ever seen. I won't make it, Elsie. I shall have you costumed like a model in one of the French magazines. And Mama will pay someone else to sew and design your dress."

"Will you take me to Gunter's for pastry the first time I wear it?" her daughter asked with the innocent ruthlessness of one who exploits a guilt she does not understand.

"Done," Winifred said, and felt heady at a chance to redesign the past into redemptive grace. "But you will have to be on your best behavior, Elsie. And do not ever catch money in your skirt again. It looks ever so common."

Chapter 11

$\mathcal{T}$he emporium was mobbed. Sir Godfrey had deigned to wait at the front counter himself, although he disliked putting himself in a servile position. He was rather perturbed that his shop had not been mentioned in the papers, his name in only one, and heaven knew one needed a magnifying glass to read the print in that. Still, orders for walking sticks and sword canes had increased, as he had anticipated.

There was a comfort in the bustle. Today, when he studied his customers, he realized that one of them could have dropped in at a recommendation of an aristocrat he had met at last night's ball.

Nobility shopped here. He decided he would personally greet each new customer for the rest of the morning, just in case.

Perhaps the irate lady who complained of spending half a crown on the sarcenet hat trimming that had faded was the dowager who had complimented his fencing skill last night. Sometimes Sir Godfrey wanted to shove his clientele out the door and stick his shoe up— Well, if the Horse Guards happened to march the lot of them into the cobbles, he would not cry into his tray of linen cravats. The people he served treated him like horse droppings. One day, when he'd made enough money to retire, and the children Violet had given him rose to prominent positions in society, he would have his revenge. He would have earned the right to be rude, and he would never stand behind a counter again, haggling over a bit of twill.

The Marchioness of Sedgecroft had come to take Violet out for the day, but not shopping.

"I'm going to pay a visit to the charity school that my husband has endowed," she explained to Francesca in the drawing room. "It is safe. I always travel with two competent footmen and an armed driver."

"I would love to visit your school," Violet said before her aunt could intervene.

Francesca smiled at Jane. "Then go. But if you don't mind, I will stay home today and save my strength for our outing tomorrow in the park."

A half hour later the stylish coach set off northeast to the charity school that had once been a church. There was only one room now, cold, badly lit, and damp, despite the coals heaped on the grate. Jane introduced Violet to the schoolmaster, and as she was about to identify the children huddled over their desks, Violet glanced out the back window and nearly dropped the basket of clothing Jane had brought for the schoolmistress to distribute.

"What is it?" Jane asked, coming up behind her.

Violet shook her head, but it was too late. Jane had spotted the tall figure at the window. "Oh, it's Fenton. The children go into raptures when he's here."

"He teaches them sword fighting?" Violet asked, smiling at the thought.

"In a school founded by the church? I shouldn't think so."

"Then what on earth *is* he doing here?"

"He and his pupils often volunteer their services as bodyguards for the schoolmaster and schoolmistress."

Violet contemplated the pale faces of the students sitting against the wall. One of them smiled at her, then ducked his head. He couldn't have been eight.

"They don't look violent," she whispered.

"Fenton isn't protecting the teachers from the class," Jane whispered back with a laugh. "He's protecting the school from the vandals who have smashed the windows and threatened to carry off the children. The fiends have gone after Mr. Dabney several times with shattered glass and bats."

"Why? Who are they?"

"Street gangs who are intimidating their younger brothers or sisters into returning home to work."

"I wouldn't have believed you once," Violet said. "I do now."

"We're hoping to move the school to a safer area

soon. Well, let's get to work." Jane directed her to a side door. "That's Mr. Dabney's closet. Why don't you put a few things away, while I sneak outside and give Fenton my regards? Unless you would like to do it for me."

Violet shook her head. "No, no. I'm sure a word from you would be more meaningful. I do think it's generous of him, however, to give his services away."

"Yes," Jane said with an arch smile, swinging around to the door. "You would not believe how many ladies I've met who wish he'd extend his generosity toward them."

Violet was mulling this remark as she proceeded toward Mr. Dabney's pantry. She opened the door and stepped into the stuffy darkness, murmuring, "Generosity toward ladies, indeed." She started to unload her basket, perceiving shelves on the left for food, and pegs to the right for clothing. "I'd like to know what kind of ladies engage his services."

"Charitable ones, I assume," he said directly behind her.

She swung around, a wheel of wrapped cheese in her hand. "Is that the only criterion?"

His eyes danced, full of wickedness. "No. Any lady who engages me has to be someone I consider a friend as well as a lover."

"I'm sure that list is very long."

"I haven't finished explaining the other criteria. Why don't I help you put that on the shelf?"

A shiver went down her backbone. "I can manage."

"It's so much easier for me," he said in an alluring voice.

His hard body bumped against hers. There was barely enough room for one person to move in the pantry as it was. She pushed a little. He gave—but only for an instant, so that when she turned, she found herself trapped in an inescapable pose.

She looked up at his face. He gave her an unabashedly sensual smile. He reached back his hand and closed the door. He lowered his other arm and pulled her against him.

"You should be ashamed of yourself," she whispered. "Following me here."

"Excuse me. I was here before you."

She laughed, enjoying the intimate amusement in his eyes. "You know perfectly well what I mean. You followed me into the pantry. It looks suspicious."

"No, it doesn't," he whispered loudly. "Her ladyship asked me to see if you needed help." His arm tightened around her waist. "Do you?"

"Absolutely." She paused. "Should I ring a bell or shout?"

"There aren't any bells," he said calmly. "And if you shout, you will frighten the children."

He had a point. "You can't keep me in here indefinitely."

He stared up at the shelves. "We have enough food to last for days."

Her heart was racing. She could not deny that

spending time alone with him sounded like a pleasant imprisonment. "So you protect children, do you?"

He shrugged. "We've chased off a few trouble-makers."

"We? Meaning the students at your academy?"

"Yes." He pressed closer to her, close enough that she felt the imprint of him through her dress. "We aren't alone. Retired soldiers stand watch in the street with us from time to time."

"How decent of you," she whispered.

"How is your aunt?"

"She seemed tired, and I worry that . . ."

He hesitated. "If there is ever anything you need, you have only to ask."

"I don't want to lose her."

"I know. I don't want to lose you again, either."

It happened in a heartbeat. He bent his head. The clean angles of his face blurred, and then his mouth covered hers. She parted her lips and felt his tongue flick against hers. It was a brief but decadent kiss. It was a kiss that scorched to the bone and set her blood on fire.

"God," he whispered, and tightened his hold on her. She lost all sense of everything but him, until a voice outside the door impinged on her awareness.

He let her go and stepped back against the wall, where the coats and cloaks hung from a row of wooden pegs. Violet released a ragged breath. How he managed to appear as innocent as he did when the marchioness squeezed inside the pantry mystified her.

She was still reeling from his kiss and suspected that it showed. She felt as if she had been baptized in flames, singed to the roots of her hair. She'd wanted to stay wrapped in his arms and never move.

"Is all well in here?" Jane asked.

"It's fine," Kit said, rehanging a cloak that he had removed from its peg a moment before.

"I've put the cheese away," Violet added, and pointed to the shelf.

Jane glanced up with a knowing smile. "I see."

"We could use some light," Kit said.

Jane looked at him. "It might help to leave the door open next time, but I suppose it won't stay unless you prop it with a brick. Weed has another delivery. Would you like to come and meet the children before we leave, Violet?"

She nodded. "I'd love to."

Kit straightened. "Should I stay to help or go back outside?"

"Go outside," Jane said, smiling at him. "The boys are already asking where you've gone. We won't stay much longer. May we drive you anywhere, Mr. Fenton, or do you have your own coach?"

"I walked, but I don't want to be a bother."

Jane turned to Violet. "Will he be a bother?"

What was a gentlewoman supposed to say? "Not at all," Violet replied.

"Splendid," the marchioness said, as if there had ever been a doubt she would be accommodated. "Then it is settled. Miss Knowlton and I might even take a peek at the fencing school. From our window, of course."

Violet followed them back into the classroom, startled when the children sighted Kit and broke into a loud cheer. He grinned, giving Violet a sheepish look, but she was cheering inside for him as well. "It seems as if he is everyone's hero," she commented quietly to Jane.

"Could he be yours?" Jane asked with a directness that rendered Violet speechless. "Oh, Violet, do not blush like that. You will have to learn that I am a tease. I did warn you of my wicked nature."

"Perhaps I should warn you of mine," Violet murmured, resisting the urge to watch Kit leave the room.

"You? I doubt it, my dear. Your aunt has raised you with great care. You have never been exposed to the vices of society."

"Perhaps I only need the chance."

Jane laughed. "Stay in London long enough."

"You are *not* wicked."

"Some people think I am," Jane said.

"Then they are envious."

"Let us read to the children for an hour," Jane said, her eyes brimming with warmth. "The wicked world will fall away as we do."

And it did. Violet sat down to read a primer with a little boy named Jack, who had dark circles under his eyes and looked up from his book every few seconds to check whether Kit was still at the window. "I'm gonna be a sword master like 'im when I grow up, miss," he whispered. "All the boys 'ere are gonna go to the academy and get training."

"Are you?" she asked, pushing a lock of hair from his eyes.

He nodded. "If we finish school. That's the pledge. And we gotta stay out of mischief. It's about . . . What's that word?"

"Honor?"

"Yeah. That's it."

She was surprised at how quickly the hour passed and how attached she had become to the few children she had met. It made her ache again for her own family. It made her grateful for what she had.

Kit was quiet during the ride to his fencing salon. So was Violet. But then, the marchioness chatted enough for three people, possibly capable of carrying on a conversation with herself. Violet wondered what Godfrey would think if he could see them. And then she felt guilty that she hadn't thought of him all day.

But how could she, with Kit to divert her? He looked at her only once during the carriage ride. His eyes had glittered like glass, so clear that she could see through to his soul.

A good soul.

A soul locked inside a man who looked dangerous indeed on the outside.

It had been a humbling day, one that had strengthened Violet's resolve to dedicate herself to good works. It gave birth to a dream that one day she would be able to endow a school in Monk's Huntley.

Even if she couldn't afford to establish it herself, she could collect donations, and Kit could— Her dream ended there. Godfrey would disapprove. He—

Kit's voice jolted her. "Well, it's back to business as usual. Pardon me, ladies. It has been a pleasure, but the sword calls."

"Do what you must," the marchioness said with a gracious nod.

Violet looked up, realizing that the carriage had stopped in front of an attractive redbrick establishment. From what she could see a sword fight was taking place on the sidewalk. A boisterous audience comprised of students, shopkeepers, and young gentlemen placing bets on the outcome obstructed the passage of traffic. A hot-pie vendor shouted that he had sold his last wares.

"Good gracious!" the marchioness said, blocking Kit's exit with her outflung arm. "One of those swordsmen is my brother-in-law, and he's promised the family he'll behave. Stay here, both of you, while I confront the rascal."

"Which rascal is it?" Kit inquired, sitting back obediently. "And are you certain I can't be of assistance?"

"It's Devon, the one who never outgrew the nursery. Just look at the big lummox. He isn't wearing any protection at all. Jocelyn will have a fainting fit when I tell her what he's up to now."

The door opened, and Jane stepped out into her senior footman's hand. Kit started to laugh. "I can't let her go into that fracas alone," he said in a low voice. He looked at Violet. "Will you promise to stay here if I leave?"

"Do you think anyone would dare harm her?"

"Not on purpose," he replied, taking his top hat from the seat. "I can't vouch for what she'll do, however."

Violet wished dearly to follow, but the moment he stepped out of the carriage a university student recognized him and shouted at the top of his voice, "Master Fenton is in our midst!"

She smiled as he made an unsuccessful dash for the *salle*. The crowd swarmed around him, bumping the coach. That a half minute later Weed handed the marchioness back inside, closed the door, and stood guard against the steps was a tribute to his dedication that Violet could only admire.

"What a rout!" Jane explained, collapsing on the seat against Violet. "That man has a following that verges on the unholy."

Violet looked over Jane's head to the window. Kit had drawn his sword and was fencing backward. Three of his students forced him to the salon door, where he slipped into a flawless lunge, disarming the trio in one move, and vanished from Violet's view.

"That was staged," Violet said in admiration. "They did that on purpose so he could escape."

But she wasn't at all surprised that Kit had a devoted following. She had been beguiled by him once herself.

"It is an amusing way to make an exit," Jane said. "I

wish I could do that at some of the affairs I attend."
Jane studied her as the carriage rocked into motion.
"Perhaps we shouldn't tell your aunt or fiancé about
this part of our excursion. I don't think I should mention it to my husband, either. Are you good at keeping
secrets?"

Violet smiled at her. "Yes. It's one of my best traits."

Chapter 12

On the following day Sir Godfrey called to take Violet and her aunt for an afternoon drive through Hyde Park. He had brought Aunt Francesca a straw bonnet decorated in silk lilies that he'd bought at a discount. When Violet caught her aunt making a face at the hat in the hallstand mirror, she decided that a day in the park might not be a good idea after all.

"I have a treat for you," Sir Godfrey insisted behind her with a mysterious air that to Violet felt more like a threat.

"What sort of treat?"

"You, my dear, will have to wait."

Violet compressed her lips. "May I have a hint?"

"No," he said, escorting her toward the door, "you may not."

"Will I like this treat?" her aunt asked, pulling off the bonnet and handing it to Twyford with a grimace of distaste.

Godfrey stared at Francesca in arrested disbelief before a respectful smile relaxed his face. "I will be disappointed if you do not, madam," he said, offering Francesca his arm.

Violet and Twyford glanced at each other before Francesca reluctantly placed her hand upon his forearm and reached back for Violet's hand. Violet hesitated. She wasn't sure what had happened between Godfrey and her beloved aunt, but she would rather stay home than serve as peacemaker between them. Moreover, if she left the house, she might miss another visit from Jane, or the message that she could never admit she was waiting for.

She would have to be careful not to bring up the subject of fencing, specifically of fencing masters, to Godfrey. She doubted she could convince him that she had developed a sudden fascination with sword fighting, after she had missed his performance at the ball.

She paused at the door to button up her aunt's short woolen spencer and followed her with Godfrey to the carriage he had parked in the middle of the street, obstructing traffic to and fro. Perhaps she should pretend that nothing was wrong, a situation rendered impossible as the three of them settled into the carriage and her aunt bent at the waist to examine one in a pile of long objects that poked out from beneath a tarpaulin under her feet.

"What in the name of creation is this?" Aunt Francesca demanded, and then proceeded to frighten the wits out of Violet by pressing the knob at the end of the

long object and releasing a sword blade in Sir Godfrey's face from the polished cylinder.

Violet swallowed a gasp as she stared at her betrothed. The blood drained from his cheeks, and small
wonder, with Aunt Francesca swiping a lethal blade at
his throat in bloodthirsty delight. "Well, look at that. It
is a sword, Violet. Your fiancé has brought a virtual
cache of the things with us to the park. How remarkable, Sir Godfrey. Do you intend to open up a shop as
we drive along Rotten Row?"

He wrested the cane from her grasp in red-faced indignation. "I have already sold them to the pupils in
the academy where I fence. Please, Lady Ashfield, give
me that stick before you stab one of us."

Aunt Francesca's voice rose in skepticism. "Is the
academy you attend located in the park?"

"It is not," he replied, his jaw tightening. "But some
of the students, including myself, are meeting there in
a few minutes, and now you have spoiled what I had
in store."

Violet subsided against the seat, afraid that she
would start to giggle and never stop if she looked either him or her aunt in the eye. But then it occurred to
her that if the other pupils of the fencing school were to
meet in the park, it wasn't unreasonable to hope that
the master of the academy might accompany them.

It wasn't unreasonable at all to hope that she would
see Kit again today, which meant that she would have
an entirely different problem on her hands than a disgruntled fiancé and meddlesome aunt. She would

have a full-blooded blackguard to contend with, an artful one, an amorous one. A person improper to know.

"I assume you have resold these sticks at a good profit," Francesca said to Godfrey with a sniff of disapproval.

Godfrey watched as the sword retracted into the stick before he answered her. "We are staging a friendly bout by the lake today. You and your niece missed my performance, Lady Ashfield. I wanted to impress you."

Violet sat in silence as he placed the cane back under the seat. So this was to be his treat. A fencing competition in the park—to honor her? Her throat grew tight. A surprise, indeed, but not what he'd had in mind. "How long have you been planning this, Godfrey?" she asked him quietly.

"For weeks," he replied, releasing a sigh that hinted she was ungrateful for not guessing.

She could only be grateful he had not guessed the truth.

For weeks. Kit *would* be there.

She could not ask Godfrey to elaborate. It was enough for her to worry that by a look she or Kit would betray the other. It was enough for her to hide her emotions from her aunt. Should she worry that Kit would break his word? How was she supposed to watch him fight Godfrey and not take sides?

"I have always been intrigued by the notion of what gentlemen consider to be a friendly match," her aunt mused in the uncomfortable silence that had fallen. "It seems to me that even in sport one can wound an opponent."

"We are professionally trained," Godfrey replied, glancing at Violet as if to implore her intervention. "We wear protective garments in the event of an accident, well-padded fencing jackets, gloves, and masks."

"I understand that," Francesca said. "But professional training does not erase every vestige of male pride. What if one of you should lose your temper? Anger can erupt even during a friendly challenge."

"Master Fenton would not allow that, madam."

Violet leaned forward, pretending a sudden fascination with the handsome team of horses that pulled another coach across the intersection. She was better off not entering into the conversation. Any opinion she ventured on the subject of Master Fenton was liable to arouse suspicion.

"I enjoyed a good sword fight in my day," her aunt said, her face meditative. "It is a skill, I must admit, that rouses a certain passion in the blood."

"Aunt Francesca," Violet murmured with a smile, "I cannot believe you would admit that. If I were to confess such a thing in public, you would reprimand me to no end."

"I think it's clear that I have been overstrict in your upbringing."

"I disagree," Godfrey said, and there was no trace of confrontation in his tone. "Violet is a perfect example of how a gentlewoman should be raised. Her demeanor is a credit to you, madam."

Violet gazed out into the street again. She and Godfrey did not know each other at all, she thought. He
wanted an unflawed wife, one who would serve as a
stage prop in his version of an unflawed world. The
realization wilted her spirits. She pictured herself
standing on a stage at a wedding altar, waiting until
the very last moment for a swordsman with a chiseled
face to rescue her. How many times in the past had Kit
rescued her and Eldbert from Ambrose or another of
their imaginary enemies? But Godfrey wasn't her enemy. And he was real.

"I hope I never embarrass you, Godfrey," she murmured.

"How could you?"

A dozen ways came to her mind.

The coach turned into the park, joining the stream of
traffic that headed toward Rotten Row. Violet glanced
past the elegant phaetons, the matched horses and liv-
eried grooms. She saw a group of ladies with plumed
hats, drifting across the grass.

"Where are they going?" Aunt Francesca asked,
peering over Violet's shoulder.

"I've no idea," she said, but she did.

She'd spotted Kit standing in his shirtsleeves and
close-fitting pantaloons as Sir Godfrey's driver was
parking behind a landau on the track. He turned, sending a detached glance in her direction. His gaze flickered once to Godfrey.

Her pulse fluttered wildly. To look at him no one
would guess she and Kit had ever shared anything

more than a dance and a charitable endeavor. She only hoped that she appeared as unmoved as he did.

She wasn't unmoved inside. His handsome elegance had sent her heart racing. The sight of him warmed her blood.

A footman helped her aunt alight from the carriage, and Violet forced herself to follow at a demure pace instead of running across the park to a swordsman she'd never been able to resist.

Whatever she did, she would not draw undue attention to Kit.

"Who is that person, Violet?" her aunt demanded in the authoritative voice that even God would be afraid to ignore. "The tall man with the group of ladies and gentlemen gathered around him? The lithesome one who is putting on a jacket and mask."

"I—"

"There is something familiar about him," her aunt continued, her suspicious nature aroused. "I have the keenest feeling I have seen him somewhere. But surely I would remember a person of such favorable appearance if we had met."

"That is my fencing master, madam," Sir Godfrey said, with a pride that strangely touched Violet. "He is the man with whom Violet opened the benefit dance the night before last."

Francesca hesitated, pulling away from Violet's hand. "Yes," she said slowly. "That must be it." But there was enough uncertainty in her voice that she stole another glance at Kit from the corner of her eye.

She looked as if she suspected there was more to his story. There was so much more, and Violet did not know most of it herself.

He *was* a sight to fluster the senses, a magnetic force caught between two worlds. Neither angel nor devil. A very human being who had suffered and proven his strength until now. Violet would not be the one to weaken him. She would be as faithful to their pact as he had been.

"Let us stand back in the shade," she said absently to her aunt. "We can see well enough from here."

"As you wish, Violet."

No. Not as she wished. What she wished for was unspeakable and disallowed. She wished to walk beside him and share their thoughts. She wished to feel his arms around her, and his mouth covering hers in kisses that took her breath away. She wished to be his best friend, to be . . . his.

She guided her aunt into the shade. She forced herself to concentrate on Godfrey as he strode across the grass. It should not have been a chore to pay attention to the gentleman who would be her husband. It should not be a temptation to compare another man's muscular shoulders and relaxed figure to her betrothed's more solid and familiar form.

But was Godfrey really the more familiar? She straightened as Kit swept a button-tipped foil in the air. Violet could have sworn she heard it sing from where she stood. The careless ease of his swing brought back a rush of memories.

She was not the only one impressed by the nimble devil. Several ladies and gentlemen halted in midconversation to regard him in wonder. Even her aunt stepped forward, risking the sun for a closer look. To Violet's astonishment Kit turned, looked straight at Aunt Francesca, and bent in a graceful bow.

"I think I like that young swordsman, Violet," her aunt said. "But I am not deceived for a moment by that bow. It was meant for you."

"He didn't even look at me."

"Exactly."

"And he is wearing a mask."

"All the better to hide his feelings for you," Francesca said drily. "You must have stirred his romantic sentiments at the ball."

"And you must have stirred sherry into your morning tea," Violet said, shaking her head. "Furthermore, if he paid any attention to me, it would be as a courtesy to Godfrey. Let us discuss Godfrey, shall we? Doesn't he look suave in his fencing jacket?"

"Not to me," Francesca replied. "But then, dear, you are going to marry him, and it is encouraging that you regard him as your champion in this bout." She paused. "I assume that Godfrey is challenging the master to duel. It *is* moving that he hopes to prove his manliness to you, Violet. Unless, of course, he is thoroughly thrashed, in which case he will prove only that he is a fool."

"Aunt Francesca, I do not know why you are suddenly so disenchanted with Godfrey, but it is something that we will have to discuss in private."

"I agree."

Kit and Godfrey now stood only a yard apart, Kit demonstrating a few directions with his foil. In all likelihood Godfrey had paid Kit for this public show. Of course he had. But did she want to see Godfrey humiliated? She wasn't sure she could watch even a congenial match between these two disparate men with an impartial heart. If she chose one as her champion, was she betraying the other? But to whom had she given herself first?

The bout started with the Grand Salute, a series of gestures by which the opponents showed respect for tradition. Violet noticed that the other pupils stopped their practice fencing by the water the instant that Kit and Godfrey engaged. The students drew together to study the master, as engrossed in Kit's strategy as she was.

It was all about control. He underplayed his parries. He might have been fastening his cuffs. His calmness never wavered.

He was controlling everyone—his opponent, his audience, and most of all Violet. Yes, he was in complete control of her attention; Aunt Francesca had not breathed a word since the salute. Kit prolonged every move. He provoked. Godfrey responded, already striving to keep up the pace. Even to Violet's amateur eye, it was obvious that Kit was manipulating Godfrey, and Godfrey, surprisingly, seemed to loosen and counter faster.

"Bash him, maestro!" a boy perched on his father's shoulders shouted.

"Yes, do," Aunt Francesca murmured.

Violet glared at her. "What did you say?"

"Achoo." Her aunt fumbled in her reticule for a clean handkerchief. "I must have sneezed. You know how grass irritates my breathing."

Violet sighed. The duel immediately absorbed her again. Kit had learned technique, she realized. There were names for the movements of the match—Godfrey had thrust a carte, which Kit parried with the carte parade. But he had been born with that skill.

A forbidden memory rose to her mind—Ambrose chasing her through the churchyard, threatening to tie her to a tree if she didn't join his army, and Kit flying after him. She was laughing, looking back as he gained on Ambrose. Her heart beat as if it would burst.

"I'll cut off your head if you touch her!" Kit bellowed with a grin.

"And I'll help him do it!" Eldbert shouted.

"Not fair," Ambrose protested, bending to draw a breath. "You're on my side today. I can't fight Kit by myself. He knows too many tricks, and he runs like a fox. He isn't civilized at all."

Violet barely broke through the boundary of the yew trees before Kit caught up with her. "He's right, you know," she whispered, staring past Kit to the broken lych-gate at which Ambrose had apparently surrendered. "You have to let him win once in a while."

"Why should I?"

"It's the decent thing to do."

"I . . . don't care about being decent."

"Then I won't stay."

"Fine." Shadows gathered in his eyes. "I'll let Little Lord Lost Pants win. On another day."

But he never did.

At times he might allow Ambrose to think he had a chance. Violet and Eldbert would wait, certain of the outcome, which typically meant that Kit would slide into a backward lunge and toss Ambrose's sword somewhere amid the broken tombs. Then Kit would clamber through the remnants of gargoyles and flying buttresses and rise up to declare that he had won the bout. And despite the pang of sympathy she felt for Ambrose, she would return home in a blissful mood for hours.

After leaving Monk's Huntley she hadn't felt that blissful since she had seen Kit again at the ball. She'd forgotten that she could feel that unadulterated abandon.

"Violet?"

"*Hmmm?*"

"Violet—why are you smiling like that?"

"What?" She shook herself, her aunt's voice intruding on her daydream. "Why am I what?"

"You were smiling, dear."

"Was I?"

"Yes. I suppose it is amusing."

"What? The fencing match?"

"That man appears to be toying with Godfrey," Aunt Francesca said with a keen air of discernment.

"Lower your tone."

"No one can hear me over all the cheering and shouting. That young man is like a beast wearing out its prey before settling down to eat it."

"I doubt that Master Fenton will be dining on Godfrey today. Besides, I think that Godfrey fences well."

"To the uneducated eye. It isn't that he fences like a schoolboy; it is that compared to his teacher . . . Oh, let us be honest: Few men could compare."

Violet could not disagree.

From the nursemaids and students to the members of the nobility who had drifted together to watch, Violet's aunt had merely voiced a collective observation.

"You must have enjoyed his performance at the benefit," her aunt said after a reflective pause.

"I missed Godfrey's scene."

"I know."

Aunt Francesca turned her head, meeting Violet's eyes. She couldn't possibly know about Kit, Violet thought. She couldn't have realized the truth after all these years. Her aunt had seen him for only a few moments, if at all, from the door, the day Violet had fallen ill and he had carried her home.

"Godfrey is showing off," Aunt Francesca said in the forthright manner she had developed since her husband's death. "I suppose most gentlemen try to do so in front of one another. I do not recall that he expressed an interest in fencing when you met him."

"He had been studying for only a few months at the time. I understand that there has been a revival of chivalry in society. I am drawn to the notion myself."

"So am I, but not when it is mere costume display. Watch that other swordsman closely."

Violet's lips firmed. She'd been struggling to do the very opposite. She wasn't sure what her aunt meant to suggest. Perhaps nothing at all. "He looks efficient, I would say."

"Efficient?" A note of disbelief quavered in her aunt's echo. "I think he looks absolutely lethal. I should have paid more attention to your dance with him at the party. He moves like no other young man I have seen."

"I cannot believe my ears, Aunt Francesca. You are going to embarrass yourself if you are overheard. All this talk of movement and—"

"See how well he lunges. Study the position of his lower body."

"I will do no such thing. You should be ashamed of yourself, a woman of your age, for even suggesting it."

"He has a natural instinct for the blade. He *does* remind me of someone, and I thought so the night of the ball. For the life of me I cannot remember who. He draws the eye."

"That is the point," Violet said in a neutral voice, "of putting on a show."

"I would argue that his talent goes beyond showmanship."

"I believe he studied fencing abroad for years."

"Where does he come from?" her aunt asked, her silver brows knitting in thought.

Violet dropped her gaze. "I couldn't tell you with any certainty. From what I've gathered he appears to be English." And thank heavens that much Violet could say in complete honesty. As far as she knew, Kit's origins remained a mystery; if he had uncovered any information about his family, he hadn't shared it with her.

Who could have given him away? she wondered. It had been painful enough for her to grow up without even a memory of her mother's face for comfort, but at least she had known that her parents had cared for her and who they were. But then, Kit had never been the sort to feel sorry for himself.

"You dance by instinct, Violet," her aunt said unexpectedly. "It is a gift, that grace of yours."

"I would have been a graceless spinning top without the years of instruction that you and Uncle Henry gave me," Violet replied. "My gift needed a guiding hand."

"But it lifted our hearts to watch you dance. Yes, in the beginning, you twirled around like a March wind, over the lawns, into the sofa, across the freshly polished floors. It often took Twyford an hour to catch you."

"I know," Violet said, and the old sense of committing other unnamed sins, of a guilt she did not understand, welled inside her. "I know I was a strain. I understand how much you both sacrificed to care for me. And yet—"

"You were the light of our lives," Aunt Francesca said, straightening her slight shoulders. "It is not always desirable, I have decided, to imprison a will-o'-

the-wisp. Some creatures lose their desire to shine when they are captured."

Violet wondered if this was her aunt's way of trying to apologize for the strictness of her upbringing. She knew her aunt and uncle had loved her. They had done their best to raise a girl who had proven unruly.

"I wasn't a magical creature. I danced because I could not bear to hold still. I heard music playing in my mind, and it made me want to dance."

"You were delightful."

"I was difficult," Violet admitted. "I always disturbed Uncle Henry when he was reading or entertaining a guest."

"Difficult?" Francesca's face crumpled, and she seemed to be on the verge of confessing a secret that Violet was not sure she wanted to know. Perhaps she'd prefer to stay in the dark indefinitely.

Before her aunt could continue, Violet returned her attention to the match. "We're going to miss Godfrey's grand moment if we don't stop chattering, and we shall never hear the end of it."

Chapter 13

$\mathcal{G}$odfrey failed to break through Kit's guard to score a single hit to the breast. Kit controlled not only his foil but the tempo of their sparring. He thwarted Godfrey at every angle of attack and kept his body in perfect alignment. Shoulder, hip, heel. He could end the match with a flick of his wrist.

In truth, he could have fallen asleep and countered Godfrey's predictable attacks. This was not sword fighting. It was the art of fencing with air.

But deciding whether to humble a pupil was a complex issue. He knew why Godfrey needed to win and whose favor he hoped to gain. Godfrey meant to impress a lady named Violet.

The trouble was that Kit shared the same male impulse, and, damn it to hell, his swordplay had spawned Violet's interest in Kit before either of them knew Sir Godfrey Maitland existed. Dark temptation threatened Kit's thoughts. A tidy bit of footwork and he could force Godfrey to perform an impromptu sword dance straight into the Serpentine.

Never mind that with one thrust of an actual small-sword, he could topple Godfrey into an early grave. No one would be entertained by such an easy act of aggression, however, least of all Kit. Murdering a paying student was anything but an honorable goal.

It would not only be illegal. It would also be immoral and offensive to the woman whom Godfrey intended to marry. Although Kit had not looked at her again since the match began, he could feel her presence as keenly he had when she'd watched him from her window.

But now, instead of fighting invisible enemies to prove his prowess, he was fighting against a rival who was all too real—one Violet had chosen to wed, which meant that there had to be some good in the man, even if Kit couldn't see it.

The intensity of the competition, the foils engaging in a blur of speed, increased without warning. Aunt Francesca took Violet's arm, drawing her a few steps closer to the match. Violet loved her aunt with all her being. She would do anything to protect her. But if Aunt Francesca kept asking questions about Kit, Violet was bound to let something slip. And if her aunt realized that he was the same boy Violet had befriended, there would be merry hell to pay.

But suddenly they both fell silent. It had become

impossible to look away or utter a word. Her aunt was right: He was deflecting poor Godfrey like a fly. He executed every response with intuitive precision, his footwork as intricate as the steps of any cotillion Violet had ever danced.

He was right, too.

There was no difference. The dynamics of a duel and of a dance derived from the same passion and purpose. Confront, conquer . . . or concede. It was all engagement and deception. Bending one's arm to elude or, if necessary, to entice. That was when nonresistance came into play. Weaving around one's partner allowed the control to attack. But you had to leave a space through which to escape.

Kit was going to lose the match.

She felt it in her bones. It infuriated her.

She bit her tongue to keep from crying out that he should win. He loved to fight. Yet she sensed that his sudden hesitation to retreat was deliberate. She sensed that he was about to sacrifice his pride to boost Godfrey's image. Of course she could not interfere. Godfrey had paid for Kit's services to impress her. Both men would be disgusted with her if she distracted them with an outburst of hysterics.

Little boys and their swords. Their pride.

Kit would survive. Violet knew he had survived much worse, and it was wrong of her to wish Godfrey ill because . . . because her secret friend was a rogue whom her fiancé aspired to imitate. What would Godfrey think if he had seen Kit's earliest fencing duels, raw and unrestrained, his wild dashes about broken gravestones?

What would Godfrey think if he had seen his betrothed dashing about in Kit's shadow? She sighed. Violet knew exactly how much Godfrey would frown upon the improper activities. But she could not undo those times, for all it might end up costing her. She would not undo them even if it *were* possible to change what had passed before.

Kit allowed his ungraceful opponent to score a hit that he could have parried with his tallywag. He ignored the groans of chagrin that rose from the happenstance observers. At the charity ball he had surpassed the expectations of strangers. Today he let them down. He shrugged as Sir Godfrey threw the crowd a victory grin, flushed with as much surprise and relief as spent effort.

Kit put more effort into not looking at Violet again to read her reaction than he had into the duel. He turned instead to his other pupils, encouraging them to dissect the bout. He had learned from witnessing other swordsmen's mistakes. He was still learning, it would seem.

Not until this moment, however, did he realize that all his years of practice, the wounds he had suffered and inflicted on others, the sum of studying under greater duelists than he, had been in the hope that one day Violet would see how accomplished he had become. And that she would cheer for him as she had when he had been outcast and alone.

He had not foreseen the day when he would throw a match to another man to prove his skill. But there it was. He sold his sword for a living. It could have been worse. And it could have been better, if she had been able to champion him again.

Violet froze in midstep as she realized that Godfrey had broken through the circle that surrounded Kit and was gesturing toward her. Surely he wasn't trying to bring Kit to her to gloat. What was she supposed to do? She could take deception only so far. Aunt Francesca might detect the strain between her and Kit, even if Godfrey did not.

"We ought to go back to the carriage and let you rest," she said, turning quickly to the track. "We have been standing on our feet too long."

Aunt Francesca brushed off the suggestion. "Nonsense."

"I'm not sure that watching a fight is beneficial to a lady who practically collapsed two days ago," Violet said, managing to keep Francesca from shaking off her hand.

"Fight? It was anything but a true contest. That young swordsman could have carved the alphabet in Godfrey's forehead had he chosen."

"Well, thank goodness for Godfrey's mask."

"I would like to meet the swordsman." Aunt Francesca gave her a wistful look. "Allow an old lady her indulgence."

Why? Violet wondered crossly. She had been discouraged from indulging her own inappropriate ways. But then, she *had* indulged in secret. She held her tongue. She stood, fettered by bonds of duty to her aunt and of affection, and bittersweet attachment to the man who sauntered closer, taking his time because he understood the power of timing. Kit also understood more about her than the gentleman to whom she would dedicate the rest of her life.

She glanced across the park at a game of pell-mell in progress, all the while aware of Kit. Kit hung his head; he appeared to be listening to whatever Godfrey was saying. Her heart leaped at the danger inherent in his approach.

She knew he was full of the devil—neither the workhouse nor his father nor his sword masters had broken his will. They had only tempered it like steel. That was it. He had grown stronger. Perhaps she hadn't. Perhaps she had grown submissive.

Mischief brightened his eyes for the quick interlude that they held hers. He placed his right hand to his heart, his mask dangling from his fingertips, and bowed low. "Ladies," he said in a deep voice that disarrayed her senses. "I trust you enjoyed the match and that none of its actions offended you."

"It was invigorating," Aunt Francesca said, and straightened as if to say that age entitled her to speak her opinion.

Kit studied Violet in curiosity. "But Miss Knowlton appears a little pale, as if—well, forgive the expression—as if she had seen a ghost."

"I assure you," Violet said in an unwavering voice, "I would not have stayed had I felt the slightest discomfort. And if I had seen—"

"I understand," Aunt Francesca broke in, "that it is not uncommon these days for ladies to take fencing lessons."

He blinked in surprise, and although Violet was annoyed at her aunt, she took Kit's reaction to mean he had conceded a point.

"It's absolutely true," he said, sliding his mask back onto his forefinger from the verge of descent. "In most cases it is an actress who seeks instruction to allow her a greater range of roles. I have given private lessons to noblewomen of independent natures."

"Miss Knowlton is no actress in the making, I assure you," Godfrey said, frowning at Kit.

"No." His light eyes flickered over her. "I wouldn't have thought so for a moment."

"What an interesting notion," Aunt Francesca mused.

He was quite an actor himself, Violet concluded, tempted to applaud him. But then, hadn't she hoped he would throw off the scent of anyone who suspected their secret history?

He folded a glove meticulously into his mask. "Certain accommodations are recommended, but in my experience, a few lessons broaden the feminine education." He gave Violet a piercing glance. "If either of you ladies is interested in light instruction, I shall be happy to leave my card."

She felt her breath catch in her throat. Offer her sword fighting lessons, would he? She wished she could remind him of the ignominious duels he had waged whirling a farmer's hoe over his attractive head. Still, even then, he had quickened the air and raised more than few drowsing spirits.

"It's terribly kind of you to offer, Mr. Fenton, but I doubt that either of us will find it necessary to fight any duels in the near future."

His mouth thinned in a fleeting smile that served to remind her he could kiss as skillfully as he fenced. "If you change her mind, you have only to ask your fiancé for a card. He has dozens of the things lying about his shop."

Sir Godfrey stared at him, aghast. "In a hundred years I could not imagine Violet wielding a sword."

"I also give command performances," Kit added, as if Godfrey hadn't spoken.

"How much do you charge?" Aunt Francesca inquired.

"No doubt more than we can afford," Violet said in an undertone.

Kit shook his head. "Didn't I mention that my fees were negotiable?"

Heaven help her. And him. One more remark like that and she would swat the audacious rascal to a fare-thee-well with her fan. She had a firm grasp on it today. But the next time she got him alone . . . *Would* there be a next time? Could she in good conscience accompany the marchioness on another mission?

Kit stared at her in a silence deep enough to herald the end of the world. *Do* not *say anything else*, she implored him with her eyes. *Not another word. Don't even think it.*

She could sense the counterattack that he ached to deliver. At length he nodded at Godfrey, dismissing the matter with a cavalier smile. "You, of course, know the lady better than I do, sir. I envy you, but such is life."

He tossed his foil over his shoulder to the assistant and three young pupils who waited within a yard of his shadow. A lace-trimmed cuff rose above the other hands to catch the master's weapon. Violet remembered how she had considered it an honor to hold Kit's sword while he climbed a tree or taught Eldbert and Ambrose how to box.

At least he had found another band of followers as dedicated to him as he deserved, even if he was more forbidden to her than ever.

Godfrey's satisfaction had begun to dissipate soon after the duel ended. By the time he returned home he felt rather foolish for showing off to Violet, whose wholehearted affection he had never seemed to capture. What had he done now to displease her? He had been convinced when they first met that her coolness had been due to her demure nature. She was quiet,

which a woman should be. She was refined, of aristocratic stock, a lady of virtue. Indeed, her composure
aroused him. She would warm his bed at night, cool or
not. Their children would carry his name and her
blood.

She would never embarrass him by conducting affairs, like other ladies of her class. Perhaps he was not
thinking clearly. Perhaps he was fatigued from the excitement of the charity ball, his long hours at his shops,
and his match against Fenton today.

The contest had taken every drop of Godfrey's
strength. After a light dinner he was reduced to soaking in a hip bath and sipping brandy to ease his rub-
bery limbs. Oddly, he'd gotten the sense that all the
swashbuckling in the world would not sway Violet to
passion toward him.

Was it possible that she had thought his display to
be vulgar? The other ladies present at the park, including her bothersome old aunt, had made no bones about
enjoying the contest. It had been meant, after all, in a
spirit of gentlemanly sport.

What did it matter that Fenton had thrown the
match in his client's favor? Godfrey wondered as he
rose from his bath to dress. He was not paid to make
himself look superior to his pupils. He put on his silk
dressing robe. He wondered again whether he had
imagined that tension between Violet and the fencing
master.

Impossible. Intriguing. How dared they, even in
Godfrey's imagination.

Fenton had never shown any excess of emotion in the entire length of his professional association with Godfrey. Should he resign himself once and for all to Violet's aloof detachment?

The benefit ball had been one thing. Violet excelled at dancing. It was not her fault that Fenton had led her off in that impromptu dance exhibition. But something had sparked the exchange between the pair of them today in the park. Antagonism? Or attraction? Godfrey had not thought Violet capable of such fire.

It was probably nothing, he thought, and turned to his chest of drawers to pick out a neck cloth for his Thursday evening at the club. Small surprise that the artful young Fenton found Violet desirable. Godfrey would not have chosen to marry a lady who lacked appeal.

Violet took her aunt upstairs to bed earlier than usual that night. The afternoon might have invigorated their spirits, but now even Violet felt the need to rest. The maid had folded down the bedcovers and closed the curtains to ward off the evening air and occasional disturbance from the street.

"Weeds are easy to grow," Aunt Francesca said without preamble after she had settled into bed. "A violet requires the right environment. How wonderful it was to watch you and your uncle dancing a quadrille with our unreliable Miss Higgins, the footman on the fiddle, and Twyford covering his false notes with a cough, and then . . ." Her voice changed as if she could see through a door to the past. "Do you remember the afternoon we caught the little gentlemen at the window?"

Violet shook her head in concern. Her aunt's mind wandered more and more. "You must mean Eldbert and Ambrose. They were at the window many afternoons."

"How they made me fear for you."

"The little *gentlemen* were laughing at me, Aunt Francesca. I do not know why you feared them. They never meant me any harm."

"Perhaps not. Eldbert was polite enough. Ambrose was always rude, as was his mother. But there was that scruffy boy who worked in the fields. That pauper. I shall never forget the day he carried you home from the churchyard. Ambrose's mother later told me that you had made a friend of him, and I called her a liar. I said that my niece would never set foot in that place. But you had."

She swung her gaze to Violet, bright, alert. "I thought the boy had killed you. I looked at you in Twyford's arms, still and white, and I thought that ruffian had brought you home dead. I thought you had been murdered and he had brought us your body."

Violet's memory of the incident was blessedly vague. Her high fever had distorted the details of that afternoon, although she could still picture Kit staring at her in horror, and she could hear his heart thudding where her cheek rested against his shirt as he carried her up the slope to the house. Eldbert had helped, but she wasn't sure how. She had begged Kit to drop her outside the door. But he had refused. She had heard her uncle talking behind him and her aunt wailing in hysterics.

"He meant well," Violet said, bending her head to extinguish the candle on the nightstand. "Ambrose didn't want to come anywhere near me. Nor did Eldbert, but at least he brought my shawl when I felt better. Ambrose suffered the most, and let everyone know it when he recovered."

"I wonder what happened to that poorhouse boy." Aunt Francesca closed her eyes. "I can't even remember the name of the man who bought him to apprentice and took him away. He was a captain, wasn't he, a widower who'd lost his own son? They never returned to Monk's Huntley, that I know. I suppose if the boy gave him trouble he could have sold him to another master. Wicked business . . . to own a person."

"Perhaps he helped the boy," Violet said, her throat constricting.

"Perhaps. How peculiar that he should come to mind when I never got a proper look at him. I would have feared for you even more had I known you had befriended a pauper."

A chill slid down her nape. Perhaps her aunt's mind was not wandering at all. Perhaps it was only coming to an inevitable conclusion. "Why did you fear so?" she asked after a pause.

"You were the only child your uncle and I would ever have. I had lost your mother when she was so young. And you . . . well, you were fearless during your earliest years."

"I was lonely."

"Were you, Violet?"

"Didn't you know?"

Francesca looked away in distress. "Not until I lost your uncle."

Chapter 14

$\mathcal{V}$iolet was surprised to find Godfrey absent from the emporium when she and her aunt went shopping early the next afternoon. The two women browsed for a good hour, admiring a number of goods as Twyford hovered nearby to be of help. Violet could have looked until the arcade closed; she was fascinated by everything from the hall clocks to the cake plates on display. But at length Aunt Francesca admitted to feeling worn.

"It's time for us to go home," Violet insisted, expecting a disagreement.

But it did not come. "Yes. This is a fine establishment. Godfrey has done well for himself. I do admire the silver tea caddy that is on display. My mother—your grandmother, Violet—had one quite similar in design."

"Then you shall have it," Violet said. "Let Twyford walk you to the carriage while I ask Mr. Cooper to put it away for us."

"I'd forgotten what good taste Godfrey has," Francesca said. "If his other shops are anything like this, he has worked hard, indeed."

As they were walking to the door a gentleman in a frock coat and buckskin pantaloons drifted toward them. He had a narrow face that at first looked youthful but showed lines of dissipation as he drew closer. He tipped his hat and murmured something in French to Violet that she did not understand.

By the heat in his eyes as they met hers, however, she decided it might have been a greeting better left untranslated. "And the same to you, I'm sure," she said quietly.

Aunt Francesca frowned at her. "That is exactly the sort of person one should avoid."

"He made me feel uncomfortable, too."

Her aunt glanced back at the throng of customers in the emporium. "I resent the way he looked at you."

"So do I. But I'll resent it more if you work yourself into a state."

"Could you have met him at the benefit ball?" Francesca asked. "He acted as though he knew you."

"Oh, I didn't think of that. I doubt it—but it *is* possible. Perhaps *I* was rude."

A few moments after Violet left her aunt with Twyford, she returned to the emporium. The gentleman who had addressed her was gone. Relieved, she caught the harried head assistant's attention. He was so obviously eager to please his employer's betrothed that Violet felt sorry for him. He climbed a tall ladder behind the counter to retrieve the caddy, and almost fell in his eagerness to do so.

"Thank you, Mr. Cooper," she said as he escorted her through the arcade. "I expect Sir Godfrey is at the wharves."

He lowered his voice. "I don't think so, miss. He ran out with his sword and his foil. I assume he's gone for lessons. Fencing has become his passion."

"So I understand."

"He fences well."

"Yes," Violet murmured, and instantly envisioned Kit walking toward her with a blade pointed at her heart. "Mention we stopped by, please."

"Oh, I won't need to do that, miss," he said earnestly.

Violet gave her hand to the footman waiting for her at the arched entrance doors. "Why not?" she asked, hesitating at his anxious expression.

"He'll notice right away that the tea caddy is missing and demand the name of the customer who bought it."

Violet gazed back into the bustling arcade. "Well, a sale is a sale."

"Yes, and your name has a good influence on his manner," he confided, stepping back to bow. "However, I beg you, do not tell him that I said so."

She laughed. "No, I—" She looked around, feeling as if a shadow had just enshrouded her.

"Is anything wrong, Miss Knowlton?"

She shook her head. "Not at all. I will sing your praises to Sir Godfrey. Thank you again."

Violet was relieved that her aunt's energy seemed to rally in the next few days. Three of the late baron's friends had sent Francesca invitations for various affairs about town. "It is moving that so many of Henry's acquaintances remember me," Francesca said, staring ruefully at the letters on her lap. "Since we have no other relatives, I'd like for you to meet them, Violet. Godfrey has offered to act as our escort."

" 'One cannot attend too many social events,' " Violet said, lowering her voice to imitate his. " 'It is good for business, and you, my dear, made a stunning impression at the ball.' "

Aunt Francesca's brow lifted. "All you need is a little mustache and a walking stick."

"I hope there is more difference between the two of us than that."

Francesca laughed, holding up another letter. "Did you read this? It's from your old friend Lord Charnwood."

"Ambrose?"

"It's an invite to a house party a month from tomorrow. Oh, my. There's to be a treasure hunt, a *fencing* performance, and a ball."

"Almost everyone will be there then."

"I beg your pardon?"

"I mean, well, Eldbert and . . . and Ambrose."

"Yes, it is Ambrose's party. One assumes he will attend."

"And Godfrey, too. If there's fencing."

"Godfrey." Her aunt set the letter on top of the others. "I take it that we are going to accept the invitation."

"I don't see how we can refuse."

"Not with Ambrose and Eldbert there," her aunt said rather slyly. "And another chance to see Godfrey's spectacular fencing skills."

"We don't have to go if you would prefer to stay home," Violet said in a neutral voice.

"I would not deprive you of the chance to see your old friends again, Violet."

Her old friends. She thought it would not be a complete reunion without Miss Higgins. But if Kit was to attend, she would do her best to resist him, or perhaps by then his interest in her would have cooled.

She saw him again at the Duke of Wenderfield's breakfast party on Berkeley Square the following week. Sir Godfrey mentioned during the drive that the academy was staging a small fencing performance for the guests on the lawn, but that he would not be participating. "Why not?" Violet asked. He did not say why, but he sounded a little miffed. For once Aunt Francesca did not venture an opinion.

Violet searched covertly for Kit in the group of handsome bucks lounging on the entrance steps. She looked for him among the younger guests drifting across the garden as she met the duke and duchess with Godfrey and her aunt. When he volunteered to take her aunt on a light stroll of the gardens with their hosts, she deliberately lagged behind.

She had just noticed a tent on the slope around which an audience had gathered to watch an Elizabethan rapier duel when she heard a cultured voice call her name.

She hesitated. Kit had emerged from the tent in a long-tailed black coat slung over a billowing white shirt and narrow brown trousers. His gaze slowly appraised the crowd. Would it be too improper of her to draw his attention? Perhaps she could walk around the tent, acting as if she'd lost her way. She could drop her fan again. No. A lady would never resort to such an obvious tactic.

But then, before she could put any plan in motion, another lady in the audience, a brazen one, who obviously didn't care what anyone thought, threw a red rose at Kit's feet. He laughed but left the flower where it had fallen.

Reluctantly Violet turned to face the person who had spoken her name again. To her relief it was the Marchioness of Sedgecroft.

Jane's green eyes sparkled with irresistible mischief. "May I borrow your company for a few moments? I am trying to elude the most boring baronet in the world. Speaking of which, where is your— Oh, dear, I wasn't referring to *your* baronet, who I'm sure is the most perfectly exciting gentleman imaginable."

Violet glanced surreptitiously over her shoulder. "Indeed."

Jane shot her a questioning look.

Violet shook her head. "I'm sorry. I was diverted."

"Fenton is too exciting," Jane said with a sigh. "You saw how the schoolchildren worship him. Well, he is who my son asks for at night before he falls asleep, and in the morning when the nursemaid tries to put on his clothes."

Violet could only smile in sympathy. She understood too well how exciting Kit could be. Even now both women subsided into silence to watch him supervise a bout. Not that anyone in the audience seemed to be paying attention to his students; when Kit performed a stylish series of disengagements to demonstrate correct positioning, a hush spread over the crowd.

He moved with a sensual grace that captivated the eye. Violet felt a secret thrill as she remembered his hard body pinning her still for his kiss. He performed a lunge that appeared physically impossible, eliciting gasps from the crowd.

"I have to have him," Jane said simply.

Violet's mouth dropped open. She realized that the fashionable world took lovers at whim, but that the marchioness could speak so fondly of her son in one moment and of "having" Kit in the next was beyond shocking. She didn't know how to react.

Jane turned to her with a laugh of apology. "Oh, my dear, your *face*. It is not at all what it sounds like. I should have told you the other day. The marquess is determined to hire Fenton as our family master-at-arms, not as *my* paramour."

Violet swallowed. "The thought never entered my mind."

"Yes, it did," Jane teased. "It's my fault for— Oh, quickly, take my arm and proceed forward. The baronet has me in his sights. I did warn you—I am shameless. I shall abandon you to his company if he catches up with us. He's forever complaining about his bowels."

Violet hastened her step. It amazed her that the marchioness could travel as fast as she did on the tiny slippers that showed in pretty glimpses through her pink silk skirts. "Do we have a destination?" she asked breathlessly.

"The pavilion."

Violet stared at the white-turreted pavilion that loomed in the distance. "It's beautiful."

"Isn't it? It is also a place that respectable people avoid at all costs, which naturally makes it a spot of great interest. You may have heard it said that there are secret passages inside that provide ideal trysting spots, as well as escape routes for the amorously inclined."

"Are there?" Violet asked.

"Oh, yes."

As it seemed unlikely that she and Jane would be accused of misconduct if they were caught together, Violet decided she had little to risk by accompanying the marchioness on her excursion.

Not that she had the wits or wherewithal to resist a woman who, a moment later, could admit with candid warmth, "It was four years ago in the pavilion that my husband kissed me insensible."

"After you were married, you mean?"

"Of course not. He was a scoundrel. Shortly after kissing me, the handsome hypocrite caught his sister Chloe in a compromising position with a young officer and brought down the wrath of God upon their heads. I'd never seen such a display of temper in my life. It was marvelous, and rather frightening."

Violet laughed at this confession. From what she had heard of the Boscastles, the scene described was not an exaggeration. The men of the family allegedly tended to overprotect their own. When it came to passion, however, they were reported to play by another set of rules.

Rather like a certain sword master who followed his own code.

Violet willed herself not to think of him, but it was useless. Would she have a chance to speak with him today? Surely if he knew that Sir Godfrey had come to the party, he would . . . Well, *what* would he do? What could he do? Rush in with sword to save the day? Kit was protecting her by acting as if they had only recently met. No weapon could break through social barriers.

"And," the marchioness continued blithely, unaware of Violet's inattention, "Grayson dared to initiate his romantic nonsense with these infamous words: 'There is a time to be wise, and a time to be wicked. Which do you suppose it is?'"

That was too much. Violet came to a halt in front of the double-porpoise fountains that flanked the pavilion entrance. Their light spray cooled her face. "I wouldn't have known how to answer."

"Neither did I," Jane admitted, urging her forward. "But it is not called the Pavilion of Pleasure without reason. A kiss from the right man renders words superfluous. Do be careful where you walk. It is dark and damp inside, as I recall."

Violet peered into the shadowed interior and felt a forbidden tug of curiosity beckon her senses. How long had it been since she had done anything daring? Not counting kissing Master Fenton. She would have adored a friend like Jane when she was younger.

"I hope you aren't one of those ladies who are afraid of the dark," Jane murmured.

"No."

"Or of enclosed spaces."

"It reminds me of a crypt."

Jane laughed in delight. "As if you had ever been in one. But then, perhaps the pavilion was designed to make us huddle closer to the wicked gentlemen who bring us here."

"Do I hear water dripping?" Violet asked, glancing around.

"That is probably one of the bathing pools. I would suggest at any other time that we soak our feet, but I shall ruin my slippers if they get wet." Jane motioned toward a staircase that was so narrow Violet might have missed it on her own. "I believe that will take us to the turret room. As I recall it has a passage inside that leads into the rear garden."

Violet climbed slowly in Jane's shadow. She couldn't help thinking that there had to be an easier way to avoid another guest.

"You are kind to help me out," Jane said over her shoulder. "It's difficult to be a lady in certain situations, isn't it? One must pretend to be polite to the oddest sorts."

"Yes," Violet agreed in a wry voice as they reached the top of the torchlit stairwell and walked into a circular chamber.

Violet stared around the tiny room in speculation. A Grecian chaise occupied most of the space, its function obvious. A light breeze entered the arched window that overlooked the garden party in progress. She glanced at the unlit fireplace. "Is the passageway in there?"

Jane nodded. "Yes. But fortunately it is well maintained, and we shall not emerge the worse for wear—"

"My lady!" a frantic voice cried up from the depths of the stairs. "Forgive this intrusion if it is not you, madam, but I am sent to fetch you!"

Violet turned in suspense.

She had to admire whoever dared to approach the marchioness in such passionate haste. A lover? A family member?

"What is it, Weed?" the marchioness demanded in a voice of exasperated affection. And then, to Violet, she added, "You did meet our senior footman, Weed, at the ball? I could not survive without him."

The marquess's stone-faced senior footman, who apparently served as Jane's personal confidant, appeared at the top of the stairs. He bowed, albeit distractedly, in Violet's direction. "The Duchess of Scarfield is aggrieved that she cannot find you."

"Well, heavens above," Jane said. "We cannot aggrieve Her Grace. Would you like to come and meet my sister-in-law, Violet?"

"I don't—"

"Good choice," Jane said before Violet could venture an opinion. "I'd hide from her, too, if I could. I can guarantee she won't complain about her bowels, but I'm bound to get a lecture for some reason or another. Weed, send a footman to escort Miss Knowlton from the pavilion to keep the gossipmongers quiet. Violet, be careful of rogues on your way down. One never knows who might be traveling through a secret passage at a party. And by the way, I never forget a favor."

"But—"

"Don't worry. I won't say a word."

"A word about what?"

"I shall call on you next week," Jane said with a blithe wave.

The footman bowed again and led the marchioness to the narrow aperture in the wall. Their voices faded. Violet went to the window, wondering how long it would take her clandestine escort to arrive, and whether she could see the fencing tent in the garden from her vantage point.

Chapter 15

$\mathscr{I}$t was all very well and good for the Marchioness of Sedgecroft to indulge in improper behavior. In society's eyes Jane and her scoundrel of a husband could do no wrong, while Violet's every move would be subject to scrutiny. She envied Jane's aplomb and doubted—

"If a lady stands in a tower window long enough, it might be assumed that she's asking to be rescued."

She spun around, her breath rushing out in surprise as she recognized the lean-hipped figure standing at the top of the stairs. "Reassure me that you are *not* my escort."

Kit gave her a guarded smile. "What are you talking about?"

"The marchioness did not send *you* here to escort me back to the party so that she could escape?"

He glanced around the tower, his hand sliding to his sword belt. "Escape from whom or from what, exactly?"

"From . . . from the gentleman who was following her at the party . . . and complaining about his bowels."

"And he followed the pair of you into the tower?" he asked in a doubtful voice.

"As far as I know, we lost him before we reached the pavilion."

His eyes danced with humor. "Is he armed and dangerous?"

She paused. "Not in comparison to you."

He took a step toward her. For countless moments she was unable to move. All she could do was stare at him, at his lean, intense face and the light eyes that seemed to lay bare her every secret.

She summoned her will and edged away from the window. Mesmerized by his presence, she did not notice the slow descent of her blue cashmere shawl from her shoulders toward the floor. Kit reacted before she did. He reached out with his sword to catch the shawl and lower it to the chaise.

His eyes lifted to hers, bright with rue. "There. Proof of how much my sword and I have improved since the day you and your shawl ensnared us."

Violet bent to pick up the wrap, lowering her head so that he would not see the emotion she was struggling to hold back. "I won't argue that."

"Don't go yet," he said, and she went still, watching his shadow advance on her across the stone floor.

Again she could not move. This time, however, a physical barrier impeded her in the form of a masterful man. Kit was not only standing in her way; he was standing so indecently close to her that a shock went down her back. She basked in the heat that radiated from his core. He magnetized, melted her.

"Go if you must," he said. "I won't stop you."

Silver glinted from the sword at his side.

She raised her gaze.

Temptation smoldered in his smile.

"That almost sounds like a challenge," she said, tossing back her hair in acceptance.

He laid his sword across the foot of the chaise. "I'd say that we were even now, except that you'll always have the advantage over me."

"Tell me the truth," she said softly. "You didn't happen to arrange this little escapade with the marchioness, did you?"

"I take offense at the suggestion. You ought to know I would never stoop to anything that low." His mouth lifted in a grudging smile. "Well, I might, but this was not a plan on my part."

"It's too coincidental that she brought me here and abandoned me as abruptly as she did."

He looked past her to the chaise. "She said nothing to me."

She studied his chiseled profile in fascination. "She speaks very highly of you." She touched his forearm, aware that it was a dangerous step for her to take. "Are you angry?"

"At you?" He turned his head and looked down at her with an unconcealed desire that took away her breath. "The entire world could send me into exile, and I wouldn't miss it if I could take you with me. The truth is that I saw you enter the pavilion, and I followed on the off chance that I would find you alone and"—he glanced at the sword on the chaise—"take you captive."

Violet stared down briefly at the length of polished steel that he had placed upon her soft blue shawl. When she looked up at him again, she knew that a hundred suitors could ask for her hand and she would never feel for one of them as she did for this man.

The flickering torchlight, his beautiful face, danced in her vision. His arms swiftly enclosed her; he had captured her as promised. She pushed without conviction at his chest in one moment. In the next she grasped a handful of his coat and drew him nearer.

Wool abraded her cheek. Beneath his coat she felt the bleached softness of his cambric shirt and the trained strength of his body. Her beloved friend. Her irresistible secret.

"Well?" he asked, and did not wait before he lowered his head to kiss her. "Are you my captive or not?"

Bittersweet pleasure sang through her. She parted her lips and felt his tongue against hers. His hands supported her even as they stole down her back with a quicksilver sensuality that left her uncertain and shivering in anticipation. The desire in his kiss drained her of her old will and filled her with one infinitely more dangerous.

"I don't want to shame you," he said against her mouth. "I don't want to be your secret friend or lover.

I don't want anything about us to be a secret. But . . . I do want you."

She closed her eyes. "I don't care about anything else."

"Yes, you do."

She twined her arms around his neck, returning his kiss until his mouth moved down her throat to the border of her bodice. Her hands fell to her sides. His breath soothed and teased her vulnerable skin, the tops of her breasts.

"I don't want to borrow you," he whispered.

He brought his hands to her bodice and tugged. She shivered, her breasts aching and exposed. His eyes, heavy lidded with sensuality, lifted to hers. "I want to be the only man who has the right to do this to you."

She took a breath.

His hands slipped under her bodice, cupping her breasts. He bent to her and drew one tender nipple into his mouth. She arched her neck, a hostage to his hunger. He nipped gently at her other breast. Her breathing quickened as he pulled his mouth away and blew on her glistening nipples.

"The only man," he repeated, as he drew her down with him on the chaise.

She submitted to an instant of panic, of pleasure; she felt his hands drift over her bottom, pressing her to his hard warmth. She had fallen in a curve against his torso. Slowly he turned her onto her back and held her prisoner beneath him. He stared down at her with a longing that flooded her veins with fire.

He kicked his sword to the floor with his foot. She heard the clatter of steel against stone, the rasp of his breath before he began moving his body against hers. Her pulse beat in her throat. She felt the thickness of him and a temptation to do . . . whatever he wished. Unbidden, she raised her hands to his shoulders. He groaned as if her touch tortured him.

"I want to be inside you," he whispered. "I want your sweetness for myself."

She was losing her hold on awareness.

"Violet. Dear God, give me the strength, or I will regret this."

She felt herself falling into darkness.

"*Violet,*" he said again, with an urgency that broke through her daze. "Get up. We cannot be found like this."

She sat up in dazed reluctance as Kit rolled onto his feet. He resheathed his sword with one hand and reached for her with the other. She rose, shivering as their eyes met. The sky had clouded up in the short time they had spent together in the pavilion. It was dark enough in the tower now to appreciate the torchlight—and the company of an armed escort.

Escort. She glanced toward the stairwell. Had Jane forgotten her promise? Violet had completely forgotten that she was waiting for safe passage from the pavilion.

She felt a pair of firm hands slide up her back. She glanced around, intending to challenge this round of mischief. But Kit was merely lifting her shawl to her shoulders. He veiled the passion in his eyes before she could fall prey to it again. The pitch of his voice vibrated in the quiet like steel cutting into stone.

"I only play games these days that I intend to play to the end. If a man challenges me with his sword, one of us is liable to die. I lived an ugly life, and you were my window to salvation. There were nights in the workhouse when I witnessed . . . when I experienced so much sin that I felt I would taint you with my company."

Her throat ached. "You never tainted me, Kit."

"Perhaps not then. Those were innocent games. There is nothing innocent about my desire for you at this moment."

She shook her head. "I didn't understand anything until Ambrose told me. I had no idea what you had to endure."

"No one wants to know what it's like in a palace. But it wasn't as bad for me as it was for the younger boys."

She cringed at the reminder of her naïveté. "You were one of the younger boys once," she said, forcing herself to grip the fringe of her shawl instead of reaching out for him. Why had she found him when it was too late to matter?

"I never think of the past," he said. "Well, that isn't true. I think about you." He paused, his smile rueful. "I've thought about Eldbert and Ambrose, too, but not in the same way."

"No," she said, smiling back in spite of herself. "You didn't scratch their names with yours into a gravestone."

He grimaced. "What a romantic placeholder for affection."

"You had affection for both of them, too."

"I certainly did not."

"I shall never forget the day Eldbert rode his new mare into the woods and it ran off with him. You had to save him, with Ambrose shouting insults I cannot repeat. And I know that you taught Ambrose how to fight. He was a miserable coward until he met you."

He shrugged. "All I will admit is that whatever I felt for them was a fraction of my regard for you."

She turned her face to the window. She was afraid of what he would say next, but she hoped he would say it anyway. "I remember sketching you as if it were yesterday. If I find the drawings, I will show them to you."

"That implies another meeting. Is there hope for us?"

She bit her lip. Was there hope? Was there any way to be released from her engagement without insulting Godfrey and breaking her aunt's heart?

"I want to do things to you that aren't proper," he confided quietly. "Ungentlemanly things to give us both pleasure."

"Kit, it's—"

"You don't understand," he said. "I need you in a different way than I did long ago. Not only as my friend, but as a lover. I want all of you."

"How do you know I don't understand?"

"You would not be alone with me if you could read my thoughts. Perhaps you're better off to forget me."

She turned to look at him. "How? I will live at least most of the year in London."

"Then we shall both live in torment, because neither of us is suited for adultery. And I will never stop wanting you."

"Adultery," she whispered, turning back to the window.

"Be mine or forget me. Make the decision before you're married."

"It would kill my aunt."

The orchestra had begun to play in the parkland. She saw a distant splash of color through the window as dancers spilled across the platform constructed for the party. Violet's heart lifted. The music stirred her. She was so wickedly tempted to ask Kit to dance with her one more time.

"I want you, too," she whispered.

She turned again, but he was gone, and a footman wearing gold-and-black livery stood politely awaiting her attention.

"Miss Knowlton?" he said as she met his gaze.

She flushed, hoping he had not heard her. Or worse, that he had not thought she had been talking to *him.* "Yes."

"The marchioness has asked me to personally attend you for the rest of the party."

The Marchioness of Sedgecroft shook out her skirts in dismay. "It's as dark as pitch in this passageway,

Weed. Remind me to inform Wenderfield that he needs to keep the torches lit below as well as above during a party. One cannot escape a tryst with a sprained ankle."

"Yes, madam."

Jane sighed. "Do you see any other cobwebs on my skirt?"

"I cannot see anything in this light. Well—"

"Wait until we're in the garden. The last thing I need is for Grayson to accuse me of having an affair."

"That day will never come, madam."

"Will you choose me, Weed, if it does?"

He pushed his long arm through the heavy mantle of ivy that concealed the pavilion's place of egress. Jane glanced up at the tower. "Don't answer, Weed. It was not a fair question. I used to think that you would choose Grayson. But now I'm not sure of that at all."

The ghost of a smile crossed his face. "I see no cobwebs in your hair or on your dress, madam."

She turned onto the hedge-enclosed path that led around the pavilion to the main garden. "Do you think my matchmaking scheme worked?"

"Only time will tell."

"They seemed so well suited for each other," she said with a sigh. "They tried hard to pretend otherwise at the school. You saw them dancing together at the ball the other night. It was as if they had known each other forever."

"Yes. One might say there was a sense of destiny between them."

"I hope so," Jane said. "Just because I sabotaged my own wedding with a wonderful result does not give me the right to ruin another woman's engagement."

"You gave destiny a helping hand, madam. Nothing more. Nothing less. It is all very romantic."

"Well, her aunt might not think so." Jane smiled. "Unless, of course, Master Fenton receives the bump in elevation that the marquess has suggested. Still, the fact is, Weed, that what I am doing could cause a scandal. The lady might lose her priggish haberdasher and be forced into Fenton's arms."

Whatever distress Godfrey might have felt when he realized that Violet had disappeared from the party was apparently soothed when she reappeared on the southwest lawn with one of the Marquess of Sedgecroft's footmen in tow.

"I was concerned, naturally, when I could not find you," he said, putting away his pocket watch. "But Pierce Carroll said he had noticed you wondering off toward the pavilion with the marchioness, and I thought to myself, 'Well, good for her. I will not interfere.'"

She nudged him toward the crowded breakfast tables. "Where is my aunt, Godfrey?"

"She went inside the house for a private tea." He cleared his throat. "I wasn't invited."

"Should I join her?"

He stepped directly into her path. "Could you spare

a moment for the man you are to marry? Have you heard *anything* I have said to you?"

No, she hadn't. She blinked, searching her brain for the first thing that she could remember from their conversation. "Yes. I heard everything. Who in the world is Pierce Carroll, and why doesn't he mind his own business?"

He looked taken aback.

"He's one of the other pupils at the salon. Thinks quite highly of himself, does Pierce. Fancies himself above the rest of us, I suspect. I don't like him. I think he may have stolen a snuffbox from my shop. Of course, I can't come out and accuse him."

"Oh."

"Did you have a pleasant time?" he inquired after a pause.

Violet gazed wistfully at the dancers on the platform. She had deceived herself into believing that she could be content with a man who cared only about his status. How could she marry a man who disliked dancing? How could she marry a man she could never love? A . . . passionless prude?

"Violet, dear, I asked you a question. Did you enjoy yourself in the pavilion?"

A blush of guilt suffused her face. "Yes, Godfrey," she answered with complete honesty. "I enjoyed myself more than I have in years."

He raised his brow. A moment passed. "I don't suppose the marchioness mentioned my name or the emporium?"

"I don't remember."

"You mentioned me, didn't you?"

She gave an evasive shrug.

"Well, you must have talked about something during all that time." He scowled, his hands clasped behind his back like a schoolmaster. "What *did* you discuss?"

"Do you really want to know?"

"Yes."

"We talked about kissing."

"About what?"

"You heard me, Godfrey."

"I couldn't have."

"She told me the story of her seduction. Well, part of it, anyway. I assume there was more."

"Good God. No wonder the nobility has a wicked reputation." He blew out a breath. "I hope you will not fall under her influence."

"I thought you wanted me to associate with high society."

"I do, but . . ." He shook his head. "I should know better than to worry about anyone putting improper ideas in your pretty head. Perhaps she is drawn to your goodness."

"I think she is good, too, Godfrey."

He glanced over his shoulder. "Can you imagine bringing your own footmen to a party? It must give one a sense of security."

She smiled up at him. He wasn't a bad person. He

deserved a wife who would love him. "It's an intrusion, in my opinion," she said softly.

He gave her a hesitant smile that filled her with remorse. "When you look at me like that, Violet, I am tempted to agree."

Chapter 16

$\mathscr{K}$it strode back to the fencing tent in a dangerous temper. His most experienced pupils recognized the look on his face and wisely did not utter a word. Ironically the only student who failed to respect his mood was Godfrey, who was not included in today's demonstrations.

Kit was leaning up against the willow tree, watching Pierce Carroll, garbed in Gypsy Rom attire, throwing knives at a target on the lawn. It was a chillingly good performance.

He felt a glimmer of suspicion. Who had taught Pierce to throw? To fence? Untrained talent was all well and good. But Kit hadn't witnessed such intensity since he had studied under his father's guidance. In fact, Pierce threw a blade with such precision that for several moments Kit forgot his foul mood, until Sir Godfrey walked up to remind him of it.

Kit tried to ignore him, but Godfrey refused to read

his cue. "May I have a moment with you in private, Master Fenton?"

He scowled. He thought he saw Violet sitting at one of the breakfast tables. And then he thought about lifting her hair from her neck and how badly he wanted to kiss that vulnerable curve where her shoulder lay bare, from there all the way to her breasts. God, her breasts.

"What do you want?" he asked Godfrey bluntly.

"It is about my fiancée," Godfrey said in a sober voice.

Kit straightened. "Has she changed her mind about fencing lessons?"

"Certainly not. May we talk inside the tent?"

Kit lifted his shoulders in a shrug and pivoted, wondering if the nincompoop was going to challenge him to a duel. Had Violet confessed? Had someone seen her with Kit in the tower and alerted Godfrey of the possible indiscretion? Kit would defend her name to the death.

"What is this about?" he demanded when he and Godfrey stood alone in the tent's musty stillness. "What do you need of me that is so important it has to interrupt a performance?"

"I will come straight to the point."

"Please do."

"I'm afraid that my fiancé does not find me attractive in the manner that she should."

Kit folded his arms across his chest. It was either that or take the man by the throat. "How does this concern me?"

"I wish to intensify the rate of my instruction. I would like to fence with more dash and danger so that at Lord Charnwood's house party I might have a chance to bedazzle her as you have."

"I have bedazzled her? Those were her words?"

"That was what the paper said about you, Fenton."

Kit rubbed his face. "Fencing is supposed to be art and sport. The theatrics are an unfortunate consequence of what is known as having to fill one's purse."

"I am willing to compensate you for your time."

"We have only three weeks until the house party. I don't know what you expect."

"I can only hope to emulate you for a few hours, Fenton. Surely you can help me out. I was not a strong boy growing up. I know that is difficult for a man of your talent to understand. My brothers tormented me until the day I left home."

"For pity's sake, Sir Godfrey, do I look like a frigging priest? Everyone has to overcome an obstacle here and there."

Godfrey swallowed. "Even if the strength I take from you turns out to be an illusion, I will be better off for studying under you than I was before."

"I cannot promise you anything," Kit said without inflection.

"I realize that. May we begin tomorrow afternoon?"

Kit gritted his teeth. He hated the weakness inside him that could never refuse a plea for help. "Fine, fine. Whether I serve as a damn governess or bodyguard, my sword can be bought at a price."

His decision did not improve his mood. Indeed, it darkened by the hour until, by the time he returned to the salon, he deemed himself unfit for anything but a good fight. Now he had agreed to train his rival to bedazzle the woman he could not have. He had given his word to Violet and to Godfrey. What sort of person bound himself to promises that were impossible to keep? He was achingly hard and angry.

It didn't make it easier that his students had appeared in force, assuming that he would observe tradition by popping corks to celebrate the day's success. Kit had not won anything today.

Still, he refused to drown his sorrows. If he took that first glass in his mood he might not be able to stop. He counseled self-discipline, and self-disciplined he would be, even if it killed him.

He practiced with his students until midnight that night in the *salle*. He criticized their clumsy footwork, their overextended lunges, their underguarded shoulders. He put them through a parade of Highland broadsword drills. He exhausted each and every one in turn until the only one left with the energy to stand up to him was Pierce Carroll.

Pierce rose to the challenge as if he'd been expecting it all along. "You aren't perfect," Kit said as their blades crossed. "But you are damned good. Why don't you study for your diploma?"

"What for?"

"Prestige."

"The devil with prestige. It takes too long to study. I

can make money now with my sword. Why don't you steal the woman you want from Godfrey?"

Kit knocked the sword from Pierce's hand and kicked it across the floor. "Don't ever say anything like that again."

Pierce held up his hands in surrender. "Forgive me. I didn't realize it was more than passion. I understand now. This is personal. I will never mention her again. A hundred pardons."

Kit hung his sword on the wall and stood in silence as Pierce retrieved his weapon and coat, exiting the salon without another word.

More than passion.

It was too obvious to hide.

It was too painful to ignore.

It was love, and it hurt, a direct hit to the heart.

How could a woman's smile render him defenseless after the trials he had survived? How could the mere act of kissing her reduce him to impoverishment again?

He was alone, and only her company would console him.

He was starving, and he could not ease his hunger for her by any acceptable means.

By the time the carriage returned to the town house, Lady Ashfield had fallen asleep. Violet gently awakened her and watched as Godfrey and Twyford escorted her up the steps. Her aunt refused to use a cane, and Violet wondered how an instrument considered by gentlemen to be a weapon was in an elderly woman's hand a sign of infirmity.

Mired in concern, she did not notice the young girl lurking between an oyster seller's cart and the lamppost until she darted forward.

She was a comely girl, and at first Violet thought she knew her. Her wide blue eyes stirred a memory. But then again, she had been thinking so often of the past.

"Miss Knowlton?" she asked, extending her hand.

Violet looked down. Grasped in the girl's gloved fingers was a folded letter. "What is this?" she asked in an undertone.

"It is from my mother, miss. She asks that if you have forgiven her, she would like to invite you to our home on Tuesday next at three o'clock in the afternoon. Her name is Winifred Higgins."

"Winifred?" Violet searched the girl's face and recognized in her piquant features a trace of her former governess's vivid charm. "She is well, and you . . . you are hers?"

The girl nodded solemnly. She seemed far older than her age—heavens, she could not be ten years old by Violet's calculation. But then, Winifred had seemed more mature than her actual age. Her womanly appearance had deceived Violet's aunt.

Still, Violet could not find it in herself to resent Winifred for her neglect. If Winifred had acted as a dutiful chaperone, Violet would never have been allowed to leave the house or make a friend. Winifred had been young herself, and vulnerable to loneliness. Had she been living in London all this time, raising her daughter alone? It could not have been easy. But who had told her that Violet was here? The first person who came to mind was Kit. Had he and Winifred kept in contact?

"What is your name?" Violet asked, biting her lip.

"Elsie, miss." The girl glanced over her shoulder, and it was then that Violet noticed a cloaked woman standing at the corner. "My mother wants to make amends," she added hurriedly. "She said to tell you that ours isn't the best neighborhood, and you should not travel there alone."

Violet nodded, strange prickles of excitement pulsing in her veins. "Of course."

"But once you're in our home, you will be safe."

What a queer postscript, Violet thought, and before she could ask another question about the invitation, the girl turned and fled toward the woman waiting for her return. Violet looked up just as Godfrey emerged from the town house onto the front steps.

He glanced down the street, shaking his head. "These street girls never miss an opportunity. I hope you did not give her anything. It only encourages them."

Violet stirred herself. "No. Not a penny."

"Damned beggars are a blight. I wish I'd wake up one morning to find every one of them gone."

Violet looked at him. It was on the tip of her tongue to say that one morning he might find her gone, too.

"Let me see you inside," he said brusquely. "I shall

not be visiting you as frequently as usual in the next few days. Intensive training for the house party, you know."

"Training?"

"With the sword," he said a trifle impatiently. "Where are your thoughts today, Violet? On the wedding, perhaps?"

She hid the letter beneath her shawl and took his hand, loath to confess that their wedding was the furthest thing from her mind. She was impatient to read Winifred's invitation. What would Aunt Francesca think if she heard that the scandalous governess she had dismissed sought to make amends? Or was there more to it than that? Violet remained unconvinced that she and Kit had not played into the marchioness's matchmaking hand earlier in the pavilion.

A proper lady would toss the invitation into the fire without opening it and turn her back on temptation. She would not open the door to past mistakes and hope that her friends would be there to save her.

Chapter 17

$\mathscr{K}$it was at home reading one of his father's trea-
tises on sword fighting when Kenneth brought
him the invitation to tea. Straight off he speculated that
Winnie was up to something. She had never sent him a
formal missive before, let alone one written on per-
fumed paper. He dropped in to visit her from time to
time, and once in a while they ran into each other at the
market. He had not seen her, though, since the day after the benefit ball.

On Tuesday afternoon, at a quarter to three, he
mounted the stairs to Winifred's rooms. The door had
been left unlocked. A note attached to the knocker by a
peacock-blue ribbon instructed anyone who called to
enter.

Anyone who called.

Which confirmed his suspicion that he was not the
only guest invited to tea.

Another note on the two-tiered table explained that

Winifred had been summoned on a few unexpected errands. Would her guests enjoy a glass of brandy and a slice of lemon bread in her absence? Kit removed his long gray coat and placed it on the hallstand with his cane and gloves.

"Anyone else here?" he called into the intriguing silence, noting that the chairs and sofa had been cleared of the usual baskets of clothes that needed mending.

His heart pounded hard against his ribs. The rose silk curtains had been drawn to let in an inch of light. The coal fire emanated a cozy glow behind the grate.

He recognized the *clip-clop* of hoofbeats, carriage wheels rolling to a stop outside. He resisted going to the window. Instead, he went to the door and listened to the echo of a lady's slippers on the stairwell. He detected heavier footsteps in the background. The lady had not arrived alone.

What if it wasn't Violet? Yet it had to be.

How had Winifred convinced Violet to come here? Did Violet realize he was waiting, hoping to see her? She would never believe that he hadn't played any part in this. She had wrongly accused him of scheming with the marchioness to lure her to the pavilion. Today he could not claim he was innocent of complicity. He was unwilling to let her go again.

Violet knocked once at the door. Twyford stood on the bottom of the stairs below her. What an unarmed elderly man could do to protect her in the event of trouble, she did not know, but he had insisted on accompanying her, and she had felt safer with his escort than she would have alone. She wasn't sure if he suspected this was more than the visit to a seamstress she had said it was. Whatever he felt, he kept it to himself. Violet knew he wouldn't betray her now any more than he would have in the past.

She lifted the knocker and let it fall. When the door opened, she was staring up into Kit's face. She shouldn't have felt any surprise, but the sight of him always flustered her. She forgot her resolve. She forgot that they were not supposed to see each other again.

He shook his head as if denying he was expecting her. He was clean shaven, his hair combed back behind his ears. He wore a white linen neck cloth against an even whiter linen shirt that bore the imprint of a fresh iron. It undid her. To think of Kit ironing his own shirt, or paying a servant from his modest income to do so.

"Believe me," he said in a husky voice, "I didn't arrange this. I admit that I hoped . . . But you shouldn't be here. I'm alone inside. Winifred isn't here yet. I don't know when or if she intends to return."

Her throat felt dry. She glanced down at Twyford, nodding to assure him that he could return to the carriage.

"You shouldn't be here," Kit said again, but she noticed that he stood aside, as if hoping she wouldn't listen, and nor did she. It was inappropriate. Neither of them had planned an assignation. The mere thought made her dizzy.

An assignation. Winifred would be her accomplice today, as she had been in the past. Except that now Violet knew her own mind. She knew what she risked losing—and she didn't want to lose him again.

"Either leave here," Kit said, as if she had any intention of doing so, "or come inside before you are seen. Whatever you decide, you can't stand in the hall."

It occurred to Kit that there had been only a flicker of surprise on her face when he had opened the door. He stood back as she stepped over the threshold.

He bolted the door as soon as she was inside. "Winnie isn't here," he said again, but stopped when she shook her head and started to laugh. "I know you won't believe me—she laid a trap."

"Without any help from you?"

"Maybe she read my mind. I'd be a liar if I said I wasn't hoping that you would come. Do you need help taking off those gloves or don't you intend to stay?"

She obediently held out her hands. "Please. This is only the second time I've been lured into a tryst. And you?"

He shook his head, his fingers deftly unfastening the buttons at her elbow. "I have to set an example these days. I could be a monk, for all the affairs I've had."

She laughed again, not convinced, he thought. "But it's true," he insisted, drawing off her long white gloves. "I lost my attraction to illicit pleasures a long time ago. But . . . I never lost my attraction to you."

"Why haven't you ever married? You would make a devoted husband and father."

"The truth?"

"You know that you can tell me anything."

"Yes," he said with a reflective smile. "That's the problem. The women who are drawn to me tend to fall into two sets. The first type is giddy over having a protector and tries to provoke me into fighting all the men who have affronted her. The other is determined to make me give up the sword and settle down into domesticity."

She looked into his eyes. For the life of her she couldn't understand why any woman would want to change him. "There must be someone who loves you as you are."

"Yes," he said, shrugging. "But I would have to love her, too. And I'd have to feel that I could trust her. And in ten years I have found only one woman who fits this description, and she is engaged to someone else."

"I don't want to marry him," she said suddenly, her eyes locking with his. "Is that a shocking thing to admit?"

He searched her face. "Nothing shocks a workhouse boy."

"It would shock my aunt, Kit. She believes she has found the ideal protector in Godfrey, and I cannot tell her otherwise. She has been so good to me, and this is all she's ever asked of me. But I don't want to marry him. You gave me the terms of our association. Why don't you give me your courage, too? I could use it."

He glanced down at her gloves, symbolic of the

challenge given. He had already accepted on her be-
half. He simply wanted to hear her say as much to his
face. "If there is any manner in which I can help, you
have to ask me. I can't overstep my bounds without
your permission."

"I should never have asked you to be proper. It
doesn't suit you. At least, not when we're alone together. Be the conqueror you are at heart." She pulled
her gloves from his hands and threw them at his feet.
"There. That is the gauntlet."

He glanced down. Then he stepped over the gloves
and pulled her into his arms. "As the one who has been
challenged, it is my right to choose the weapons we
shall use."

"According to whom?"

He smiled slowly. "According to the dueling code."

"Very well." She laid her head against his shoulder,
allowing herself to savor his protective strength. "You
aren't wearing your sword today, Master Fenton."

"I didn't think it would be appropriate for tea. I
have other weapons, I assure you," he said, and
reached up his hand to unfasten the frog of her pelisse,
catching it before it slid to the floor. "As you do," he
said, his eyes teasing. "But I noticed that you haven't
brought your fan. Does that mean you won't discourage my advances?"

"Kit—"

He dropped the pelisse on a chair behind him. "It is
also my privilege," he continued, dipping his head to
hers, "to name the time and place of the duel."

She gave a breathless laugh. "You always did make up the rules as you went along. To your advantage, I remember."

"Are you sure," he asked, his lips hovering above hers, "that you're willing to break the rules again to be with me?"

"Name the time," she whispered.

"Now."

"And the place."

His lips touched hers. "In the bedroom, but not yet."

She lowered her eyes. "When?"

"After I've undressed you and kissed you until you are too weak to put up any resistance."

"But—"

He brushed against her. She swayed, and his left hand shot out to encircle her waist. "Wait," he instructed her.

"When?" she whispered, her body molding to his.

"I can't predict the exact time," he murmured as his right hand unhooked the back of her dress. "This is a different kind of match than I usually fight. Moreover, a maestro knows how to prolong the moment."

Her lips parted. Kit not only believed in prolonging a moment; he also knew when to seize it. He gripped her against him and kissed her until she was clinging to his neck by one hand and half sliding down the length of him. He could have fallen to his knees himself for want of her. Wordlessly he lifted her into his arms and carried her into the bedroom.

He laid Violet upon the sturdy iron bedstead. Then,

layer by layer, he unfastened her sleeves and under-garments until at last all that was left was to pull out the comb that held back her hair. Her breasts, pale and heavy, rose as she drew a deep, nervous breath. He smiled to calm her. He felt anything but calm himself. Her nude body brought his blood to a boil.

She had undone his self-discipline without even try-ing. He wanted her for his own. He wanted her to him-self, here, on the flocked mattress, before anyone could take her away from him again.

She was still the most beautiful creature he had ever seen. He would still crawl through black tunnels to be with her. He would fight for her. She had been his light once, and he would do anything to prove he was wor-thy of her. She was offering him the ultimate gift—herself.

He leaned over her, carefully unknotting his neck cloth. He let his eyes wander from her lush mouth to the delta of her thighs. Her soft vulnerability aroused his animal instincts—the need to mate, to make her his. He traced his fingers from her delectable mouth down the curve of her shoulder and stroked the underside of her breasts. His heartbeat escalated as her nipples darkened, responsive to his touch. He lowered his head to lick each engorged tip in turn.

She gave a moan and arched against his mouth. He placed one hand upon her belly, stilling her, and with the other unbuttoned his shirt. She closed her eyes, her breathing ragged. He allowed his hand to drop to the hollow between her legs. His fingers parted her wet folds, slipping inside to find pulsing heat. She swallowed a groan.

She shivered and opened her eyes. Awakened sensuality smoldered in their depths. As he pressed another finger inside her, his own sex thickened. He felt the ache of it all the way up through his teeth.

"Conquer me," she said, lifting her hand to his face. "Be my champion."

"A lady is not supposed to marry a boy who begins life as a pauper, no matter how high he rises in the world. I will never be respectable."

"I will never belong to anybody else but you."

For a moment he did not react. But then he broke. He drew back on the bed and swiftly tore off his neck cloth, waistcoat, and shirt. It would be bliss to get out of his breeches, but he resisted. The need to thrust inside her warm flesh was too strong. She gasped as he covered her with his body, her hands instinctively clasping his shoulders.

Instinct. He followed it as he gently forced her back against the bed. Her breasts lifted, and she smiled, raising one knee, a natural tease, a temptress. He was harder than he had ever been, desperate for her, afraid that he would explode the instant he put himself inside her.

Still he waited; still he understood that to master her was to prolong the moment. He stroked her nipples slowly. "Don't move."

"I'm not sure that I can," she whispered.

He drew a breath, ignoring the unbearable tension

that built in his body, and kissed her mouth, the creamy skin of her throat, the pointed tips of her breasts. He kissed her belly and below, his tongue parting the sweet lips and then sucking gently on the sensitive bud above.

Instinct.

Destiny.

They had not been merely a lonely girl and an ill-begotten boy once upon a time. They had been friends and enemies, champions and critics, drawn each to the other. Kit was a romantic. He did not believe in passion without love.

Chapter 18

She felt immodest. She felt unfettered. She felt afraid until his deep voice soothed her. He was different from the Kit she had known, and yet still familiar. The wicked strength of those hands. His beguiling mouth. It became a duel between them, yes, and it was dangerous. But it was more—an intimate dance to heaven.

His tongue stabbed deep and dominant inside where she ached and had never been touched. The purity of the pleasure she felt forbade that she know shame. His hands forced her farther apart. She was unguarded, exposed, unable, unwilling to escape the happiness she found with him.

"Sweet," she thought she heard him whisper, but his voice was muffled, his face buried between her thighs.

Her back arched. She begged silently for mercy. She pressed her wrist to her mouth to keep from crying out. The sensations he unleashed inside her became too intense to bear. She fought against them. For a terrifying moment she thought her heart had stopped, and a black mist swam in her mind. His tongue quickened, speared deeper. He sucked at her bud.

She flexed her body, a final objection or surrender, perhaps both at once. She splintered and gave herself to the sublime pleasure that shivered through her blood and into her belly.

Overcome, she opened her eyes as he slipped back to remove his trousers and then lowered himself over her, bracing his arms on either side of her shoulders.

"Beautiful," he said, his voice wickedly deep. "I want to devour every inch of you."

She stared at his bare form and felt defenseless against his masculinity. He was lean and lithe, with taut muscle defining his shoulders and torso.

He grinned. "Do you like looking at me in the raw?"

She blushed. "I wasn't doing any such thing."

"You were. It's all right. I like looking at you, too."

"You've a wicked tongue."

"Did you like what I did to you?" he asked. "What are you ashamed of?"

"Do people talk about things like that?"

He kissed her softly on the mouth. "I've no idea what other people talk about in bed. I'm glad enough that I can be myself with you."

Perhaps she was still in shock as he kissed her, the scent of her own desire on his mouth. But even the intimate act he had just performed did not prepare her for the raw desire that raked her as his shaft prodded her sensitive cleft.

"I could sink into you and never leave," he said, his eyes holding her spellbound. "I could break this damned bed—" He broke off with a deep-throated growl. "But I'm going to do what is right even if it kills me."

Kit wasn't sure how he summoned the willpower to stop himself in time. Maybe it was the innocent trust in Violet's eyes. Maybe it was the memory of carrying her home the day she'd taken ill, the horror on her uncle's face when he realized that his niece had made friends with a workhouse boy. In his mind Kit could still hear her aunt's hysterical shrieks from inside the house.

What has he done to her?

He would like to believe it was more than guilt that stopped him. He would prefer to think that his control had come from the code of honor that he had studied and taught.

Whatever the reason, he somehow found the strength to lift himself from her alluring warmth. His prick stood as stiff as a poker. He ached with primal impulses. Yet he knew what he had to do if she were to be his. Not his secret lover. But his for all time.

He stepped away from the bed and stood in silence until he was able to gather full control of himself. He wanted her for his wife. She wasn't going to be disgraced. When he took her, it would be on their wedding night.

"I care too much about you to bear," he said at last.

He cast a longing glance at her tempting body where she lay on the bed before picking up their garments from the floor. "I want you to go home."

"I wouldn't have stopped you," she whispered. "I love you, Kit. I wanted to show you what I felt."

He closed his eyes, her confession eroding his resolve. "I'll do the right thing by you. I promised myself in Monk's Huntley that I wouldn't drag you into the mire."

"You're not in the mire now."

He opened his eyes, stealing another illicit look at her tousled beauty. Violet unveiled. "Please," he said. "You tempt me more than I can take. Fencing has given me control of my body, but it has not made me able to resist you."

"What are you going to do now?" she whispered, sitting up slowly.

He put on his shirt and helped her back into her clothes, aware of the clock ticking in the hall. When she had finished dressing and combed back her hair, he took her hand and led her to the door. She clung to him.

"Answer me, Kit. What are we going to do?"

"We have a term for it in sword fighting." He stared down at her in possessive yearning. She had no idea what it cost him to let her go, but he swore that this would be the last time. "It is called a change of engagement."

Her eyes widened. "You're going to confront Godfrey?"

"One of us has to."

"You are his hero, Kit."

He frowned. "Not for long."

"Godfrey is the least of our worries. My aunt cannot withstand another heartbreak. All she has ever wanted is my happiness."

He took her face in his hands and kissed her lightly. "Then I'll have to prove my worth to her. Would you be ashamed to be my wife?"

"I've never been ashamed of you. Nor can I live without you any longer. I'm going to tell her as soon as I get home. I know I can make her understand. She has softened since my uncle died."

"Then I will manage all the rest."

Chapter 19

$\mathscr{G}$odfrey had taken a cab to the shop that morning, certain that there was rain in the air. He followed his usual ritual of sequestering himself in his counting-house to check on his money box before he inspected the clerks for untidy attire. He spent another three hours reviewing his accounts. He found that he had been overcharged on his last shipment of silver lace. The sales of walking sticks, however, had exceeded his expectations. His association with the fencing academy was paying off in more ways than one.

A little past noon he entered the emporium, right in the midst of a gentleman complaining about the exorbitant price of a fish fork the assistant had shown him. Godfrey forced a smile and approached the counter, only to notice another man coming through the door. It was Mr. Pierce Carroll, arguably Fenton's best pupil, although no one at the salon cared much for him.

Jealousy, Godfrey expected. Godfrey did not care

for him, either. Pierce struck him as a person who paid his bills at the last moment, if at all. He fenced better than the other pupils. He disregarded rules as it suited him, and he was attracted to the vulgar women who chased Fenton at performances. Godfrey thought he was not an asset to the school at all.

"What can I do for you, Mr. Carroll?" he said in his most professional manner. "Do you wish to make a purchase?"

Pierce glanced around the shop. He was an attractive young man, neatly dressed, but not one Godfrey would like to meet after dark. To his credit, though, he seemed to be impressed by the well-lit, airy atmosphere. "I was in the neighborhood, on my way to the academy, actually, and thought I might look for a watch. I lost mine last night."

"How unfortunate," Godfrey said, already gesturing at a clerk.

Pierce smiled, leaning against the counter. "In a sword fight. A duel."

Godfrey froze. "Not in an actual duel? You didn't."

"I'm afraid I did."

"Fenton will *not* be pleased."

Pierce pursed his lips. "Fenton does not know what happened. I haven't told him yet."

Godfrey looked him over. "You won, I assume?"

"Oh, of course." Pierce brushed around him to view the tortoiseshell-encased timepiece that the clerk had placed upon the counter. He examined it and shook his head. "I shall have to return when I'm not in such a rush. I have to put in an hour or two at the salon. I feel a little stiff in the shoulder from last night. There's nothing worse than coddling a sore arm."

Godfrey frowned. He had the feeling that Pierce never intended to make a purchase in the first place. He had probably just come here to brag. "I have a lesson myself at five."

"The master posted a message that he will be gone for most of the day."

"But I paid my subscription in advance. Where has he gone? He never misses a lesson, and this week is especially important to me."

Pierce's narrow shoulders lifted in a shrug. He had arrogant mannerisms, Godfrey thought distractedly. He would probably like the French walking stick that concealed a brandy flask in its ebony handle. "I hope this has nothing to do with your duel last night. Notoriety is acceptable to a point. But a gentleman does not seek genuine bloodshed."

At least, that was what Fenton had taught his pupils. It would be a ghastly embarrassment if Godfrey were connected with a fencing instructor who violated the law.

"I don't think Fenton is engaged in a fencing matter at the moment," Pierce said, nodding toward the door. "I think he's engaged in a personal affair. You ought to practice with me. Fenton is too easy on you."

Godfrey took a step forward. A well-dressed couple had alighted from a coach. "If Fenton is not at the salon, I think I shall stay here for the rest of the afternoon. I want lessons from the master, not mere practice."

"Suit yourself." Pierce tipped his hat. "Where is your enchanting fiancée today, if you do not mind my asking? The last time she went missing, so did our illustrious sword master."

"Missing? What the devil are you talking about?"

"At Wenderfield's party. You were upset yourself that Violet disappeared. Don't you remember?"

Godfrey bristled. The unmitigated nerve of the man. Who did Pierce think he was? Should Godfrey report this impoliteness to Fenton? Was there, truly, anything of consequence to report? Fenton despised pupils who carried tales like little children.

Fenton and Violet. Violet had been in the pavilion with the marchioness during the breakfast party. Godfrey had seen the two ladies together with his own eyes.

Was Pierce insinuating that Violet and Fenton were engaged at this very moment in a liaison? Impossible. Outrageous . . . and yet it wasn't as if Godfrey had not sensed a tension between his fiancée and the fencing master.

"Where my fiancée spends her time, Mr. Carroll," he said, giving Pierce the shoulder, "is not anyone else's affair."

Pierce smiled, polite now, perhaps even penitent. "You are correct, sir. My sincerest apology. It is her affair, not mine."

Dear Twyford had not said a word to Violet during the drive back to Mayfair. There had been no recrimination in his eyes, only his ever-present concern. She did not doubt that he would lie to protect her. His devotion to her took nothing from his loyalty to her aunt, but he had been butler since Violet was a baby, and no matter what society said, they felt a deep affection for each other. She did not want to land him in trouble with Aunt Francesca over Kit. What had happened today wasn't Twyford's fault. Violet had gone of her own free will to Winifred's rooms.

She had gone knowing that Kit would be there. Yes, she wished she could have seen Winifred, to assure her that she held no grudge, but it was Kit who had drawn her there, Kit she needed and who had accepted her challenge. But was that challenge as easy for him to conquer as he made it seem?

She bathed in warm rose-scented water, preparing to face her aunt, but it did not help. She had no idea how to confess the truth. She knew only that after today she would never belong to anyone else, and concern for her reputation paled in comparison to her passion for Kit.

But if any scandal reached Aunt Francesca, or if Kit confronted her aunt with the truth, the damage inflicted would be unthinkable. Violet had to make her aunt understand. Aunt Francesca had dedicated her life to sheltering Violet.

How ungrateful Violet would seem when she admitted that she could not marry the gentleman her aunt had chosen to be her protector. She needed passion and laughter in her life. Godfrey cared too much for the unimportant things in the world. She wanted the imperfection and inconvenience of children. But most of all she wanted a love built on a foundation of friendship and a man strong enough to defy the world's limitations and win.

A man who knew her heart.

She dressed slowly and made her way through the hall to the upstairs drawing room. In surprise she noticed a tall, bearded gentleman sitting next to Francesca by the window.

"I didn't know we had a guest," she said, hesitating at the door.

He rose from his chair. "Miss Knowlton?"

She noticed the bottles on the tea table, the fashionable cut of his frock coat, his professional tone of voice. "I am the physician to the Marquess of Sedgecroft," he said. "If I may talk to you in private . . ."

She glanced again at her aunt, who appeared to be drifting into a peaceful doze. "What is it?" she asked when she and the doctor faced each other in the hall.

"Your aunt's malaise comes from angina, I am sure."

"From where?"

"From what. It has been suspected by my fellows for some time that excitability of the nerves can cause disorders."

"What is her disorder?"

"It concerns her heart."

"Is she going to—"

"I do not believe so. It all depends on the condition of the valves. It will help, however, to keep her calm

when she feels any distress. Have her drink pepper-
mint tea before her meals. Call for me if she grows pale
or feeble at any time. She may take laudanum if she
feels pain, and the drops of digitalis that I have pre-
scribed."

"Then she cannot leave the house?"

"Good God, of course she can. She must. Light activity is beneficial. What lifts the spirit heals the heart.
She is resting now."

She trailed him to the top of the stairs. "We are supposed to attend a house party together."

He nodded. "Enjoy yourselves."

"But her heart . . . Isn't there anything else I can do?"

He looked down at the butler standing in the hall
below. "Yes. You can keep her bundled up in cold
weather and discourage her from eating rich foods.
Above all, you must not be maudlin about this. Be
cheerful, for her sake and your own."

"Thank you," Violet said, sighing as he descended
the stairs.

To think she'd been so content in Kit's arms only
hours ago. She would never have forgiven herself if
anything had happened while she was gone. But by
the same token she couldn't deceive her aunt any longer. She would have to wait now until an opening presented itself. Would she find the words to convince
Francesca to accept Kit? To persuade her that the man
Violet had chosen for herself was better than Francesca's choice?

Chapter 20

A change of engagement.

His sword would not win this battle for him. Kit would need the devil's luck to pull this off.

He might end up in a duel himself if Godfrey would not release Violet from their betrothal.

He had watched from the window until he saw Twyford escort Violet to the carriage. A few minutes later he took a hackney to his own lodgings to change. From there he went to the Bond Street office of the solicitor that one of his patrons, the Duke of Gravenhurst, had suggested he visit should he ever need legal guidance. He carried the sealed letter that the duke had given him to use as an entrée. He had trained the duke personally in the use of the sword throughout the years of their acquaintance.

The reception room was crowded with men and women from various walks of life. When Kit was finally called to Mr. Thurber's office, he had worked up a speech to introduce himself.

"I gave His Grace fencing instruction here in London and at his Dartmoor estate, sir. My name is—"

"Fenton. Yes, yes. *The* Fenton. The duke thinks highly of you. I hope you are not here because you have killed a person."

Kit laughed and withdrew the letter from his pocket. The solicitor took and dropped it, unread, into a portfolio that appeared to be filled with similar missives. "I was led to believe that the duke's letter entitled me to legal advice and perhaps a small favor."

"Not a small favor at all, Mr. Fenton," he said, sinking back in his chair. "A sealed letter like yours is basically carte blanche from His Grace. What is it that you need? You do not appear to be in a desperate situation, but then, appearances mislead."

Kit slid forward in his chair, balancing his walking stick between his knees. "I am rather desperate."

"Have you killed an aristocrat in a duel?"

"No."

"Have you been caught cuckolding a prominent husband?"

"Certainly not."

"Creditors?"

"None."

"Then?"

"I am desperately in love with a lady who is engaged to another man. I would like a license to marry her as soon as legally possible."

"Is the lady in an urgent position?"

"In my opinion, yes. We both are."

"I meant could she be carrying your child?"

Kit paused. If not for the self-control he had summoned at the last moment today, he would not have been able to answer that question. "No."

The solicitor stared at him across the desk. Kit had the sense that he wasn't shocked by the request. But then, working as the scandalous Duke of Gravenhurst's solicitor, he was probably well-versed in controversy.

"Please submit your name and address to my clerk before you leave, Mr. Fenton. And the same information about the lady, if you please."

Kit's walking stick tilted forward. He caught it before it hit the desk. "That is all there is to it?"

"Unless the lady's betrothed brings legal action, then yes. If he withdraws with grace, that will be the end of the matter. If not, I shall appeal to his finer instincts, and if that does not work, then I shall appeal to his purse."

"And your fee?"

"That has been covered by His Grace."

Kit stood, shaking his head. "I don't know how to thank you. Both of you."

"In the duke's case, the less said of him the better. He would prefer that his favors be kept private."

"On my honor, sir."

"I hope, then, that you and this lady will be happy together. You will receive the special license shortly at your address."

"Thank you, Mr. Thurber. And thank His Grace for me."

The solicitor nodded. "Please let me not read in the papers that your engagement is followed by a duel."

It was late by the time Kit returned home to wash and dress. He could not show up on Violet's doorstep to announce his intentions at this hour. And his intentions were to make her his wife before he fulfilled his obligation to perform at the upcoming house party. He could not think of an easy way to tell Godfrey that he was stealing his fiancée. Godfrey would have to accept the loss like a man. Godfrey could demand satisfaction, but knowing what he did about the baronet, Kit thought it more likely he would demand his subscription money back.

Violet's aunt was a different matter. The thought of facing her terrified Kit. It was doubtful that Lady Ashfield would challenge him to a duel. But at least he could approach her with a relatively clean conscience.

He had left Violet with her virtue intact, and even though his body ached with regret, refusing to take her maidenhead today had been the right thing to do. He had meant it when he'd told her that he was finished with stolen moments and separations.

He went to the academy later that night. He'd missed several lessons today, and with the house party rapidly approaching he could not afford to lose time necessary for last-minute training.

Almost nightly a pupil, current or former, would wander in, pick one of the foils from the wall, and fence with an adversary he might or might not know until he had warded off whatever demon had driven him to the school. A few left money on the hallstand, a sign of the success they had achieved in life, or of respect to the master.

Some helped themselves to whatever happened to be left around: a forgotten cloak, a good sword, a half-drunk pint. The rule was to take only what you needed and return it when you could.

There were more returns than thefts.

But on most nights at least one swordsman came by and ended up spending the night at Kit's lodging house. Some had gotten into trouble at home and needed advice. Some had no home. Some were looking for trouble.

Kit heard laughter drifting from his private dressing room.

He detected a female's scent in the air, not cheap, but the costly perfume of a Mayfair wife. It reeked of explicit passion. He walked past the small gallery stairs and saw a woman's cloak lying over a chair.

He knew right away that his visitor was not Violet. He would have been furious if she had come to this part of London at this hour without a damned good reason. He pushed open the door of his dressing room, where a lamp burned low.

His mouth thinned in disgust. It took his eyes a few moments to adjust to the darkness and identify the half-naked figure straddling the young man who sat spread-legged on the armchair.

Although all Kit could make out was her bare back and loosened red hair, he knew he had seen her before.

It was a strict rule of the school that ladies, either visitors or pupils, must be under escort at all times. If an actress arrived for lessons to prepare for a part, she did so in daylight and laughed off the insinuations of disrepute that such activity engendered.

The woman turned at the waist, one hand coyly covering her breasts.

"Master Fenton?" she whispered.

He stared at her, recognizing that cloying voice. Not any Mayfair wife, but Viscountess Bennett.

"Where have you been?" she said, petulant now. "You missed several scheduled lessons. My servant has been watching the salon for hours."

"Then he can see you back to your husband." He entered the cramped room in cold fury, recognizing the man lounging back in the chair. "I should have known you'd be involved."

Pierce glanced up, casually refastening his shirt and trousers. "I took the liberty of covering for you. I didn't think you'd mind. The other students needed practice. And Lady Bennett had other needs."

He stood unmoving as she approached, relacing her gown. "What are you doing here?"

She shook her head, the answer obvious. "This is your place of business. Name the price."

He gave an incredulous laugh. "Do you think I am a male whore to be bought?"

She slowly pulled up her sleeves. "We both know you are not a wealthy man. I desire you."

"I have never shown the slightest interest in you. Why should you desire a commoner who disdains you?"

"Christopher Fenton is no ordinary commoner," she

said. "He can ward off a man with his sword and pleasure a woman at the same time."

He leaned back against the door. "That is the most
ludicrous statement I have ever heard."

"It is also said that you are a master in more ways
than one."

A cab rattled by in the street. Kit's patience was
dwindling. It would be just his luck if a group of his
younger pupils burst in to witness what could easily
be mistaken as a ménage à trois.

"What kind of woman," Lady Bennett asked, her
gaze still riveted to his face, "do you desire?"

He thought instantly of Violet, and his body responded.

"What kind of woman," Lady Bennett asked, her
hand lifting, "tempts a man who is dedicated to his art?"

He caught her wrist before she could touch his belt.
"Since you have shown an interest in the art, let me
explain a basic rule in fencing. A man does not leave
his blade or any other part of his body unguarded."

She looked rather pleased that she had at least provoked some physical reaction from him. "I will be
waiting if you change your mind. I could make you a
very wealthy and satisfied man."

He released her hand and looked past her to the man
sitting motionless on the chair. "Walk her to the door,"
he said curtly. "And don't bring a woman here again."

Pierce laughed. "I didn't bring her here. She wanted
you. I was keeping her company to be polite."

A moment later Pierce returned to the salon. Kit was

standing in front of the stairs to the fencing gallery. "Why are you the only student here?" he asked suddenly, realizing that his rooms had been empty when he returned home. "Where has everyone gone?"

"They're probably at Wilton's house, sir. We ran into a spot of trouble outside his club last night. Kenneth and Tilly had to take him to his mother's house. We tried to find you, sir, but no one knew where you'd gone."

Kit could not hide his reproach. "Do not tell me that you and Wilton got into a public fight."

"Sir, we answered an insult. Wilton required the services of a surgeon, but he held his own against the men who disrespected us. You would not have wanted us to slink off like cowards."

Kit stared at him in contempt. For a moment he could have sworn he saw a flash of malice in Carroll's eyes. The bastard had a taste for blood. There was trouble in a pupil like that.

"I've no interest in training gentlemen who use their skill as an excuse to kill, unless they are pursuing honor. I take it that honor had nothing to do with what happened last night?"

"Master," Carroll replied with a woeful smile, "isn't honor a personal matter to decide?"

"You are going to ruin my reputation," Kit said through his teeth. "I can only hope no one will die as a result of your rash behavior."

Pierce put his hand to his heart in feigned remorse. "I give you my word that I will not take up a sword again in anger unless it is for honor's sake."

Chapter 21

*V*iolet and her aunt were viewing fashion plates together the next morning in the drawing room when Twyford announced that a gentleman visitor wished to be received. The caller had declined to give his card. From the twinkle in the butler's eye, Violet knew that this person could not be a stranger.

"A stranger?" Aunt Francesca mused, looking remarkably well after a good night's rest.

It was unthinkable that Twyford would allow a notorious figure, a fencing master with Kit's history, into the house. Twyford would never risk upsetting the baroness with such a bold action. But then, Twyford had become bolder with age. He had escorted Violet only yesterday to a scandalous encounter.

Violet had taken advantage of her butler's tenderness too many times to count. She rose from her chair and headed to the door, stepping on the plate that had slipped from her lap. She looked down at the picture of the bridal dress she had been admiring. She'd torn it with the heel of her shoe. It reminded her that she had bought only a pair of long white gloves for her trousseau. The lonely purchase didn't say much for her enthusiasm. How would she ever be able to look at Godfrey again?

"Violet," her aunt said in concern. "What is wrong with you today?"

"I . . ." She shook her head.

"Do you have something to tell me?"

"Yes, but . . . I don't know how to start."

"Well, then—"

"Madam," Twyford called from the hall.

"Who is it, Twyford?" her aunt asked in disconcertment.

"The gentleman would like his identity to be a surprise."

The baroness hesitated. She looked again at Violet, her face contemplative, and gave a shrug. "You had best not bring a scoundrel into this house, Twyford, or I shall put you out onto the streets to beg."

"If it pleases your ladyship," he said, and moments later he escorted the unidentified gentleman into the room.

Violet stared in silence at the man who approached her and bowed before she could steal a look at his face. He was husky, overdressed, and too dark to be mistaken for Kit. But as he straightened, he became familiar. A friend. She drew a breath.

One of her beloved friends. He wasn't Kit, but he *was* second-best. She broke into a delighted smile and cried inelegantly, "*Eldie*! Oh, Eldie! Look at you! You're so distinguished and lovely and— Do come closer. I'd no idea it was you. Why didn't you let me know you were coming? Why haven't you answered my last three letters?"

"Eldie?" her aunt said in a baffled undertone, and then he stepped closer to the window and the light glinted on his silver-rimmed spectacles. "Dear life, it is *you*, Eldbert Tomkinson. And what a pleasant surprise you are, indeed. Violet has mentioned many times that you distinguished yourself in the infantry. I cannot believe it was a decade ago that I watched your father riding you around the ring."

Eldbert's color mounted, as if he were embarrassed to death; Violet wondered how he had ever withstood the rigors of the British army. He said, "The memories of our past friendship in Monk's Huntley sustained me during many a dark night."

"How gratifying, Eldbert," the baroness said, glancing at Twyford, who stood as if he could not be seen outside the door. "Tea and strawberry cheesecake, Twyford. Bring a little porter for our guest, too. Have you been back to Monk's Huntley, Eldbert? Has it changed much since we have been gone?"

Eldbert lifted his broad shoulders, cutting such an impressive figure that Violet ached to dance in glee around the room. His appearance today had to be a good omen. "It is remarkably unchanged, Lady Ashfield. I was hoping, in fact, that we all might return for a Christmas reunion."

"Christmas?" Violet had not thought past her end-of-summer wedding, and now that would not take place. She envisioned her old house, haunted by her uncle's spirit and days that could never be recaptured. Would she and Kit be together this coming Christmas? Would her aunt understand and allow him into their lives? How could she ever choose? She dearly loved both of them.

"Eldbert." She shook her head, restraining herself from embracing him.

She had no desire to sit sipping tea with him, acting as though the past had not happened, stiff tailed and clucking like pigeons in a park. But then, perhaps he would pretend to have no knowledge of their forbidden history. How dreadful to think he might even be ashamed of the escapades they had gone on with Kit. Could he have forgotten? He was an officer who had fought a war.

The quick smile he sent her when Aunt Francesca reached around for her lap robe indicated that he remembered. And that he and Violet still had secrets to share. She shook her head. "How good to see you again."

He lifted his brow. "Is that all?"

"I have missed you—I have missed your brains and your instinct for getting me out of mischief," she whispered.

"Well," he said, clearing his throat, "I have missed your getting me into mischief. I am happy to say, though, that I've never made a blood pact with anyone else in my life."

She grimaced at the reminder. "Neither have I. But those were good times."

"Grand ones."

"It is rude to whisper, Violet," her aunt said, beckoning Eldbert to her chair. "Sit, the pair of you. Your father is still alive, Eldbert?"

He came toward her, Violet leading the way. "Yes, and he is well, thank you. But Lord Ashfield, madam, I—"

"He died almost two years ago."

"I am sorry. I didn't know. I have been away for such a long time."

"How could you know? I have made Violet visit all the places of my youth. We have been traveling ever since we left Monk's Huntley."

The tea arrived, and Violet sat, curbing her impatience, as her aunt asked Eldbert endless questions about the village. It was her aunt's way, she assumed, of recalling her own grand memories, and Violet thought it entirely innocent until unexpectedly Francesca asked Eldbert what he remembered about the churchyard below the old manor house.

Eldbert glanced at Violet, who slowly lowered her cup to the table. "The old churchyard, Lady Ashfield," he said. "The ruins, you mean?"

"I wondered if it remained as desolate as ever," she said. "Or if the parish had carried through on its threat to raze the ruins and erect a school upon the site."

"No one is going to build upon it for as long as the rumors persist."

"Rumors?"

"There has always been talk of treasures buried in the forsaken graves. The grounds will be sacked into eternity."

Francesca stared at him, intrigued. "What sort of treasures do you mean?"

"Those of a reclusive earl who had amassed a fortune during the Restoration and swore he would take it with him when he died. His relations pillaged the crypts, but I believe they were looking in the wrong place, as he intended them to do."

Francesca appeared to be fascinated. "What manner of fortune do you think one might find?"

"Assuming a person knew where to look," Eldbert answered, "you could unearth several chalices embedded with rubies, and gold plates from Jacobean days. The countess owned a casket of jewels that allegedly disappeared upon her death."

"Why were these valuables buried with the family?" inquired Francesca, her manner alert.

Violet stared at Eldbert, silently imploring him to stop before he revealed anything that could implicate either of them in their past misdeeds. She half rose to ring for fresh tea, but Aunt Francesca raised her hand, the motion forbidding Violet to interrupt.

"The earl's family was stricken by the plague, as were a great many of the other persons buried improperly in the churchyard," Eldbert said. "There was fear of contamination."

Francesca looked at him in horror. "And you played

in the place? I shudder to think of what might have happened to the three of you. Digging in graves, my soul."

"I never dug in a grave," Violet said before Eldbert could be led into revealing the existence of Kit and the tunnels by which he traveled.

Eldbert blinked behind his spectacles. "We explored," he said carefully. "We followed the maps I had made, which followed the streams—"

"And Violet sketched," Aunt Francesca said with a thoughtful frown. "She drew sketches of your adventures, and there was another boy."

"That would have been Ambrose," Eldbert said, as Violet held her breath, dreading his response. "His father is also deceased, Lady Ashfield, and he has inherited."

"I am perfectly aware of that," Francesca said in a subdued voice. "We are to attend his house party soon and I shall have to make peace with his mother."

Eldbert looked down at the plate of cheesecake Violet quickly offered him. He shook his head. "I'm sorry. Talking of graves and those we have lost, over tea, was not my intention."

Francesca gave him a forgiving smile and rose without warning from her chair. Violet and Eldbert stood, each extending an arm toward her; Francesca deigned to give Eldbert her hand. "Nor was it mine. It is all right, Eldbert. I am glad to see you well. Now, why don't the two of you go out into the garden while the sun is shining? If I can find my warm shawl, I might even join you."

Violet gave vent to a sigh.

A minute or so later she and Eldbert had strolled to the end of the small garden, past the small pond to a low bench that sat against a wall smothered in old-world sweet peas.

"My father disliked Ambrose when we were young," Eldbert said, remaining on his feet until Violet sat down.

"My aunt didn't warm to him, either. He was a spiteful boy."

"I believe he might be a spiteful man," Eldbert said. "I'm not sure what will happen at his party. I'd hate to think he was planning revenge."

"Revenge for what?" Violet asked, frowning at him.

"For not giving him his due. He always resented us for not doing what he told us to."

"That was ten years ago."

"Well, I don't think he's changed all that much."

"Is that what you came here to tell me?"

"In part."

"Then what else is there?"

Or who else?

Between them hung the unvoiced question.

Nothing, no hidden treasure, no person in heaven or below, not Ambrose or the earl's ghost, could engender in them the concern or curiosity that Kit did. He was a creation ex nihilo that an abandoned cemetery had pushed forth for the world to notice.

He was the reason that Eldbert and Violet had run through another garden, and he was the reason they sat here today. He was all they had talked about in the old days.

His appearance in the churchyard had brought them together. His departure had broken their band apart. "What else could Ambrose do to hurt us, Eldbert? Brag of his title? Parade about in new trousers?"

He sat down beside her; the abstract air that had made him appear odd as a boy gave him dignity now. "I have something else to tell you. I assume it is still acceptable for us to share a confidence?"

She stared into his spectacles. "Always, Eldbert. To the end of time."

"I found out myself only last month, when I visited London for a few days. It was shortly afterward that I finally received the last letter you had sent me. I know this will come as a shock, but Kit is here, Violet. He is in London, and he's made a new man of himself."

She turned away.

"Do you remember the retired captain who bought Kit's indenture from the palace?" he asked her.

The palace. She cringed at how naive she had ever been to believe the euphemism.

"Do you remember," he went on, "that we were afraid he would sell Kit to pirates or do him unspeakable harm?"

She stared down at a cobweb that a spider had built between the strands of sweet peas whose tendrils curled like question marks in the sun. The silk appeared fragile to the eye, too delicate to sustain the slightest damage.

"Yes, I do," she said. "But—"

"Violet," he said in an urgent voice, "I visited his *academy*. He runs a fencing school, and I have seen no finer swordsman in the years I served at war. He did not notice my presence in his crowd of admirers. But I know that if he had glanced my way, he would have recognized me. And my only thought was to call out my congratulations for what he had overcome."

She turned her head. "You *didn't*?"

He paused, clearly taken aback by the passion she had not been able to hide. "No. I realized before I could push my way through the crowd that public acknowledgment could lead to questions neither of us wanted to answer."

She put her hand on his. "I understand."

"Do you?" He shook his head. "I left as he finished his demonstration, but later that night I returned to the school to see if I could find him alone. There were people there even then. Violet, I did not go back."

She stared past him, her gaze lifting to the rear of the house. What was that shadow in her bedroom window? Someone moving in her room? She felt a twinge of concern. Had she left Kit's card where Delphine could see it? She reassured herself that she'd put it in a safe place—under the Bible on her nightstand. No one would think to look there.

"I felt as if I'd betrayed him," Eldbert said, staring down uncomfortably at her hand. "But I thought of you, and of what might happen if you met him by chance before your wedding. How would you explain your friendship with Kit to your fiancé? I didn't know whether Kit would give you away."

"And this is your secret?"

"Yes—I thought I ought to come to you immediately and prepare you in case you were caught unaware in his company." He gave her a grim smile. "I could too easily imagine Kit with his fencing skill meeting you and your fiancé."

"Yes, Eldbert," she said simply, nodding in agreement, biting her lip to discourage a smile.

"Violet," he said in a suspicious voice, "you are taking this well. Do you think I've made too much over nothing?"

She broke into an irrepressible smile. "Oh, Eldbert."

"You already knew," he said in astonishment. "You let me ramble on, and all the time you knew."

She released his hand and glanced up again at the house. Her bedroom curtains hung unmoving. Perhaps she had imagined that furtive shadow. "It is a dangerous situation," she said, instinctively lowering her voice. "I don't know what to do. Kit and I have seen each other. We are . . . in love."

She expected him to gasp, to shake his head in chagrin or give her a long lecture, as the young Eldbert would have done. Now, he merely frowned; the surprise had already gone from his face, replaced by concern.

"A dangerous situation, indeed," he said. "Then my fears were not unfounded."

"My aunt doesn't know yet, Eldbert, and I'm afraid of what will happen when I tell her the truth."

"I am afraid of what will happen when Ambrose brings us back together. It could easily come out that we knew Kit as he was once the four of us are in attendance at his party. I can tell you this much—I will stand by you and Kit no matter what."

Francesca convinced Delphine that she needed to borrow Violet's shawl. It pained Francesca to invade her niece's privacy. She had never done so before, even though she had been tempted on occasion. Fear of discovery, unfortunately, and not respect had stopped her.

Francesca had always been afraid of what she would find if she pried into Violet's life too deeply. Even now she braced herself as she entered the room. As if it were yesterday she could see her sister lying still on her bed against a vivid wash of blood. And a baby in the midwife's arm. A living, monkey-faced creature who had been spawned by sin through no fault of her own.

From that moment onward Francesca had felt she was protecting her niece against possible dangers that had been set into motion on the day of her birth.

Francesca had manipulated Violet's world to shield her from the sins that might tempt her. She thought she had succeeded. Her niece was betrothed to a respectable gentleman, and Francesca should be able to attend their wedding day with a happy heart. But her instincts said the opposite. She crept to the window and studied the two people in the garden. Violet seemed animated now, as she had been while watching that mock fencing contest in the park.

But how could the match have made her happy?

How could comparing Godfrey's stilted jabs to the other swordsman's exquisite parries have failed to make her miserable? To know she was marrying a handsome oaf when there were beautiful knights in the world? Had she really convinced Violet that respectability was more important than a love match? Perhaps Francesca no longer believed it herself.

She could die knowing her duty had been fulfilled when she was convinced that Violet had found the protector she deserved.

But first she had to know *why* she felt that she had met that young swordsman before, or at least whom he resembled.

And she had to find out why he had made Violet seem happier than she had been since her childhood, since the days when they had lived in Monk's Huntley.

The answer lay directly in front of Francesca once she turned from the window. She did not have to hunt for it. The answer lay upon Violet's desk, in an old sketch atop a tidy pile of thank-you letters to be posted.

Violet was no great artist. But she *had* captured the boy's face in its defiant youth. Francesca reached out for the drawing. If she tore it into shreds it would not change a thing. Violet was her mother, Anne-Marie, all over again, letting romance lead her and not practicality. Nothing that Francesca had done had thwarted the girl's true nature.

Nothing had destroyed the passion in her soul. And, unexpectedly, the realization brought Francesca great relief.

Chapter 22

Ambrose, third Viscount Charnwood, examined his shaven face in the mirror for evidence of the heavy jowls he had inherited along with his title and affluence. Despite his wife Clarinda's reassurances that he did not show any sign of the family dewlaps yet, Ambrose noted the slack skin that hung beneath his jaw. Clarinda saw no flaws in either her snorting pack of pug dogs or the two sons she had provided Ambrose and abandoned to their exhausted governess.

Dogs.

Boisterous offspring.

Which of them had made a puddle on the pair of cashmere trousers that Ambrose had discovered under the bed this morning? His eyes watered at the lingering aroma. He feared it had permeated the wallpaper. How could he debut at a club smelling like a chamber pot? Or at least smelling one in his mind. The maids had not mopped it all up. He pressed a scented hankie to his nose.

He heard the boys, ages six and seven, creating an unearthly commotion on the formal terrace in the gardens below his bedchamber. He wandered to the window. Every article his children discovered, be it a twig or a chop knife, became a weapon of some sort. Had he behaved with such uncouth abandon as a child? He preferred to believe not. He had been bullied into walking through wild places.

It was no use trying to forget his childhood. The memories of Monk's Huntley assaulted Ambrose at the most inconvenient moments. When he cheated at cards with the boys, for instance, he could hear Eldbert reprimanding him. When he was demonstrating to his sons the correct way to hold a sword, he could hear Kit snorting in derision or see him reaching out to position Ambrose's thumb on the grip.

His face darkened in resentment. The old criticism still stung. What gall. A beggar correcting a Charnwood. An inmate touching Ambrose's clean gloves when who knew what diseases besides the measles he carried on his person? It might be true that Kit's influence had given Ambrose some advantage later in life. Ambrose's fencing master at school had twice remarked that Ambrose showed a flair for the sword.

Which he hadn't. Kit had taught him a few tricks with the blade, and Ambrose had been quick enough to use them to confound his opponents. In his opinion, however, a sword remained an instrument of slow tor-

ture. Take his own children, for example. Scars, bloody
knees, a beheaded bust in the foyer. The boys should
learn to shoot small animals at the hunt and become
proper sportsman. All the noise, the practice, and for
what? To score points in a salon? Elegance was out-
dated.

"Gentlemen still admire the art of swordsmanship,"
Eldbert had said when they last met. It was a subtle
insult, Ambrose knew. As if Eldbert's military experience made him an expert on manhood, while Ambrose
had dutifully attended his estate affairs.

Yes, yes, yes. Ambrose appreciated those who had
fought for England. But how could England continue to
conquer the world if the titled few were not respected?
Rules were not meant for those who ruled. The aristoc-
racy understood the idiosyncrasies and double stan-
dards that others were obliged to obey. One agreed to
the proper order of things, or propriety perished.

At times Ambrose was afraid that even his wife,
who claimed that royal blood ran weakly in her veins,
had defected from her heritage. It was Clarinda who
had suggested the house party at their Kent estate instead of in Monk's Huntley. It was Clarinda who, after
he consented to her suggestion, began studying the society papers for hints on how to plan an unforgettable
first party. Now his wife had decided on the Marquess
of Sedgecroft's benefit ball as the model to which she
and Ambrose must socially aspire.

Clarinda viewed the house party as the beginning of
her rise in the upper crust, a foothold for the two hea-

then children she had brought into the world. Ambrose saw it as a descent into bankruptcy, but there was no doubt that it was a necessary evil. If a lord meant to maintain any appearance at all, he was compelled to entertain.

In the end Ambrose had been forced to assert himself in regard to the planning. "A house party is one thing," he had informed his wife after meekly submitting to her request to host the event. "But, dearest, we need not outdo the Marquess of Sedgecroft's lavish ball. An amateur theatrical, a small orchestra for the dance, and one of Eldbert's treasure hunts will suffice."

A party could have only one host. A band needed only one leader. To this day Ambrose was unsure whether he had been led astray by Kit or by Violet. It was preferable to think he had fallen under a young criminal's influence. It was unendurable to think that an English lord had allowed a girl to rule the roost—or that Kit had carved out a name for himself and risen high.

"Ambrose! Ambrose!"

He sighed, turning, to see his wife sail through the door. As always the sight of her uplifted him. She was perfection, with her short blond curls, huge brown eyes, and appealing plumpness, draped in an ivory silk promenade dress.

"There you are," she said, coming to the window before he could get out a word.

But then, he was often at a loss for words in her

presence. She laid her head on his shoulder. He restrained the urge to warn her that she would leave powder marks on his coat. "Ambrose," she said in a whispery voice that melted his annoyance. "You always pretend to have no affection for the boys. And yet here I catch you, watching them in pride."

"I do love them," he said, sighing.

"That pleases me to no end."

He glanced at the window, lifting his left hand to draw the blinds. Before he could block his view to the garden, he saw his eldest son shove his brother into an urn overflowing with ivy and geraniums. The governess shot across the terrace, skirts flying, to intervene. Ambrose stared at his howling youngest in grave sympathy.

His wife's hand slipped under his outer garments to his bare stomach. His muscles contracted in anticipation. He felt his manhood thicken. If only the governess could stop Parker from that unholy wailing. If only the boy would stand up for himself—if only Parker would take revenge instead of letting Landon bully him about all day.

"Ambrose," Clarinda whispered, and drew him by the tail of his waistcoat to the bed, where she proceeded to disarrange his attire and smother him with kisses. "Give me passion," she said, nudging his coat to the floor with her foot. "Give me—"

He rolled onto his side to object, but she was stronger-willed and he was too starved for her attention to wager a fight. But his sons were still fighting and he could not concentrate on lovemaking with that racket in the background. Either Parker or the governess had punished Landon, for he was howling now, too.

"The boys," he said between catching his breath and his wife's deep, ardent kisses. "That infernal noise has to end."

She had unfastened her gown at the shoulders, and her white breasts shimmered above the confines of her corset. He had undone his pantaloons and worked them down to his knees. "Am I your lord and master?" he asked meekly.

She arched her back, slowly lifting her skirts to her hips. There was a blessed silence from below. "You are, indeed," she said in a breathless voice, and slid to take him inside her.

"Give me a daughter, Ambrose," she said in abandon, and when she addressed him in that breathy voice, he felt potent enough to fulfill her every wish.

But at the crucial moment of intercourse, as he had barely penetrated Clarinda's body, a memory crept into his mind. He saw its image as vividly as if it had happened yesterday. He saw two boys dueling in a derelict churchyard—a profane act that disrespected not only the dead but the aristocratic living. He saw Kit's sword flash in the air, and he quailed, shrank in resentment, in awe. How could a human being move that fast? It was a sin against nature.

"Ambrose!" Clarinda's cry reached him as if from the end of a tunnel, an echo of Kit's impatience. "Ambrose, pay attention! One cannot found a dynasty upon daydreams."

A dynasty. Daydreams. A daughter. It occurred to him that his wife resembled a doll. If only she did not talk.

So the pauper believed he had overcome his past. Kit had aspired high. Ambrose could ruin him with a remark. He could ruin Violet, too, on the eve of her wedding to another nobody. He could pay both of them back for past humiliations. It wasn't as if he cared about a stupid, secret pact—well, he could show them all if he liked. This could be the most memorable house party ever held. It could even rival the Boscastle family's for scandal.

Such plans for restoring his honor among his childhood rivals cheered him immeasurably, and he returned his attentions to his wife with renewed vigor.

Chapter 23

ime could not pass fast enough for Violet. It had been two days since she had seen Kit, and the house party loomed in another week. Godfrey had not contacted her, and she was afraid of what would happen when he did. But even if Kit would not intervene to prevent her from marrying Godfrey, she was determined to save herself. She had worked up the courage to endure a scandal. She had told her aunt over breakfast that she wished to talk to her at length after they had eaten. Strangely Aunt Francesca had not appeared surprised or upset at the pronouncement.

Understanding might not change her aunt's point of view. But it could ease the strain between the two women. It could lift the guilt from Violet's heart. She wanted this dishonesty to end.

Her aunt was taking tea in the downstairs parlor when Violet slipped into the room. They looked at each other in trepidation and in trust. She glanced down at the sketching paper in her aunt's hand and knew indeed that the time for truth had come.

She recognized her amateurish pencil marks, remembering the very day she had attempted to catch Kit on paper. He had refused to stand in place long enough for her to do a decent job, and she had scolded him for being so uncooperative. But she had done her best. Judging by her aunt's face, she had depicted him well enough.

"Do you want to tell me about him, Violet?"

"I do. Very much."

"How could this happen?"

"I never meant to hurt you."

"All these years," Francesca said. "All that I did to discourage you from following your mother's path, and it was for naught."

"What did my mother do that made you so afraid for me?" Violet asked in a thick voice. "What curse did I inherit that you and Uncle Henry stopped talking whenever I came into the room? Was she a monster? Did she commit a sin so unspeakable that it was passed on to me when I was born?"

"You can't condemn me for the sacrifices I have made. Who is this boy in the sketch, Violet? What does he mean to you?"

Godfrey had selected half a dozen snuffboxes to show off at the house party. Violet detested it whenever he took a sniff, and Godfrey himself disliked the sensation of a drippy nose. But quite a few aristocrats collected the boxes. He couldn't miss the chance to impress possible clientele.

He wished for a pinch of something stronger than snuff when he walked uninvited into Lady Ashfield's town house. He wondered at the greeting he would receive. No one had answered his knock at the front door. He had been busy at the emporium all week, and hadn't so much as sent a message to Violet in days. Nor had she contacted him.

He had pushed Pierce Carroll's nasty insinuation to the back of his mind. But now it resurfaced, and he resented it. How dared the rascal hint that Violet was anything but the virtuous lady Godfrey had chosen to be his wife.

Godfrey had put Pierce in the right peg from the start. He was a bad sort. He'd let him know as much the next time he saw Pierce at the salon. It was obvious that Pierce had hoped to stir up trouble, for God only knew what reason.

Godfrey was ashamed of himself for listening to such claptrap, and— Where was Twyford? Why was the front door unlocked?

He walked resolutely to the drawing room, recognizing the voices conversing within. He had never paid Violet a surprise visit before. It was unforgivably rude of him to intrude.

He thought of how Fenton would make a dramatic entrance. Perhaps Godfrey should imitate his dash. But the house was unusually quiet, and when he reached the drawing room, he paused to listen to the drifts of conversation inside before he entered.

"I've been afraid of displeasing you all my life," Violet said, her voice steadier than she felt.

"I've wanted to tell you about your mother for a long time," Francesca said. "While your uncle was alive, he would not hear her name spoken in his house. Henry disapproved of her, even though he adored and accepted you as his own."

Violet drew her chair closer to her aunt. "Don't cry, Aunt Francesca. The doctor said you have to stay calm."

"I need to cry. Every woman needs to have a good weep now and then." She dabbed at her cheeks with the handkerchief she had pulled from her lacy cuff. "You are Anne-Marie all over again."

"How is that?" Violet asked, her gaze slipping to the sketch of Kit.

"You have inherited the headstrong nature that leads a young woman to heartbreak. I should have known that I was only delaying the inevitable."

Violet looked away. "She died in childbirth because of me. That is it, isn't it?"

"Yes, but—"

"And my father grieved so deeply when she died that he blamed me and went off to war. He didn't care if he was killed after he lost her. He wanted to be with his wife. This is what you told me when I was little."

She had believed the story and recounted it to herself whenever her mother came to mind.

Francesca's face twisted with guilt. "I am too old to bother with lies. It doesn't matter that my intentions have been to protect you—instead I am forcing you to marry an unlikable man."

"You didn't force me."

"Your mother loved your father enough to defy our parents, and decency," Francesca said, her face clouded with pain. "She loved him, but he did not love her."

"He didn't?" Violet asked, shaking her head. "Are you certain?"

"More than certain," Francesca said with a bitter smile. "He was anything but an honorable man. When Lord Lambeth learned that your mother had conceived you, he not only denied a romance between them, but he paid three other men to swear they had been intimate with her."

"What a weasel!"

"Your uncle wanted to call him out, but a public scandal was not in your best interest."

"But how?" Violet asked in a disbelieving voice. "How could he hide their courtship? You told me he had courted her."

"In secret, Violet, and I was their accomplice. He was engaged to another woman, but neither Anne-Marie nor I had any notion. He deceived us both."

"What did she do?" Violet asked slowly.

"What could she do? My parents sent her to an older cousin for the confinement. I went along, too, so that it would appear we were traveling together to care for an ailing relative. As Anne-Marie increased, our cousin made arrangements to place you in another home."

Violet stared at her in unquestioning acceptance. Had she suspected all along? It wasn't possible. "I might have been a foundling," Violet said.

"You had a family," Francesca said. "I was years older than Anne-Marie, and I would not let anyone give you away. The baron was courting me during this dreadful time. I had married him two months before your birth, and he agreed that we would adopt you."

Violet breathed out a sigh. "I always knew that something was wrong with me. And now I know what. No wonder you worried about me. I am not a lady. I am an illicit lie."

"You needn't sound so relieved, Violet," Francesca said, laughing despite her tears.

"It *is* a relief. I don't have to pretend I am the epitome of feminine perfection."

Her aunt sniffed. "That sounds altogether ominous. Don't you dare take this to mean that you can engage in wanton misconduct."

"I'm not a lady," Violet mused, a smile curling her mouth. "I could have started my life in an orphanage. I could have ended up being a courtesan."

"Violet!"

She bit her lip. "Please don't get upset. I'm sorry, and I wasn't serious. But . . . I'm not ashamed. My poor mother. How she must have resented me."

"Never. She loved you and worried until her death that you would carry the weight of her sins."

"I don't belong in proper society."

Francesca frowned at her. "No one has to know. Your uncle had forged documents made of your mother's marriage to a gentleman who never existed. He paid a handsome bribe to have your name entered in a birth registry."

Violet raised her head. "You should have told me a long time ago."

"You should have told *me*," a man's voice thundered through the room. Sir Godfrey banged open the door in a passionate outburst. "This is the sort of secret a gentleman should know before he marries shabby goods."

"How dare you," Francesca said, struggling to rise from her chair.

Violet surged to her feet, wrapping an arm around her aunt to hold Francesca at bay. "Do not get up, Aunt Francesca. I don't want you upset."

"What about me?" Godfrey demanded. "Does anyone care that I have been deceived?"

"Not particularly," Aunt Francesca said, sitting back in her chair.

He strode up to Violet, his face contorted in a mask of contempt. "I should have known the night I saw you dancing at the ball. You were a natural wanton."

Violet raised her chin. "I shall hit you if you say anything like that again. I mean it, Godfrey. Passion is in my true nature, and if you push me far enough . . . Well, you don't want to know what I might do."

He backed up a step. "I-I thought I was marrying the genuine thing. What am I supposed to say when people ask me about our broken engagement?"

"I don't know, Godfrey." She felt a flash of pity for him. "It's better that you find out now."

He grasped his walking stick. "To think I spent all that money on flowers to impress you."

"The flowers did impress me, Godfrey. It was your pettiness that put me off."

He pivoted, turning to the door, where Twyford stood, his brow arched in disdain. "You are leaving, sir?"

"And not fast enough."

"Godfrey . . ."

He looked back at Violet in wrath. "What is it?"

"Here." She pulled the half-dead nosegay he had sent her aunt from the vase and tucked it into his coat pocket. "You might as well get your money's worth."

Then he was gone.

"That was wicked of you, Violet," her aunt said in the lull of silence that followed Godfrey's angry departure. "I wish I had done it myself."

Chapter 24

It was eleven o'clock at night. The patrons of the corner pub had gathered outside the fencing salon for a free performance. In the street behind them a more well-heeled audience enjoyed the show from the comfort of their carriages. It was always a treat to watch the maestro train his pupils. His friendly curses often rose over the clash of blades or thunder of footsteps on the stairs as he took out his stopwatch to time a run.

He felt anything but friendly when he recognized the sallow-faced gentleman pushing his way through the crowd at the door as if he owned the place. "God help me," he muttered.

The Duke of Wynfield, a former pupil and an old friend, who had lost his father in the last year, and his wife three years before that, glanced around in amusement. "Ah, the haberdasher is here. He looks a little pale. I think he needs your shoulder to cry on, maestro."

"Shut up," Kit said with a reluctant laugh, turning back to the stairs as Godfrey stumbled like a sleep-walker into the chaos around him. What the blazes had happened to him now? He looked as if he'd ingested a fatal dose of poison.

"Watch where you're going, Sir Godfrey!" a voice shouted at him. "I almost beheaded you."

Godfrey reached Kit's side, wiping his face with his handkerchief. "Master Fenton, I need a word in private."

"Not now."

"Yes, now."

"Not—"

"It's about Violet. I *must* talk to you alone."

Kit stared at his stopwatch. "My dressing room. And this will be the last time; I swear it." He glanced up at the tall figure who stood by the door, examining the tip of his fleuret. "Excuse us, Pierce."

"By all means." Pierce turned, opening the dressing room door and closing it with a decisive click the moment Godfrey followed Kit inside.

"What is it?"

"I have found out the truth about my fiancée."

The Duke of Wynfield stared across the salon at the raven-haired man lounging against the dressing room door.

Their eyes met and clashed in silence. The duke made it clear by his look that he disliked Pierce. In fact, he stared at him until Pierce pushed off the door and sauntered past him, fleuret in hand.

"I think Sir Godfrey has cooked his own goose," he said, as if he and Wynfield were in on a private joke.

"It isn't our business."

"No, of course not. I wouldn't say a word to anyone but you. I know Fenton can trust you."

"Yes." Wynfield turned away. "With his life, if necessary."

Kit stared at the dagger that lay on the dressing table behind Godfrey. Fake prop or not, he had never been as tempted to use a weapon in his entire life. "Why did you eavesdrop in the first place?" he asked in disgust.

Sir Godfrey pulled the half-dead nosegay out from the pocket of his coat. "Here. Take the foul things. They are a symbol of what I felt for her."

"Your feelings have mended fast."

"I am the injured party."

"If you dig in any one spot deep enough, you are bound to find a skeleton. What possessed you to sneak into her house uninvited?"

Godfrey averted his gaze, and Kit knew that the next thing out of his mouth would be a lie. "I was worried when no one answered the door. Lady Ashfield has not been well, and Violet has neglected her for her charity work."

"How shameful, Sir Godfrey. To criticize a lady with a caring heart."

"But she *isn't* a lady; that's the point. And she didn't care about breaking my heart with her deceit."

"You said she was unaware herself of her past."

"A fabricated past, indeed. Who would have dreamed that such a lovely face had been born of vice and not the virtue she pretended?"

Kit felt the fire of rage building inside him. "Who would have dreamed that you were a toad unworthy of her trust?"

Godfrey swallowed. "You don't expect me to marry her now that I am aware of her disgraceful beginnings?"

"*Croak, croak,*" Kit said softly. "I hope no one steps on you before you leave this room."

"But . . ." Godfrey's eyes bulged. "I can't withdraw my suit without causing a stink."

"And what," Kit asked in a pitiless voice, "do you expect me to do? I have a suggestion."

Godfrey blinked furiously. "Does it involve a sword?"

"Not if you prefer a pistol."

"I came to you for sympathy, Fenton."

Kit tossed the flowers into the dustbin. Had the baroness kept this secret from Violet, or was it even true? "The only sympathy I can offer," he said, walking Godfrey to the door, "is to make your demise as quick and quiet as possible. To spare you the scandal, of course."

Godfrey closed his eyes. "I half wish that you would. I wish that you and she—"

Kit froze. "Go on."

"—would be spared any unnecessary scandal, also." His breathing grew raspy. "Will you keep this a secret between us, Fenton?"

"Will I *what*?"

"I can't afford for anyone to find out why I broke the engagement. It has to die a quiet death."

"Why do you think you can trust me?"

"Because you are an honorable man, and I am a miserable coward."

Kit smiled slowly. "Under one condition."

"Anything," Godfrey said, gray faced and flattened against the door.

Kit sighed. It was too tempting to forget that in the end only two things mattered—Violet and his honor. He couldn't toy with Godfrey, as much as the cad deserved it. "I will keep your secret—"

"Bless you," Godfrey breathed, clasping his hands under his chin.

"Unclasp your hands this instant."

"Is that the condition?"

"The condition," Kit said between his teeth, "is that you are never to mention Violet in a derogatory manner again. In fact, you are to forget that you ever knew each other. Don't darken her doorway again. I will also find a way to kill you if you say one word against her."

Godfrey nodded. "I knew you would understand."

"I understand that you're a fool." Kit elbowed him aside to open the door. "Not a word to anyone. And, Godfrey—"

"Sir?"

"I'm canceling your subscription as of now. Without a refund."

Godfrey shrank away as Kit reached out to open the door. He strode out into the salon, scowling at the sullen quiet that greeted his appearance. Every pair of eyes followed Godfrey's undignified escape to the front door.

"Well?" Kit challenged. "Why are you all standing about like tin soldiers? Engage."

"Fenton."

He turned at the sound of Wynfield's voice. "What is it?"

"How long have you known Pierce Carroll?" Wynfield asked as they met by the stairs.

"I'd say six or seven months at the most. Why? Where is he?"

Both men glanced around the salon, searching for the lightning-fast figure in the noisy mélange. "He's gone," Wynfield said.

"What of it?"

"I don't like him. I mistrust his intentions around you. Did you know that he was French?"

"I may have heard him speak the language, but then so do I. The fencing terms are in French, and every serious student of the art has to learn them sooner or later, or—"

"His name isn't Pierce Carroll. I think he's hiding something from his past."

"I'm not exactly proud of my origins, either."

"But you overcame them."

Kit shook his head in dismissal. "I've been a criminal. I've known more sinners than I can count. But for the grace of God and my father's intervention, I would be in lockup. Who do you think Pierce is?"

"I saw the name de Soubise on a letter that fell from his jacket the last time we changed for practice. I wouldn't have thought anything of it if he hadn't snatched it up—"

"De Soubise. Are you certain?"

"Yes."

Kit was silent as he looked up to the sword mounted above the rack of foils on the wall. "My father," he said finally, lowering his gaze in understanding, "had one bitter enemy: the Chevalier de Soubise, who had a son several years older than me. I should have known the day I saw Pierce throwing knives that he was not who he claimed to be."

"Do you think he'll be back?"

"Count on it," Kit said with certainty.

"When?"

"When I least expect him."

"What can I do to help you?" Wynfield asked.

"Watch over my woman if I am distracted. Take care of her when I do what I have to do. I will address any threat the chevalier's son might pose once and for all."

Chapter 25

$\mathscr{V}$iolet had fallen asleep that night at the bottom of her aunt's bed. She opened her eyes and saw her aunt bending over her, her face wreathed in a smile. "Wake up. We have to pick out your wardrobe for the house party. It isn't too early to start."

Violet stretched, feeling like a familiar weight inside her had been lifted, and . . . "Where did all those roses come from?" she demanded, gazing at the vases of long-stemmed blooms that occupied every surface imaginable and filled the room with the heady perfume of romance.

"It looks like a hothouse in here," she marveled. "Who sent them to you? Not . . . not Godfrey? Oh, please, don't say that he wants another chance."

"It was not Godfrey," her aunt said with a wry smile. "Your secret knight sent them. And, I have to admit, it is a favorable strategy on his part."

"Was there a note?"

"Yes. He has asked to meet me at a house party."

"And?"

"And we shall have to see."

Despite the drama of her broken engagement, Violet looked forward to the house party. It would be the reunion that she and her friends had promised one another, even if Miss Higgins could be present only in spirit. Violet had written to her before leaving London and asked if they could take a proper tea together when she returned. But for now she looked forward to hours of dancing and of being with Kit, whose company she craved with a happy desperation that she no longer had to hide.

She searched for him amid the guests milling around the other gigs, carriages, and post chaises that crowded the driveway to the estate. She sought a glimpse of him in the couples drifting across the lawn to stroll down secluded avenues provided by the tall privet hedges.

Every so often another carriage rumbled through the wrought-iron gates. Footmen raced forth to attend new arrivals. A majordomo in a scarlet coat stood on the front steps between— Violet stared through the carriage at the gentleman in a top hat and the lady in turquoise silk standing at his side.

"Is he here?" Francesca inquired as the footmen opened the carriage door.

There was no point in pretending that she didn't know whom her aunt was talking about. It felt wonderful to be able to finally share her fondest secret. "No. I think that's Ambrose on the steps, though. The gentleman in the top hat. Kit wouldn't be with the other guests. He hasn't been formally invited to the party." She subsided against the seat. "And perhaps this will be the last one I shall ever attend."

Her aunt reached for her hand. "But you have friends like Mr. Tomkinson, who rode behind us from London. And if you are never invited to another party, it will not matter."

"We will have our own parties," Violet said, smiling at the thought.

"Yes. And I will dance with Twyford, if I can get out of my chair."

Violet turned her head as a footman opened the carriage door.

She *was* willing to turn her back on the fashionable world to become part of Kit's. Besides, if society learned the truth of her low origins, she would be judged, deemed unworthy, and instantly banished from it for the rest of her days.

"Where is Delphine?" her aunt asked as she stepped gingerly from the carriage.

"You gave her orders to make sure our rooms are closed off to drafts and drunken gentlemen who might wander about in the dark."

"Ah. That was sensible of me. Shall we wait for Eldbert?"

"He's parked a half mile behind us. Besides, I am dying to see what kind of man Ambrose has become."

*   *   *

Ambrose stared at the man who had quietly walked past the receiving line that started on the steps. Unannounced as yet, unadorned, except for the sword that sat at his hip like a calling card, he attracted the notice of more guests at the party than the host and hostess.

At last he looked up at Ambrose, who was half tempted to greet him. He saw recognition in Kit's eyes, but he wasn't sure he saw any respect. Hadn't the man learned any manners after all these years? Who did he think had paid him to perform at the party?

Was it proper for a viscount to acknowledge a fencing master? His guests seemed to think so. Was this the right moment for a public greeting? Suddenly Ambrose hadn't a clue whether he wanted to pay Kit back for the old taunts or thank him for lessons learned.

"Who is *that*?" Clarinda asked in a curious voice.

Ambrose shrugged. "Must be someone from the fencing academy."

"Ask him."

"Now?"

"Please, darling. He is a very fetching person."

"We have *important* guests to greet."

"The boys have begged to meet him, Ambrose," Clarinda whispered. "And he is a looker, I must say."

Someone gave a cry from the receiving line. "It's Master Fenton!"

"God," Ambrose said. "How inappropriate."

"Yes," his wife said in a dreamy voice. "I'll bet he is."

His face grim, Ambrose muttered an apology to the guests waiting in line on the steps and made his way down the other side onto the drive. Kit had started toward the garden, but he hesitated as Ambrose approached him.

"Viscount Charnwood," he said, his tone deferential.

Ambrose wavered. He could sense Clarinda—in fact, he could sense nearly everyone—watching this exchange. "My good man," he said, "you flatter yourself if you think you have ever made my acquaintance. What is your name?"

He bowed, his face impassive. "Christopher Fenton."

"I don't believe we have met."

"My mistake, your lordship." Kit turned.

"Fenton, you say?"

"Yes, my lord."

"I have never met anyone by that name."

Kit did not reply. In fact, he gave no reaction at all. But at least Ambrose had the satisfaction of the last word, although as he watched Kit bow again and walk away as if he owned the place, he felt an irrational urge to call him back and . . . Well, he didn't know what he would do. Kit had always been good at taking Ambrose off guard.

Chapter 26

"Violet," Ambrose said, his eyes brightening as he noticed her in the line. "I almost didn't recognize you. I would never have made you wait if I had known it was you."

She smiled self-consciously, as if she were surprised by his warmth. "It is good to see you. What a beautiful estate."

"It'll do, I suppose. Better than the old heap at Monk's Huntley."

"This is my . . ." He turned to introduce his wife, but Clarinda was engaged in conversation with another guest. He glanced to the silver-haired woman who stood in dignified silence behind Violet, a hat adorned with black plumes shading her face. "Lady Ashfield, I did not recognize you, either. How decent of you to come."

"You haven't changed at all," she said, deigning to give him her hand. "You look just like your father, especially around the chin."

"She's tired, Ambrose," Violet said, sending her aunt a frown. "Would you mind if we went upstairs to rest before we are officially arrived?"

He couldn't stop looking at her. When had Violet become a beauty? She had grown out of her awkwardness into something altogether compelling. "Not at all," he said, motioning to the footmen in the doorway. "There will be a moonlight supper later if you're game. The fountains will be filled with champagne."

"I don't know," she said, not anything like the girl he remembered. "We'll have to see."

"If not," he said, his gaze following her retreat into the house, "I shall look forward to tomorrow, when everyone is introduced in the great room."

She gathered her skirts, giving Clarinda a curious glance. "Until then, Ambrose."

Violet saw her aunt to her assigned chamber, where she left her to her maid, Delphine, and walked across the hall to her room. The footman opened the door and disappeared before she could tip him. She walked slowly into the spacious room. Warm sunlight streamed through the leaded casement windows, gilding the man who stood waiting for her to notice him. As if any female could ignore such a handsome figure.

"Master Fenton."

"Miss Knowlton."

She took a breath and was swept up against him before she could exhale. His body felt like tempered steel, and, hoyden that she was, she surrendered without any sign of resistance. "This is a surprise," she said, as she hooked her arms around his neck. "I didn't think I'd—"

He kissed her.

"—see you until—"

He deepened the sensual attack.

"—tonight," she whispered between his dizzying kisses.

"I couldn't wait," he said, smoothing his hands down her back, his breath flirting like a flame with her mouth. "You have the sweetest lips I have ever kissed."

"Yours are the most sinful."

"Compared to . . . ?"

She sighed, her eyes teasing. "No one. Never. You're the first."

"The only," he corrected her. "From today to forever."

"There's going to be a moonlight supper in the park."

"I don't need moonlight," he said, pulling her toward the chair behind them. "I have your love to lead me through the dark."

"And champagne," she whispered. "Ambrose is extravagantly filling the fountains with champagne."

"I don't need champagne," he said, falling into the chair with her on his lap. "I'm going to get very drunk on you tonight."

"I wondered when you'd arrive," she said, her voice uneven. She combed her fingers through his silky hair.

"Eldbert followed our carriage here to guard us on the road."

"I know," he said, his eyes glinting. "I trailed behind him to guard both of you."

"How noble of you, Kit. And how noble of you to be hiding in my room like this."

His hands stole around her waist and locked her against him. "I have a reason to be here. I have several reasons, actually. Most are pleasant. One is not."

"The bad news first," Violet said, laying her head upon his chest.

His tapered fingers stroked almost absently down her neck. She felt wondrous shivers in their wake. "It seems I have an enemy," he said. "A person from the past who wishes to avenge an old offense."

"That you committed?" she whispered.

"No. My father did," he said, his face composed.

She lifted her head from his shoulder. "Is this person here?"

"Not as far as anyone knows. He calls himself Pierce Carroll. That is not his true name."

"Oh," she said, "the man who does not mind his own business."

His eyes searched her face. "You have met him?"

"Godfrey made a remark about him at the breakfast party. It was meant to stir up trouble, as I recall."

The hand that had been caressing her stilled. Kit's eyes darkened with purpose. "I should have listened to my instincts then," he said, "Even Godfrey recognized a threat."

"Godfrey left me," she whispered, burrowing back into his firm shoulder and the folds of his Irish linen shirt.

"I know. He told me. Are you sad?" he asked, his hand slowly resuming its seductive quest.

"Do you think less of me because my mother wasn't married when I was born?"

"Did you think less of me because my mother left me at an orphanage and I wore the same shirt for weeks at a time when we were young?"

"You never looked scruffy to me, Kit."

"I washed my shirt in the stream and wore it back to the workhouse wet whenever I saw you. I didn't want you to know how wretched I was. I wanted to look like a person worthy of your admiration."

"Kit," she whispered, raising her head to look up at him. "You're the bravest person I have ever known."

"Do you think so?"

"I do."

"Then marry me."

"Yes," she said. "And yes. Yes. And in case I wasn't clear the first three times, my answer is yes. When?"

He laughed. "I'll be damned if I'll leave anything to chance again. Can you be ready in an hour?"

"You've lost your mind," she said, struggling to break free. "We can't have a ceremony in Ambrose's house—and I don't have a dress. My aunt would have to know—Kit . . ." She wriggled to her feet, staring down at him in dismay. "How can we get married at a house party? What happened to an old-fashioned courtship?"

"I think a decade of friendship counts for something. Even in medieval days I doubt they went any longer than that, and if they did, that explains all the besieged castles and stolen brides that never made much sense to me from a historical perspective; but from the point of a man desperately in love, I now understand."

"What?"

"The wooing is over. Except for your aunt."

"You aren't serious. I don't have a dress."

"Look inside your wardrobe."

She did, opening the heavy rosewood door to see a dress that looked as if it were made of clouds and spun sugar, with water pearls and fine embroidery on the sleeves and a low-cut bodice. It was the most beautiful bridal gown she had ever seen, but . . . "This is from Winifred?"

"Well, I certainly didn't make it."

"Do you think it will fit me?" she asked, biting her lip.

He grinned. "It should. I described your proportions to her."

"You didn't."

"No."

"She couldn't have made it for me in such a short time. Was it hers?"

"I think so. Wish me luck facing your aunt."

"Luck," she whispered, lifting the gown down to admire it in the light.

*　　*　　*

Kit charged up the stairs to the long gallery, bowing and muttering, "Pardon me," to the startled guests he bumped against. He wondered why no one so much as replied, "I should think so," or whether Ambrose had invited an exceptionally polite crowd, or if the fact that he was one of few men present wearing a sword gave the impression that he was late to a duel.

He turned at the top of the stairs and addressed the two ladies staring up at him from the landing. "Excuse me, ladies, but I'm going to propose marriage."

"Marriage?" The ladies giggled in delight.

"To one or both of us?" the younger inquired.

"You'll have to choose, maestro," the eldest said with a saucy look. "You can't marry both of us."

"What a pity," he said, his eyes lowering in playful woe.

The Duke of Wynfield came running up the stairs alongside Kit. "Does either of you ladies require assistance?"

Kit cut him a droll look. "Not unless you want to marry one of them."

Wynfield smiled uneasily. "Not today, thank you." He started to edge away. "And thank you, Fenton, for the warning. I think I'll use the other stairs."

"No. Stay with me."

Wynfield glanced up at the long gallery. "Any maidens up there in need of comfort?"

"I doubt it. Their caretakers presumably dropped the bolts when they saw us coming up the stairs."

The duke walked up behind Kit to the portrait-hung

long gallery. "I see more footmen at this party than young ladies. Where are the debutantes?"

"Sequestered in the north tower under the guard of their dragonesses," Kit replied, studying the small figure sweeping majestically toward the staircase from the end of the gallery. A pair of servants flanked her at either side of the wings.

"Isn't that a dragoness flying toward us?" the duke asked.

Kit put his hand to his sword. "Yes, but don't worry."

"Why not?"

"Because she's my dragoness, not yours, and it is my duty to confront her."

Wynfield recoiled in shock. "But she's an elderly woman."

"Her advanced age is a weapon."

The duke slowed another step. "But you cannot *fight* a lady of her years."

"Did I give you the impression that I intended to challenge her?"

"Well, I saw your hand go to your sword when you noticed her—"

"For luck, Wynfield. I'm not about to do battle with a baroness."

The duke glanced down the gallery. "By the look on her face, she might not feel the same way."

"I appreciate the show of support," Kit said stoutly.

"I've never acted as a second in a duel between a man and woman before."

Kit threw out his arm to impede Wynfield's progress. "One more encouraging remark like that and you and I are going to have it out right here."

"What do you want me to do?" Wynfield asked distractedly, eyeing a chambermaid who had just appeared with a basket of soap balls and sachets swinging in her hand.

"It's like walking to one's execution," Kit said, lowering his arm.

"That's not a promising way to view a proposal," the duke said, following the chambermaid with his eyes. "Where is the maidservant going?"

Kit had to laugh. "Thank you for the reminder. There's nothing morbid about marriage, assuming I get that far. What harm can an elderly woman inflict on me that I haven't already experienced? I've lived through every manner of shame. The worst thing she can do is refuse me. Or go into hysterics again."

"Did you say something, Fenton?"

"I said a lot of things that I'm not going to repeat. But thank you for pretending to pay attention."

Kit lifted his shoulders, mentally girding his loins for battle. The baroness had him in her sights, making him glad he had changed into his black tailed coat and formal trousers. He had performed before princes and dukes, Gypsies and greater masters than he could ever hope to be. But he had never felt as unsure of himself as he did as he approached the frail, silver-haired woman whose shrieks had haunted him for years.

She walked straight toward him, her gait slow but confident. She knew who he was. She wasn't going to back out of this encounter. She was going to give him a chance. His future depended on their duel. He would live or die today by how well he fought for what he wanted.

"Here." He impulsively unsheathed his sword and passed it back to the duke, who was lagging farther and farther behind. "Hold this for me."

He turned.

And swept into a bow before the baroness. "My lady," he said, "I am honored to meet you again under these circumstances."

"Which are more favorable than the last," the baroness said, her eyes sparkling as he straightened. "I am on my way to tea. Would you care to join me?"

He smiled. "With your permission, I am on my way to my wedding. Do you think that tea could wait until tomorrow?"

Pascal de Soubise had packed into his portmanteau several pairs of gloves, a change of clothing, and the snuffbox he had stolen from the emporium. He would carry his dagger with him when he made his escape from the country house to the coast. He disliked the necessity of wearing a wig as a disguise for the Channel crossing. But he was close to ending his chase and fulfilling the pledge he'd made to his father. He looked forward to prowling the Parisian boulevards. Perhaps, in a few months, he would travel to Louisiana or the Carolinas, where dueling was the rage.

He had no particular desire to cross blades with Fenton at a house party. Then again, the challenge posed added heat to what he had considered a lukewarm kill. He abhorred the rules of polite fencing, the use of the foil. A swordsman fought duels, and he fought to draw blood.

Chapter 27

*T*he baroness had accepted Kit's offer for Violet's hand and agreed to the necessity of a whirl-wind wedding. The pupils of Kit's academy who had been invited to the house party stood guard outside the manor gates as Kit, Eldbert, the duke, and Twyford whisked the bride-to-be and her aunt into Kit's mud-splattered traveling coach.

It appeared to Kit that they would make a clean escape. Most of the guests were engrossed in a late-afternoon cricket game on the lawn. Two of Kit's students were giving free fencing instructions on the terrace. As far as the other ladies at the party knew, Violet and the baroness had decided not to appear for tea. Master Fenton had been briefly spotted outside the billiards room, and a small congregation stood outside the closed doors in the hope that he would soon emerge.

"I can't believe that nobody saw us," Violet said

breathlessly, her eyes shining as the coach clattered over a sturdy stone bridge toward the tiny chapel that Eldbert had found on one of his maps.

Kit pulled his head back in the window. He wasn't sure now that they'd made a clean escape at all. A gentleman in a top hat was striding down the drive, his gloved hands on his hips. "I wonder if we should have invited him."

"Who?" Violet asked softly.

He stared at her, shaking his head. She looked so winsome in the voluminous tulle gown Winifred had created that he couldn't remember his own name for a moment. She was a Christmas present wrapped up in so many billowing layers of lace and loveliness that he couldn't wait to open her. She was wearing elbow-length white gloves, holding Eldbert's hand on one side, and her aunt's on the other. And soon she would be his wife.

Kit turned his head, glancing at the duke. He liked Wynfield well enough, but somehow it felt wrong to be sitting beside him at a moment like this. Should he have invited Ambrose? Why? Because he and Violet had escaped without permission from his party? Why should Ambrose come? So that he could spoil their wedding as he had spoiled their adventures?

Violet uncrossed her satin-shod feet. "Who was that in the driveway?" she whispered. "Did we forget someone?"

Eldbert glanced at Kit across the coach.

"Was it Ambrose?" Violet guessed, bending toward

the window like a summer blossom in the breeze. "Shouldn't we go back and invite him?"

"Why?" the duke and Lady Ashfield asked at the same time.

"It is his party," Eldbert said, moving to give Violet's gown more room. "We probably should have told him where we are going and that we'd be back."

Kit frowned. "You're the one who thought he was planning something spiteful."

"I thought he was. But now I wonder if he wasn't just showing off. He's done better than all of us."

"Not than me," the duke said.

Eldbert nodded. "But you're not one of us."

"I beg your pardon."

"Never mind," the baroness said. "It's a long story and a secret. We can let you in on it after the wedding."

Ambrose watched the coach rattle out through the gates and veer toward the village road. Not for a moment did the impromptu fencing display in the driveway deceive him. Kit had run off with Eldbert, Violet, and God only knew who else. Wherever they were going, they meant to exclude Ambrose. Kit had looked right at him when he'd stuck his head out the window.

He should have made a cutting remark about Fenton's background earlier. Or about Violet's unladylike youth. He was a fool for feeling any loyalty to Eldbert, or for imagining true friendship between them. Just as he was a fool for thinking Kit could teach his sons a few tricks to keep them from getting fagged at school.

And where was Violet's button-seller fiancé in all this? Any gentleman would be mortified to see his betrothed trundling off in a coach with three unmarried men. Ambrose wouldn't be surprised to hear she was in the market for a new protector on Monday, her value considerably decreased as a result of this little escapade.

Friendship.

Did Ambrose need it, anyway?

"Ambrose!" a petulant voice called to him from the steps. "What are you doing standing there all by yourself when there are guests in the house?"

He sighed, turning to see first his mother, dressed like a wraith in gray, and beside her his wife, in a yellow-striped taffeta dress that hurt his eyes.

"Why are you alone, darling?" Clarinda asked, grabbing his sleeve to steady herself in the gravel.

"I was watching the students practice a sword fight." He indicated the group of young men scattering across the drive. "It's over now."

"Who left in that coach?" his mother demanded.

"I—"

"It looked like Eldbert and Violet. Are they teasing you again, Ambrose?"

"No, Mother, they are—"

"They're coming back!" Clarinda cried, standing on the tips of her shoes. "They're turning back and waving at you from the window, Ambrose. I think they're asking you to go with them."

He shook his head, his hands buried in his pockets. "No. No. That's the bend in the road. The coach is turning onto it."

"No. It isn't, Rosie," his mother said, pointing with her cane. "They're coming straight back toward you. I'd turn and pretend I didn't see them if I were you. Quickly. Go and talk to the other important guests. I've no idea why you invited them in the first place. Where did that duke go?"

Lady Charnwood looked up at her husband's face. "Ambrose? What do you want to do? Someone told me this morning that by this time next year Christopher Fenton will be made a baronet due to the influence of the Boscastle family."

"I wouldn't be surprised if he didn't rise higher," he said, smiling reluctantly as he recognized Kit's head halfway out the coach window. "He has the devil's confidence, Clarinda."

"Viscount Charnwood!" Kit shouted from the slowing coach. "Would you and the viscountess care to slip away for a whirlwind wedding?"

Ambrose wavered. "May I bring my mother?"

"Mothers are always welcome," Kit replied, even though the baroness made a sour face and refused to give up her seat when, a half minute later, the old viscountess climbed inside the coach.

"This is perfect," Clarinda announced, crowded between Kit and the duke, who wedged her in like a pair of bookends. "I only wish I'd known earlier so I could have brought champagne."

"I've brought champagne," the duke said.

Ambrose laughed. "Only one bottle?"

"Hell, no."

They'd opened two before they reached the tiny twelfth-century chapel where a jovial vicar was waiting to perform the ceremony. Clarinda insisted that she serve as a bridesmaid, and she talked up until it was time for Violet and Kit to exchange vows.

"This will be more than a house party now," she said, straightening the train of Violet's gown. "It will be an event. It's only Thursday and we've had our guests elope in a whirlwind wedding. It's ever so much more exciting than the puppet show planned in the rotunda."

"Be quiet," Ambrose whispered, patting her fondly on the bum. "The minister is beginning the ceremony."

"Don't do that," she whispered. "Fenton saw you. He'll think you're ill behaved."

"He knows I am."

But Fenton had eyes only for his bride, Ambrose decided. He couldn't deny that Violet and Kit made an attractive pair, a dashing swordsman dressed in a long black coat and his own elegant trousers. His bride looked as radiant as an angel.

And Eldbert—he was stout but ever so dignified.

His friends.

Ambrose realized how profoundly they had influenced his life. What kind of person would he have become without them? Well, whatever he was, he could strive to better. If Kit could pull himself out of his private hell, then perhaps Ambrose could lend a hand to others in a similar unfortunate position.

His mother, who hated the baroness, was collapsed on Francesca's shoulder, weeping her head off. The baroness was consoling her, all in black, her wrinkled face woeful but kindly. His mother was crying for no reason, really, except perhaps that she had drunk too much champagne.

But at last the ceremony began, and there was quiet as Kit and Violet exchanged their vows. They kissed, clearly so much in love that even Ambrose felt his eyes fill. It was an inspiration to realize his old friends had fallen in love. It was distressing to think he'd ever resented them when they could have been in touch all these years, instead of his waiting to prove to them he was better off than they would ever be.

Of course, that wasn't true.

Kit and Violet would be content and prosper and pursue their own adventures in the future as they had in the past. Ambrose considered it an honor to be counted in their circle of friends. His sons had declared Fenton to be their personal hero.

Until this moment Ambrose would have denied that he had kept company with a common workhouse boy. But now it was an honor.

The servants of Charnwood House had been alerted to expect a wedding party. So, unfortunately, had the guests. Kit had hoped to keep the marriage a secret from the main body of the manor until morning. But the scandal broth had spilled; a group of ladies and gentlemen stood waiting in the hall off the great salon to offer congratulations and catch a glimpse of the bride and groom.

It wasn't every day, after all, that a demure young lady eloped with a fencing master. And, the whisperers asked, wasn't she engaged to the gentleman who owned the emporium where most of them shopped? Come to think of it, what *had* happened to Sir Godfrey Maitland?

Christopher Fenton might be as handsome as sin, but he had a reputation for being an honorable man. He didn't fight a duel at the drop of a glove. He could not have challenged Sir Godfrey without the sensation showing up in the papers.

"We shall have to wait until Monday to read the news," one lady remarked to her companion. "Maybe there will be a duel when we return to London."

"Would you look at that," her companion replied. "I think he's carrying her up the stairs. What a handsome couple they make."

Chapter 28

$\mathcal{K}$it ignored the bystanders. He merely smiled and accepted their congratulations, Violet clasped firmly to him for the climb. Her skirts flowed behind them.

"Everyone likes you," Violet whispered. "I think I'm jealous."

He glanced up. Only one face in the crowd drew his attention. His pulse jumped in fury as he spotted Pierce pushing people aside to reach the stairs.

"Not everyone likes me, darling."

"What is it?"

Pierce advanced, his eyes moving past Kit to his wife. "She doesn't have to leave on my account. Consider this my wedding present to you both."

Kit had lowered Violet to the floor of the main staircase and quickly stepped in front of her.

"Find Wynfield or any of my pupils," he ordered Violet. "Stay with them.

"At dawn," he said to Pierce, reaching to touch his sword, only to realize that he had not seen it since handing it to the duke.

The man who called himself Pierce unsheathed his sword. "No, maestro. Now."

Kit sighed, shrugged out of his coat, and removed his vest. He glanced toward the stairs and spotted Wynfield waiting, Kit's sword at his side.

Kit nodded.

The other guests drew back against the wall in silence as the duke strode across the hall. A cloud of uncertain anticipation had darkened their excited chatter.

"Don't be alarmed, ladies and gentlemen," Wynfield said, his stride unhurried. "Your host has promised this will be a house party that no one will forget." And under his breath, he said to Kit, "Do you think I can convince them this is part of the entertainment?"

"You can try," Kit said, reassured by the familiar weight of the weapon in his hand.

He glanced around at his wife, whose eyes held his in understanding. He was glad he had warned her that this was not a game he wished her to witness. "Go with the others, darling. I'll be with you again as soon as I can."

She nodded in obvious reluctance. "Don't be long. And . . . be careful."

"Wynfield, do you mind moving the assembly into the great room and watching over Violet until I finish here?"

"Not at all."

The duke cut across the hall, Violet at his side, and

the instant they crossed out of view, Kit refocused his energy on the man who thought to challenge him. A long-planned revenge, indeed. Kit would fight to defend his father's honor. At least he was not facing some hothead who hoped to prove his manhood and ended up making a mockery of the sword.

Pierce had stripped down to his shirt in palpable anticipation. He stood in the middle of the hall like a conqueror. "Well?" he said, his dark eyes full of contempt. "Is the master going to defend his reputation or forfeit?"

Voices rose from the far end of the hall. Kit could have laughed at his luck. From the shadows came another convention of guests, led by Eldbert and Ambrose, who had gotten into a dispute right after the wedding ceremony and were now arguing with each other over the top of Clarinda's head.

"I tell you again, Ambrose," Eldbert said, "the fumes from unventilated pipes will kill you."

"This is a house party, for the love of heaven. Talk about something more pleasant than plumbing."

They broke off, gaping at Kit.

He knew what they were thinking. He saw Eldbert's arms wave up and down like an orchestra conductor to hold back the crowd. As if that weren't distracting enough, he spotted the baroness and Ambrose's mother bringing up the rear of the group. It crossed his mind that of all the ladies he wished could witness him wage the fight of his life, it would be Violet, and not her aunt.

A hiss of steel in the air captured his attention. His rival's blade whispered below his left ear, not close enough for a piercing but close enough that his anger spiked, and instinctively he engaged, and sliced a crimson slash down Pierce's wrist.

Pierce blinked. "Well, that's better. You do have it in you."

"Yes. And I was hoping to save it for my wedding night."

"My name is Pascal de Soubise."

"Is that supposed to mean something? Or are you letting me know how you want your epitaph inscribed on your grave?"

The tang of blood.

The ring of metal.

It was better to think of it as a game. Better to pretend that a girl being held for ransom was watching him from her window. Or that he was fighting to prove his worth to Captain Fenton. Pascal beat at him again and again, his mouth a taut line as Kit dodged every attack.

Kit pivoted, jumping over a tray that a terrified footman had dropped when the duel began. It might have indeed been a tombstone. He might have been trying to impress his friends with bravado and ballocks as he had in the past. He danced in a semicircle, remembering how much his father had taught him when he was arrogant and thought he knew it all.

Weave a web of steel around him, Kit. Economy of movement.

I'm running away, old man.

The doors are locked.

Locked doors never stopped me. I could scale the garden wall and be halfway through the woods before you'd notice.

Perhaps, Kit.

Why should I study? You said yourself I'm a born swordsman, the best you've ever seen.

In Monk's Huntley. That isn't saying much.

"Reviewing the code?" Pascal taunted, beating at Kit until his boot heels touched the tiles of the white marble fireplace. "Hit to the breast," he added, and kicked the ornamental fire basket in Kit's face. "Some skills can't be taught in school, *master*."

"I know," Kit said with all sincerity, deflecting the basket with his free arm.

"How do you know, you who follow every rule and stay inside the circle?"

"Let me show you," said the master to his challenger. "Extend your damned leg and deliver."

Pascal laughed. "Give me an elegant kill and get it over with."

"You're as slow as a grandfather clock."

"You're as slow as my grandfather's cock," Pascal shot back, drawing a gasp of shock from the audience as he swooped down with his left hand for the poker lying on the hearth.

He swung it at Kit's head.

Kit ducked, frowning in irritation. He had just married the woman of his dreams, and he had no intention of being carried incapacitated to his wedding bed. Still, he had a reputation to maintain, and the partygoers, who he hoped thought that this was a staged duel, expected to see it fought to the end.

"No padded vests!" Pascal taunted. "No rules! No romantic performance for the faint of heart!" He slashed at Kit's knees, the swish of steel a whisper in the silence.

Kit executed a volte, a half turn to escape the blade before he thrust in quarte. Pascal slashed again. Where was his weakness?

Wait for another attack. Control. Provoke a response. Pascal made a feint. Kit answered with a circle in prime.

"I should have guessed," he said with a disdainful smile. "You're too impatient to perfect an attack."

"Perfection won't matter much when you're dead."

"True." Kit shot a glance at the awestruck spectators. "Ladies, my regrets. Pupils of the academy, pay attention. You will not see a lesson like this again in a very long time."

Sweat glistened on Pascal's forehead. "At least my father died fighting—despite the fact that yours had crippled him."

"The chevalier instigated the duel. He wouldn't leave the serving girl who worked for my father alone. He demeaned her in front of witnesses."

"And in front of witnesses, I am taking the revenge I promised him." He spit at Kit's feet. "Fenton was a half-mad drunk."

"Who died with honor."

Unhittable, Kit began to score hits, thrusting and circling, remaining beyond the other sword's reach until the time was right to attack. There. An opening.

He slid into a lunge, crossing his blade hard and fast against the hilt of Pascal's sword. He jerked hard. The other sword flew into the air. Kit caught it by the grip in his free hand and backed Pascal into the fireplace.

"Strike like lightning," Kit said, passing both swords to the first gentleman in the hall who approached him—not surprisingly Eldbert. "Honor is met."

Pascal exhaled, his face pale, and bowed. "I would rather that you had killed me."

"Well, it is my wedding day, and I want my wife to have only good memories of it."

He glanced around. The pupils of his academy had formed an inescapable semicircle around the man who had betrayed their code.

"Let the authorities deal with him," Kit said, pulling down his sleeves.

Violet had slipped outside from the great room into the garden when the duke wasn't looking and had reentered the house. She thought Wynfield was chasing her, but by the time she had jostled through the knot of onlookers to reach her aunt, there wasn't much he could do to stop her without causing another scene. Not that anyone would have paid attention.

The hall was as tightly packed as the zoological exhibition of tigers at the Tower of London. Except that one of the beasts on display was her husband, and if he had to heed his instincts, then so did she.

As a girl, she had often watched him fight, sometimes over her and sometimes over nothing. But this was different. This was danger. Swords crossed. Steel flashed. And it was not a game. Honor meant everything to the man she had married.

"Stop them," she heard Clarinda say to Ambrose. "Do something to make them stop or go outside before they put a hole in the wall. I thought we had agreed they should either perform on the terrace or inside the ballroom when it is clear."

Ambrose shook his head slowly. "Leave them be. And, dear, do be quiet. He'll never forgive us if we interfere."

"Lord Charnwood is quite right," the baroness remarked to no one in particular, but in a softer voice she said to Violet, "I told you that Master Fenton had a way with the sword."

He had a way with Violet, too, and he would be having his way with her right now if his vengeful pupil had not chosen this inopportune moment to challenge him. But she understood what he had to do.

She grasped her aunt by the arm to steady her, or perhaps they steadied each other, allied at last in truth and their support for the man who was their honorable protector.

Chapter 29

She stood by the window in her wedding gown, waiting. It seemed that she had waited for Kit all her life. But when he entered the room she was caught by surprise. And when, casually, he began to remove his neck cloth, shirt, and finally his trousers, she was rendered speechless. It was twilight, and the fading light that filtered through the leaded casement windows burnished the contours of his face and form. But he was hers, and from the glimpses she stole, she decided that there wasn't a tamed inch on his beautiful body. She was eager to test his wildness for herself.

"Boys with their swords," she said with a rueful sigh, rousing herself from her trance to approach him. "Are you all right?"

"Are you?" he asked, his smile so explicit that her heart began to race.

She nodded, and the next thing she knew she was trapped in his arms, her hand looped around his neck.

His erection rose thick and rampant through the folds of her gown. "I couldn't leave you."

"I know."

"Did I distract you very much?"

"Not as much as you do now."

He drew back briefly and dropped his clothes on the carpet. "Let me help you out of that dress."

"Why did you take so long?"

"Just making sure that no one else needs me tonight. I don't want to be interrupted."

She shivered as she felt his hands slide down her back in blatant ownership. "I need you," she whispered. "This is the first time we haven't met in secret, and . . . that you've held still long enough for me to get a proper look at you."

"Fair play," he said, and slipped back another step, lifting his hands in what appeared to be surrender—only to reach for her before she could absorb the full impact of his naked perfection.

He unfastened the buttons at the back of her gown. He untied the small bows at each of her shoulders and the big silk bow at her back. The skirts of satin and tulle fell open like petals. Moments later he took off her stays and muslin chemise, her garters, stockings, and slippers, until at last her beauty was unveiled, exposed for his pleasure alone.

His gaze dropped from her face to her bare feet. "I don't think we're going to spend much time at the party."

"We'll be missed," she whispered. "There's a treasure hunt planned for the morning."

His eyes studied her with a promise to possess. "I'd rather play with you."

He saw softness everywhere. He studied her curved shoulders and her full breasts with the blushing peaks. He wrapped his hand around her waist and slowly drew her against him. Flesh to flesh. Man and wife. She felt as vulnerable, as virginal, as she appeared.

He felt hard and hungry, and no doubt looked it.

Violet stared up into his eyes. She felt indecent and desired. But she refused to cover herself from her husband's scrutiny. Her breasts tingled with a warm arousal that was spreading down to her ankles. A flush of excitement flooded her entire body. Her smile invited him to look his fill.

He led her across the room and lowered her beneath him onto the bed. He was a man who lived by instinct, her husband. He had known her for a long time. He knew what she needed now.

"I love you," she said, swallowing over the knot of emotion in her throat. She smiled up at him. "I love you so much."

"I know," he said, and kissed her, his mouth branding hers in heated anticipation, his muscular arms imprisoning her on either side. "I love you, too, but your mouth is too sultry. You should smile like that only at me."

She moaned; the hard pressure of his body heightened her arousal. His kisses inflamed her blood. He settled beside her, pinioning her wrists with one hand to the pillow. She felt herself grow warm and damp for desire of him. His mouth strayed down her throat, past her shoulder, and lingered at her breasts. She arched her back as he drew an aching nipple between his teeth.

"Kit—" Her belly contracted at the wrench of pleasure that took her without warning. As if he sensed and sought to increase her desire, he plunged his fingers deep inside her sex at the same instant that he drew hardest on the tender peak. As he suckled, the indecent sensation inside her intensified.

She lost her focus, shattering into fragments, sobbing as she gave herself to the primal force he had unleashed. Even then, even before she could recover, he wanted more.

"I've waited so long for you. I can't wait another moment."

"Neither can I," she whispered. "Master me. Fully engage. And . . . let me move. Let me touch you."

"Wrap your legs around me, sweetheart. I'll be your sword and your shield."

He released her wrists, his mouth tightening as she ran her fingers down his back. Her naked flesh looked like sensuality incarnate against the bedcover, a scarlet that matched the deep hue of her mouth and the nipples he had kissed into swollen tenderness. His.

His gaze strayed lower, to the tempting cleft between her thighs. He stroked his knuckles against her flesh in carnal enticement. She raised one knee, following her intuition. Her eyes flickered to his, encouraging him to take his pleasure. He was Kit, and he was something more, infinitely capable of taking her prisoner with whatever game he wanted to play.

He knew that, too.

He placed his hands under her hips, pulled her upward, and impaled her with a swift determination that bolted her to the bed. "Sweet," he murmured soothingly, withdrawing and slamming back inside her before she could take a breath.

She arched her back, her tissue breached and stretching to take the thickness of him.

He drove into her, unrestrained, possessed by only one need—to make her his own, to seal their pact. He penetrated and pushed as deeply as she could take and then pushed deeper still. He moved against her, sensation building, insatiable.

She whimpered, but he couldn't hold back. He thrust harder, the unstoppable, perfect thrusts that he had dreamed of. He filled her and overflowed her so that she was bound to him alone for all time.

Kit lay content in the gathering shadows, his bride in his arms. There was supposed to be a champagne supper at midnight in the park to informally open the party. Right now, however, he could hear laughter from the gardens, children fighting and getting scolded by their governesses. In a few years he might be chasing his own offspring across Monk's Huntley.

Anything was possible, he mused.

It wasn't even Friday, when the house party officially began, and he had married the love of his life, patched up a feud with an old friend, and fought a duel against a young fool.

Who could predict what the future held?

"Kit?" she whispered, as moonlight spilled into the room. The fire had burned to embers. She slid her hand down his side and between his thighs; a few hours of pleasure had made her more comfortable communicating in this manner.

He nudged his knee between hers and sank his hard shaft deep into her swollen depths. "I'll have to be gentle with you this time," he said softly, undulating his hips. "You're going to ache at the dance tomorrow night."

She liked the idea. But she liked the idea of taking even more of him inside her. "I took dance lessons for years with a demanding master. I can manage."

"Maybe." He withdrew, smiling down at her before he fastened her to the bed. "But I'm a different kind of master. This training is a little more intensive."

Chapter 30

*W*inifred had not wanted to bring her daughter along with her to see the baroness. An invitation from Lady Ashfield could mean another reprimand, and there was no reason for the child to hear any stinging words. But at the last minute Winifred's sister had been called away from the shop in the back room of which Elsie could have waited. Winnie could hardly leave her little girl at the fencing academy.

"Now, you mind yourself, Elsie," she whispered as they stood together on the steps of the town house. She squeezed her daughter's gloved hand and checked her chin for crumbs. "The baroness is a fierce lady at times," she added, lifting her hand away to raise the brass knocker. "And she can be frightening. Just play with your dolls in the garden or in the kitchen if she gives you permission to—"

The door swung open.

Winifred blinked in surprise at the old butler's face.

The creases were engraved a decade deeper. His smile was so welcoming it left her at a loss for words.

"Miss Higgins," he said with a deep bow. "Please come into the drawing room. The baroness is expecting you." He gestured to an open door in the first of two hallways. "And, *you*, Miss Higgins," he said with a courteous bow to Elsie, "are expected in the kitchen for tea with Cook."

Elsie turned to her mother. "May I?"

Winifred nodded. A maidservant had appeared in the other corridor and beckoned Elsie with a friendly smile. Winifred looked up into Twyford's face, her courage faltering. "I expect I'm about to get what I deserve," she said quietly.

"No doubt, miss."

A footman arrived to take her gloves, jacket, and beaded reticule. Whatever warmth she had seen on Twyford's face must have been her imagination. She could not detect a spark of emotion in his eyes as he led her into the baroness's presence.

Frightening?

No. Lady Ashfield looked small and vulnerable on her tapestry chair by the window. Again Winifred wondered if she was imagining things. It seemed to her that a smile crossed the old woman's face before the solemnity Winnie recognized took its place. Still, she didn't imagine Lady Ashfield's voice, as dignified as ever, when it resounded across the room.

"Dear me, Miss Higgins. Was that your daughter who just went past like a ghost?"

"Yes, madam," she replied with a curtsy.

"She is how old?"

Winifred rose, swallowing hard. "Nine, madam," she said, waiting for the woman to question her about the husband she didn't have and likely never would. Then she reminded herself that Lady Ashfield had lost the baron not that long ago.

"You must be curious why I have invited you here today. Do sit down."

Winifred considered bolting for the door. But something held her. Not curiosity. Perhaps it was a need to let go of old grievances. "I did wonder, yes."

"As you might have heard, my niece was recently married to her childhood sweetheart."

Winifred reached behind her for the chair, afraid she would collapse in an undignified heap on the carpet. Twyford darted from the doorway to whisk the chair against her sinking weight. Before she could thank him, he returned to his post, she straightened her back, and the baroness resumed the conversation.

"I will be returning to Monk's Huntley in a month or two, Miss Higgins, and I am in need of a companion."

"A companion?"

"If you are available. I have plenty of room for you and your young girl in that house."

Almost a month had gone by since the house party. Godfrey was still unmarried, a sorrowful condition for a man his age. On the other hand, business at the emporium had never been better. His connection to the Boscastle family, however tenuous, had vastly improved the flow of customers through his doors. One of them might be a well-off lady who would make a suitable wife.

Indeed, quite a few ladies had stopped by the emporium to offer their sympathy for his broken engagement and to state that Fenton must be a rogue to have stolen Godfrey's bride from him in such a brash manner. But Godfrey suspected otherwise.

He suspected that Fenton had married Violet to save her from ruin, and for that he had earned Godfrey's respect. And if they had been meant to be together all along?

Well, life went on. Godfrey took to heart one customer's advice that he should stand firm under the circumstances and that fate had a way of rewarding gentlemen like him in the long run.

Really, that was all that counted, Godfrey thought. To be regarded as a gentleman. To keep stepping up in society. And now, because of losing Violet, he hadn't fallen down the ladder; he had only climbed up a little higher, and his aspirations seemed unlimited. Why, Miss Charlotte Boscastle, the headmistress of the Scarfield Academy for Young Ladies here in London, had stopped by the emporium today with her mentor, the Duchess of Scarfield, to shop, and no sooner had Godfrey hastened to serve her than that young rogue from the fencing school, the Duke of Wynfield, strolled into the shop as if he owned the place.

Godfrey had little time to lament what he had lost. Nobility shopped here.

Violet strolled with Jane through the well-maintained gardens of the marchioness's Park Lane mansion. She had just passed her husband, fencing with his private student in the summerhouse, the senior footman, Weed, cheering on his young master. The marquess stood on the steps, watching his son with equal parts pride and anxiety.

The pungent sweetness of herbs rose from the sunlit path the two women followed. "Can you smell the rosemary?" Jane asked, lifting her skirts. "It stays on your slippers forever. What was it that Shakespeare said? Something about rosemary being for remembrance." And she paused, giving Violet a conspiratorial smile. "I read the most outrageous story last week that claimed you and your talented husband had fallen in love at the Duke of Wenderfield's picnic breakfast."

"An utter falsehood."

"And," Jane continued, "that the pair of you had conducted an assignation in the pavilion, arranged by an unnamed marchioness."

"What will people say next?"

Jane feigned a look of complete innocence. "What they will no doubt be talking about, and what *I* should not tell you until it is formally announced, is that the marquess has petitioned for your husband's baronetcy and that his patent has been approved. With prestige will come prosperity. But you can't tell anyone I've told you this yet. I've never been good at keeping secrets, but didn't you say that it was one of your best traits?"

Violet bit her bottom lip to stifle a guilty smile. "I've kept a few," she said after a moment.

Jane shook her head. "Intriguing ones, I gather. Ah, I think the gentlemen are finished. Grayson was going to break the good news to your husband after the lesson. Don't forget—I didn't mention a thing. I shall leave you alone to talk."

Violet stood for a moment. "Jane?"

"Yes?"

"You might not be good at keeping secrets, but you are skilled at matchmaking."

"Am I?"

"*Hmm.*"

"My husband has accused me of the same thing. I can't imagine why."

It wasn't long after Jane returned to the house with the marquess, Weed bringing the young heir by the hand, that Kit sauntered across the garden to meet Violet.

She restrained herself from running into his arms and taking his foil hostage, as he had done her heart. "Nice to see you," he said, lowering his head to kiss her in full view of anyone who happened to be watching from the house. "I do believe we've come up in the world."

"Have we?" she asked, remembering her promise to Jane. "And what does that mean?"

He reached with his hand for hers. "For one thing, we are moving to a fancier part of town. For another, we will not be called Mr. and Mrs. Fenton for too much longer."

"No?" she asked, her eyes glittering at the pleased grin he gave her.

"How does Sir Christopher Fenton and Lady Fenton sound to you?"

She looked up at him, unable to conceal the happiness she felt that he had received his due. "I can't think of anyone in the world who deserves it more than you, Kit. But the truth is, I knew you were a knight from the moment I saw you chasing dragons in the churchyard."

He smiled down at her, the subtle scent of rosemary, of remembrance, wafting in the air around them. "And you were the lady I fought for and wanted to win."

"With help from our friends."

He laced his fingers with hers. "Sometimes I used to make up endings for my life. I'd imagine that I had a family who would find me. But nothing could have turned out better than this."

"Maybe they will find you, Kit."

He laughed. "We'll have our own family by then if they do."

Epilogue

$\mathcal{H}$ome for Christmas at Monk's Huntley. Kit had never thought, years ago, to see this day. He hadn't dreamed that he would return as Sir Christopher Fenton to the place that held his strongest memories. He stood at the garden gate through which he had carried Violet and given her up for what he'd feared would be forever.

He listened to the voices of friends and family, *his* family behind him, and he felt the restraints of the past slipping away.

"I lost the present I had for Eldbert," Violet said, beautiful against a background of snow in her cranberry silk gown and matching cloak. "I know it was sitting by the door and now it's gone."

"No, it isn't," Kit said, putting his hands in his pockets to keep from touching her. Even though she was his wife, he had to subdue certain instincts in the presence of others. "I helped Twyford load everything in the carriage before we delivered the pies and gifts to the workhouse." And he'd made sure that the children got their share first.

Winifred's daughter came dashing through the garden from the rear of the house. Moments later the baroness and Winifred appeared at the front door, bundled up for the drive to Lord Charnwood's Christmas dinner.

"Elsie, stop!" Winifred called in exasperation. "Don't you dare leave this garden without me."

"I only wanted to walk to the slope and see what the churchyard looks like in the snow."

"Not by yourself, miss!" her mother cried in alarm. "And where are your gloves?"

Elsie danced off in the direction of the garden gate, twirling around Kit and Violet. "It's snowing." She lifted her face and stuck her tongue into the air. "I love winter. I love snow."

"You won't love a cold bum if you slip on the ice," the baroness called after her. "Watch where you are going, child. Where is my walking cane?"

"Right here, ma'am." Kit pivoted and strode up beside her, hooking his arm around hers.

"That is good of you, Sir Christopher. But what about Violet?"

"I have another arm," he answered, looking past her to his wife.

Francesca glanced up at him in approval. "And what will you do when the child Violet is expecting arrives?"

He smiled. "I have shoulders, ma'am."

"Strong shoulders," Violet said, and took his other arm. "To go with his character."

Kit said nothing, but the look they exchanged could well have melted every snowflake falling from the sky. He heard the jingle of harnesses in the winter stillness, and Eldbert singing from the driver's box of his lumbering coach.

> *O come, all ye faithful*
> *Joyful and triumphant*
> *O come ye, o come ye to*
> *Eldbert's car-riage!*

He sang as they squeezed into his coach with his father, Dr. Tomkinson, Twyford and the footman heavily muffled and hanging on the back for the short drive. By the time the driver deposited the group outside the wreath-festooned doors of Viscount Charnwood's mansion, every voice was raised in song.

Kit hesitated before he followed the others into the house. But Violet stopped on the entrance steps to wait for him, her expression worried. "What have you forgotten?"

He shook his head. "Nothing. It's something I remembered. Go in from the cold."

"You— Oh." She laughed, her face clearing. "The trousers."

"Yes. Scene of a past sin. I haven't been here since."

"Well, Ambrose is waiting in the hall for you, and if it's any consolation, he appears to be fully dressed."

He bounded up the stairs and grasped her hand. "This is the first genuine Christmas I've ever had. A family Christmas."

"Think of next year," she whispered as they walked into the happy mayhem of dogs, children, and old friends gathered to make another decade of memories.

Kit took it all in as he seated Violet and her aunt beside the log fire popping in the grate, and a man-servant brought him a cup of buttered wassail. He drank in the warm glow of the candles and good cheer.

"Eldbert is serving on the board of guardians for the poorhouse," Ambrose said, raising his cup to Kit's. "To your health, Sir Christopher."

"And to yours, my lord."

"The thing is," Dr. Tomkinson was saying to Eldbert and another guest as they drifted toward the hearth, "nobody likes the notion of building a school next to a churchyard or, God forbid, upon it."

"When are we going to have dinner?" one of Lord Charnwood's sons demanded from the doorway.

His mother, Lady Charnwood, rose from her chair in vexation. "Do not let those slobbering hounds in here, Parker. Where is your governess?"

"We locked her in the coach house. Can we go out-side?"

"Indeed not," Lady Charnwood said. "You are to stay in the kitchen, where it is warm."

Winifred appeared in the doorway behind the child. "I'll watch them in the garden for a few minutes."

Eldbert turned from the fire. "Shall I come with you? Parker, have you ever gone on a treasure hunt?"

"Dinner will be served in two hours," Lady Charnwood said, looking relieved at the offer. "I want everyone at the table in time. Do you hear me, Eldbert?"

"Let me see if your father has a compass in his study," Eldbert said, obviously not hearing her.

"Somebody let the governess back in," Dr. Tomkinson said.

"Are you sure you won't have any wassail, Violet?" Ambrose asked. "We've got rum punch or lemonade, if you like."

"I'll have lemonade, thank you."

"Is that mince pie I smell?" Kit asked. "What a divine aroma."

"There's roast turkey and venison and plum pudding," Lady Charnwood said.

"What is that banging coming from the outbuildings?" asked Dr. Tomkinson.

It washed over Kit in a rush, the warmth. He went to the window and spotted Eldbert cutting through the garden with Miss Higgins, Elsie, Landon, and Parker running ahead. He gave a laugh, turning to see Violet rising from her chair. She was radiant, bathed in the glow of the innumerable candles that cast shadows on the deep-red walls. Together they watched until the five figures vanished into the white landscape and snow gently fell like a veil to shield them from view.

"Will they ever find treasure, do you suppose?" she asked.

"Why not?" He lowered his head to hers. "I did," he said. "I found you."

"Look up," she whispered.

"Is there a bough of mistletoe above us? I hope so, because I am desperate to kiss you, and I know that it is an improper act."

She smiled, her eyes glinting. "Don't you dare. Just look above the fireplace. Do you remember—"

"No. I can't remember anything when you smile at me like that."

"*Kit.*"

He glanced up, recognizing the two smallswords that held a place of honor on the wall. "Very nice," he said, meeting her gaze. "But I still want to kiss my wife."

Another family came to visit, and soon the house overflowed. Someone started a game of charades that ended abruptly with the announcement that dinner, at last, was served.

"But Eldbert isn't even here," Ambrose said, glancing at his guests. "Neither are the—"

The hallway door flew open; a blast of winter's breath gusted over the assembly. The footman hastened forth to attend the shivering arrivals.

"Mama!" Landon exclaimed, bursting into the cluster of guests like a cannonball. "Look what we found! Buried treasure. It wasn't the filthy stupid lie that Papa keeps saying it was. It's real. Here. Look for yourself if you don't believe me."

He held up a silver chalice encrusted with soil and rubies. Kit blinked. Those stones looked real to his eye.

Ambrose strode up to his son. "What the devil? That is the chalice that belonged to the collection of—"

"—the dead earl," Eldbert said, his voice challenging Ambrose to disagree. "It is quite remarkable that the children have found what we searched for when we were their age."

"Fancy that," Violet said with one of those smiles that provoked Kit to no end.

After a decadent dinner at a table set with polished silverware and an enormous Christmas cake in the middle decorated with sprigs of holly, Kit caught Violet again as the company drifted off to play more games and open gifts by the fire.

"I've got a present for you, Kit."

"Is it a kiss?"

"Not in the parlor."

"Look up, Lady Fenton. That is mistletoe above our heads."

He kissed her then in front of the baroness, Eldbert, Ambrose, and the others. He wrapped his arms around her waist and kissed with such concentration that he didn't even notice when everyone paraded back into the dining room to take a piece of Christmas cake.

"Sir Christopher," Ambrose said from the doorway, "would you leave off kissing your wife long enough to do the honor of cutting the cake?"

"With his sword!" one of his sons suggested from the staircase, peering through the balustrade like a prisoner behind bars.

Violet took Kit's hand. "It seems only fitting that you should be the one."

His gaze traveled to the dining room, where the guests had gathered. It was the reunion that five young friends had promised one another long ago. It was a pledge fulfilled. With a loving glance at his wife, Kit shook off the bonds of the past and stepped forward to embrace the future.

Read on for a glimpse of the
next captivating romance in
the Bridal Pleasures series
by Jillian Hunter

The Duchess Diaries

Available from Signet Select in January.

*I*t was the best of balls; it was the worst of balls. It was the annual graduation ball honoring the Scarfield Academy for Young Ladies in London. It was an evening of hope, which Miss Charlotte Boscastle had resolved would not end in disgrace. It was an evening of beginnings and farewells.

As the academy's headmistress, Charlotte would receive accolades for her efforts in training another class of young ladies to enter society. She would be praised for any marriage proposals offered to her students as a result of their elite schooling.

She would also be blamed for any scandals that she allowed to besmirch the academy's name. Her archenemy, Lady Clipstone, the headmistress of a lesser school, had predicted to the newspapers that some social misfortune was bound to occur during the event. Charlotte took little comfort in the knowledge that she was surrounded by members of her own family—

everyone in the *ton* knew how controversy tended to follow the Boscastles. It was said that whenever more than two of them were gathered in one place, the devil came into active play.

Still, she was grateful that the Marquess of Sedgecroft, her cousin, had agreed to host the affair at his Park Lane mansion. She appreciated the fact that he had invited his battalion of friends to fill the ballroom and impress the girls.

Perhaps, after tonight, she might be able to draw a breath. For good or for evil, the graduates would venture forth into the world. Until dawn broke over the occasion, however, she was obligated to stand guard against any rogues who thought to take advantage of an inexperienced girl. She had her eye on one rogue in particular. He had looked at her only once. The Duke of Wynfield was without question the most intimidating guest at the ball, and Charlotte wasn't about to let him steal her glory.

She wondered if he even remembered the last time they had seen each other, at the emporium in the Strand. They hadn't exchanged a single word. Charlotte had been shopping for the academy that day. He had been shopping for the pair of strumpets draped over either of his elbows.

He had kissed one of the tarts on the neck—and merely smiled when Charlotte, at the opposite end of the counter, had gasped in shock.

She had returned to the academy hours later to record the incident in her diary, changing a detail here and there until, *en fin*, the actual event bore little resemblance to her fabricated but far more satisfying version.

Fancy. Yes, she knew. Her diaries simmered with illicit truths and vicarious pleasures. She had been keeping a journal ever since she could hold a pen, but it was only recently that she'd decided to record her family's history. Not that those chronicles needed any enhancement.

Unfortunately her private life did. In the pages of her secret musings, the duke not only adored her; he had been pursuing her for months. In actual life, he was domineering, indecent, and inexcusably taken with disgraceful women. In his fictional encounters with Charlotte, he was domineering, indecent, and inexplicably taken with her alone.

In Charlotte's revision of the incident in the emporium, the duke had noticed her across the counter and had immediately dismissed the other women. He had walked straight up to Charlotte and, without a word, grasped her hand.

"My carriage is outside," he said, his sinful smile mesmerizing her. "May I take you away?"

His face receded. Another voice, breathy and excited, was whispering in her ear. "That's the Duke of Wynfield you're staring at, Miss Boscastle. Do be careful. Everyone is saying that he's in the market for a mistress."

Charlotte gripped her fan and turned to regard her favorite student in dismay. "Lydia Butterfield, reassure me that he has not found one in you."

Lydia gave her a wistful grin. "Dear Miss Boscastle, I shall miss you with all my heart."

"You shall miss my guidance—that is clear."

"I won't need it any longer," Lydia said in regret. "But I will miss your history lessons."

"All the battles and beheadings?" Charlotte asked, stepping to the side to stop Lydia from staring at the duke. Or him from noticing her. "But don't be so melodramatic, or I shall start to cry. Your family still lives in London. You may visit the academy whenever you wish."

"My family— Well, my *betrothed's* family lives in Dorset, and he is eager to start a family—"

"Your betrothed?" Charlotte said faintly.

Lydia bit her lip, nodding toward the short gentleman standing a few feet behind her. "Sir Adam Richardson, the architect."

"Lydia, I am so—" Envious? Overcome? Relieved? "—proud," she said firmly. "He appears to be a fine gentleman."

Lydia laughed, her gaze drifting to the duke, who was *not* known to be a gentleman at all. "I was told that he is a wildly jealous lover."

"Your fiancé?"

"The duke," Lydia said, laughing again. "He has a reputation for being a possessive suitor."

"*Lydia.*" Charlotte attempted to look shocked, although the same rumors had not escaped her attention. Such gossip should have stamped the duke as an unacceptable person instead of engendering wicked daydreams about him in Charlotte's imagination. Why did it feel so pleasant to picture him tearing off his long-tailed evening coat to defend her from . . . ? Oh, since it was *her* flight of fancy, the other man might as well be Marcus Moreland, the cad who had broken her heart years ago.

She could picture it so vividly. The ballroom would be cleared for a duel; the duke had studied swordfighting at Fenton's School of Arms. Charlotte had watched him perform at a benefit ball in this very mansion. She'd had nothing to do with him on that past night, and it was doubtful that she would capture his interest in the future.

"I don't think that either of us need worry about the duke's amorous proclivities," she assured Lydia, thus uttering the fateful words that would come back to mock her before morning came. . . .

New York Times bestselling author

Jillian Hunter

A DUKE'S
TEMPATION
The Bridal Pleasures Series

The Duke of Gravenhurst, a notorious author
of dark romances, is accused of corrupting the
morals of the public. But among his most
devoted fans is the well-born Lily Boscastle,
who seeks employment as the duke's personal
housekeeper. Only then does she discover
scandalous secrets about the man that she
never could have imagined.

**Available wherever books are sold or at
penguin.com**

Christina Dodd

In Bed with the Duke

Demure lady's companion Emma Chegwidden never defies society's rules. Until the night she runs right into the arms of the mysterious and menacing Reaper—a masked man who rides the night-shadowed countryside. His goal is justice…or is it vengeance?

Cynical, dangerous, and ruthless, Michael Durant, long-lost heir to the duke of Nevitt, is the last man Emma should defy. But some challenges are too tempting to resist. Soon Michael discovers a woman whose beauty and courage reach through to his tortured soul. And he will defy anything, even fate itself, to claim her.

Available wherever books are sold or at
penguin.com

S0171

Sara Lindsey

Promise Me Tonight

Isabella Weston has loved James Sheffield for as long as she can remember. Her débutante ball seems the perfect chance to make him see her in a new light.

James is stunned to find that the impish girl he once knew has blossomed into a sensual goddess. And if he remember his lessons correctly, goddesses always spell trouble for mortal men.

When Izzie kisses James, her artless ardor turns to a masterful seduction that drives him mad with desire. But, no stranger to heartbreak, James is determined never to love, and thus never to lose. Can Isabella convince him that a life without love might be the biggest loss of all?

"A real love story...A perfect escape."
—*New York Times* bestselling author Eloisa James

**Available wherever books are sold or at
penguin.com**